Wildwood

Colleen Wait

CONTENTS

Acknowledgements

Over the years, writing has become an extension of me. My life, my family, my thoughts, feelings, beliefs, hopes and dreams. It's all on paper for the world to read. I have written a blog, done free-lance for a local magazine, and now my twelfth book is here for you to enjoy. I acknowledge you, the reader. Thank you for reading, I hope and pray that something touches your heart. My one desire is to please God, not man. If you enjoy the book, it's a bonus!

Chapter 1

Soft white candles in mason jars hung from white lace ribbons which were carefully tied to branches of the tall, majestic oaks on a clear moonlit night. Their flickering lights gave the wooded park a fuzzy, ethereal glow. Soft music played off in the distance, wafting through the air. It mingled gently with the breezes, swaying the lavender and roses to and fro. Whispers of 'beautiful', 'magical', and 'lovely', were barely audible when a delicate hand reached up and placed a finger on the man's cheek. It traced his strong jaw line ever so slowly then one finger stopped for a brief moment on his lips for him to kiss it, reached up to touch his soft brown eyes, one at a time, before the hand rested on his heart. The hand patted the tune of his heartbeat in time with it's own. The love in his dark brown eyes spoke to her soul.

"I, Michael, promise to be fully committed to you," said the young man in uniform. "To love you, protect you, honor you above all others. You, Camille, own my heart. To you, I freely give my love, my life. We will hold hands through fields of flowers and the flames of fire. I will protect you until the day I die and then I will still love you, forever."

The view widened to include the young bride dressed in antique white lace. Her long auburn hair fell in ringlets over her shoulders. Their faces were aglow in the candlelight as they gazed into each other's eyes.

1

"I, Camille," said the bride with tears in her eyes. Her voice shook, yet her soft hazel eyes never left his, "promise to love, honor, and respect you every moment I'm alive, with every breath I take, and with every beat of my heart. To you, Michael, I freely give myself to you for the rest of my life. I will love you forever."

"I will love you forever, forever…"

"Mommy?" asked a small voice from the doorway. "You awake?" Lacey moved her gaze from the small TV on her mother's dresser to the woman's face. She quickly wiped away the tears that had emerged at the sight of her father.

Camille pressed a button on the remote and gave small, loving smile to her daughter.

"I thought I heard you talking to someone," said the little girl, in her little girl trying to sound grown up voice, anxiously wanting to be invited in. The r's and l's were still difficult, and noticeably absent when she was sleepy or stressed.

"Come." Camille patted the comforter beside her in the big king-sized bed. "I was just talking to Daddy."

"Daddy?" The girl's eyes grew large as she ran and dove onto the bed. "Where?"

"No, honey, just his picture," answered Camille in a soft voice. She put her left arm around her daughter, held the small laptop computer with the other, barely holding back tears. "I'm sorry, Lacey. I didn't mean to…"

"It's okay, Mommy." Lacey wrapped her tiny arms around her mother while looking at the picture on the laptop screen. "That's my favorite picture of him. I…I wish I had been there," she said. Her words cracked while trying to hold back her emotions.

"You weren't born yet, silly," stated Camille. She kissed her daughter on the top of her red curls then stated, "I still remember our wedding day like it was yesterday even though it was eleven years ago."

"When will he come home, Mommy?" asked Lacey, rubbing away the remaining tears with the back of her hand. She remembered what they had been told, but didn't want to believe it was real.

"Lacey, you know what happened," stated her mother with a soft whisper.

"I think the man was fibbing. It isn't true," she said with a stubborn pout.

"Do you remember that day?" asked Camille.

Lacey nodded her head. She thought hard to recall that horrible day. Sometimes the memories came to her in dreams, whether she wanted them to or not. When they came, she tried to stay in her dream for a very long time.

Lacey was barely 6 years old and it was a week before Christmas. Her daddy had gotten permission to do a video chat several days prior to let Lacey and Mommy know he would be home in time to celebrate the holidays with the family. His job as a Captain in the Marine Corps took him into the line of fire on the front lines as the war had escalated. Contact with home had been sparse at best over the past six months. Mommy and Lacey were putting the finishing touches on the 6-foot fir Christmas tree when the doorbell rang.

"I'll be right back," stated Camille. She pointed to two gifts on the fireplace hearth. "Put Daddy's presents under the tree for me okay?"

"No, Mommy. I'll get it. It's Daddy. I know it's Daddy come to surprise us," answered Lacey while twirling in her red and green dress, embroidered with presents and candy canes- an early present from her grandmother.

Lacey's smile dropped the moment she opened the door. Two big, tall men in uniform stood on her front porch. They didn't look happy. "Mommy!" Lacey called out without taking her eyes off the men. With her small hand still on the doorknob, she turned toward her mother when she approached. By the look on her mother's face, Lacey knew

3

something was wrong.

Camille froze in the foyer. Lacey looked back and forth from soldier to mother wondering what was going on.

"Ma'am," said the young man in uniform, hat in hand. "I'm sorry..."

The rest of the words were a blur. Lacey's mother's knees buckled as a loud wail erupted from her lips. The man spoke gently, handed her mother a letter, spoke something more to her, then slowly walked away. The biggest man patted a confused Lacey gently on the shoulder, said he was sorry, then turned to join his partner.

"Daddy's helicopter crashed," Camille said. She stroked her daughter's head then flipped the computer screen to the next picture. "Remember when we took this picture?"

"That's me when I was five," answered Lacey. "Daddy took us around and around to see all the 'copters. Is that the one that crashed?"

"I don't think so, but one like it. Daddy was working, trying to get his squadron to safety that day," she said, meaning the day of the crash.

"Like that one time? When that big man wearing all those shiny medals gave Daddy an award?" Lacey pressed the arrow key to see the next picture. "He said Daddy is a hero." She pointed to the general in the picture.

"He was...is," stammered Camille. She gently touched her pendant.

"Daddy gave you that, right?" asked Lacey.

"Yes, it was the first present your daddy ever gave me. I still wear it because it reminds me of him."

"But, he can't be in heaven," argued Lacey. She reached up to touch the gold anchor hanging from a delicate chain around her mother's neck. "The man said they couldn't find him. Right? I think so, he said that. I heard people say that he was just lost."

"We've had this discussion before, baby girl," stated Camille.

"Well, I'll never believe it!" cried Lacey who then began to cough.

"I know," cooed Camille as she rolled Lacey over onto her stomach and began patting her back. "Take a deep breath. School tomorrow and you have homework to turn in."

Lacey continued to cough, which made her nose run. The coughing and running nose began the cycle which started shortly after the news about her father. Coughing, followed by vomiting and then fever. There would be no school for Lacey the next day. She had been drug to many doctors and to their church's family minister, who was also a psychologist. They all determined Lacey's constant illnesses were psychosomatic. Death of a parent affects children emotionally, Lacey remembered hearing them say over and over again. "It will pass with time," they all told her mother.

It had been a year since the news of the presumed fatal accident and the illnesses continued. Lacey, a once vibrant, happy child who loved to play with her friends and be involved in her Sunday School class was gone. In her place was a sickly, sad, unsocial child who became ill at any form of change. The first telltale incident was when she walked into her classroom a mere week after returning to school after the memorial service and came face to face with a substitute teacher.

"Who are you?" Lacey asked the strange woman standing in the doorway of her classroom.

"Good morning. I'm Mrs. Watson. Your teacher is out today."

"Gone? She's not here?" Lacey began to breathe heavily. Her stomach churned. "Call her. Call her now!" insisted Lacey. "She is my teacher. Not you! I don't know you." Tears began to flow down the little cheeks as the teacher tried to explain to deaf ears. The coughing started when Mrs. Watson moved her hand from the doorknob to her shoulder. "No!" Lacey cried through coughs then ran to the bathroom just inside the

5

classroom. She aimed for the toilet but missed.

"Mrs. Andreas, come quick," Lacey heard an older student cry out from down the hall at her mother's classroom door. "Lacey..."

Embarrassed, scared, and confused, Lacey shut her eyes tight, curled up in the corner under the sink. She wished everyone would just go away and she was back at home. Purple vomit from grape jelly and juice at breakfast covered the floor and her dress. Kids from class walked by and giggled while Mrs. Watson tried, in a very loud voice, to control the classroom.

"Honey, what's wrong?" asked Camille as calmly as she could.

The frightened little girl was scooped up by her mother and carried out the door without explanation to anyone. Lacey's chest heaved, her stomach dry wretched, and then she fainted in her mother's arms in the school parking lot. She woke up in a strange place, the emergency room her mother told her. Immediately the little girl felt better, safe. Calm was restored.

"That lady," Lacey stated. "Stranger. Mrs. Campbell wasn't there."

"Mrs. Campbell is sick today, sweetheart. It happens sometimes," explained Lacey's mother. "That lady is a substitute teacher. Whenever a teacher can't go to work, somebody has to take her place. You know that."

"You're a teacher," said Lacey, a little confused.

"That's right. And right now, someone else is teaching my class."

"So, I can go to your class when Mrs. Campbell is sick?" Lacey stated more than asked.

"No. You have to stay with your own class. I will be right down the hall, honey, so you will be safe. And, I'll talk to Mrs. Campbell, if it will make you feel better. If she knows ahead of time that she is going to miss school she'll let me know and that way you won't be surprised. It will happen again, Lacey."

That answer seemed to satisfy Lacey. That is, until a month later when Mrs. Campbell left suddenly in the middle of the school day. Lacey began to sneeze. Her nose began to run, and then the fever. Initially thinking she was sneezing to get to go home, Camille had Lacey spend the rest of the day in the nurse's clinic. By the time they got home, Lacey's fever was 102.

"Lacey, honey," Camille said to the frail girl in her arms the following night. "Let's ask God to make you well so we can go to school tomorrow." Camille gently laid her daughter on her own bed and pulled the sheet up to the girl's chin.

"Okay, Mommy," said Lacey in a faint, weak voice. She hugged her favorite teddy bear, the one her father had given to her as a baby, while her mother began to pray.

"Lord," began Camille. She stroked her daughter's forehead while she prayed, "my baby girl needs your healing hand. She's hurting and has missed another day of school. Please heal Lacey's body and her heart."

"And bring Daddy home," added Lacey as she always did.

"Amen," they said together.

"Is Gramma coming for Christmas?" asked Lacey through a yawn.

"I think so," answered Camille with a smile that didn't match her sad eyes. "Christmas is soon, isn't it? Good night, sweet girl."

Lacey sighed a deep, sorrowful sigh. She didn't want to think about Christmas. She wished she could make it go away. Her mother gave her a light kiss on the cheek then tiptoed to the living room. Lacey followed, knowing where her mother was going. On the mantle, where they had been placed a year ago, were the two gifts, unopened, untouched. It had too painful for either of them to remove the packages. Neither had spoken of the gifts since that day. Lacey's mother picked up each box, one at a time, held them to her heart, then returned them to their spot. This time, however, there would be no tree, no decorations, no joy, nothing to celebrate.

The classroom in the large elementary school the following week was a stark contrast to the sad living room. Brightly colored decorations were taped to every available wall space while giggles from anxious children filled the room. Mrs. Campbell tried her best to keep the children on task the last day of school before winter break. It was a futile effort. Was every year.

"Settle down, boys and girls," said Mrs. Campbell in her commanding teacher's voice. "I have a very important assignment to give you before you leave for break. It is due the day you return to school. Put this note I am passing out in your planner and give it to your parents so they can help you with the assignment." Mrs. Campbell waited until the groans stopped and all eyes were on the teacher. "Now, the assignment is to write what it means to celebrate. A birthday, a holiday, a good grade," she said, pausing with emphasis. "Be specific, define the word. What does it mean to you? Secondly, while you are on holiday, write about your experience. Did you celebrate? What and why? Did you not celebrate? Why? Were you disappointed? Pleasantly surprised? Happy? Sad? Was it just another day off from school? You choose what to write about. Alternatively..." Mrs. Campbell began after looking at the artwork on the wall.

"What does that mean?" asked a boy in the back row.

"It means instead of." Mrs. Campbell continued, "Alternatively, you may draw your answers. Be creative. Draw what you did on Christmas day. Show me how you celebrated. You may also do both."

"Like a story book?" asked another classmate.

"Exactly."

"Will you celebrate Christmas?" Katie, who sat next to Lacey, whispered when Mrs. Campbell's back was turned. She had been Lacey's friend ever since her mother transferred to the military base. The two had been inseparable until the day of the memorial service.

Lacey shrugged without looking up.

"You coming to Sunday School this time?" she asked.

Lacey shrugged.

"Come see Sprinkles on Saturday," Katie urged. "She's bigger than the last time you came over. You can come over after lunch. I'm going to Cassie's, um, her… in the morning …" Katie started to say more but stopped mid sentence and pretended to do her schoolwork.

"No," said Lacey quietly with her eyes glued to her desk. Fighting tears she whispered, "Cats make me sneeze." Lacey wished Katie would be quiet. How could she be so cheerful? Lacey could only think of the assignment Mrs. Campbell had just given and what her mother might say after finding out she didn't do it. How could Mrs. Campbell make her write about the most horrible time of year? They will both just have to understand, she decided.

After school Lacey sat down quietly in the library in her usual spot, a corner rarely used. The year before she had played with her friends as they waited for the bus or for their parents to pick them up. Now, every day after school while Mommy did her end-of-day duties, Lacey sat alone and read.

"Ready to go, honey?" asked Camille. "Gramma should be here by dinner time."

"I'm ready," Lacey said with a nonchalant shrug.

"What's wrong?" Camille picked up Lacey's backpack and waited.

"Oh, nothing." Lacey pushed her ginger curls out of her face revealing red eyes.

"Something happen in class?"

"No."

Camille gently grasped her daughter's hand and began to lead her to the car. "Talk to me."

"I…it doesn't matter. I didn't wanna go anyway."

"But you weren't invited."

"No."

"You haven't gone to anything you've been invited to all year," stated Camille in a soft but matter-of-fact tone. "Maybe that's why the girls stopped inviting you."

"I know."

"So, maybe you could invite your friends over during winter break."

"No, that's okay. I think so I'd rather play with Gramma." She didn't really, but staying home with her grandmother was preferred over girls giggling and bragging about their Christmas presents.

Gramma, or Mrs. Amaryllis Blythe, was waiting in her dirty, old, dreadfully old van when Camille and Lacey pulled into the driveway.

"Well now, look what the cat finally drug home," exclaimed Amaryllis. She picked up a slightly uncomfortable Lacey and gave her a giant hug.

"You're early, Mother," stated Camille. "We didn't expect you for another few hours."

"Well, I decided not to stop at the flea market. I can go later in the week with you two." Amaryllis dropped Lacey to the ground, opened up the back of the van and pulled out an old ice chest. "I brought dinner so y'all don't have to cook," she stated.

"Mother, you didn't need to do that."

"Well, I know your hands are full and you could use a break. Me and little Lacey can talk while we cook and you can go buy yourself a new attitude, missy," said Amaryllis with a wink to her granddaughter. "Go on and put your school things away. Don't mind me. I'll be in the kitchen."

"Yes, Mother. Come on Lacey, let's put your backpack in your room," stated Camille. She unlocked the front door and led the way.

"Gramma smells weird," stated Lacey once behind closed doors in her bedroom.

"Shh," Camille gestured with a not so serious frown on her face.

"I don't remember her hair being that long. She likes that weird, fluffy skirt a lot, too," she said, almost with a laugh. "Didn't Gramma wear it last Christmas?"

"Mother is set in her ways. I don't think she's bought new clothes or cut her hair in at least a decade," stated Camille. "Plus, she likes to be comfortable when she drives. Let's go see what she brought for dinner."

"Do I hav'ta eat it?" Lacey scrunched up her nose at the smell that came from the kitchen.

"Mother, what have you got there?" asked Camille as they entered the room.

"Well now, let's see. Dandelion salad, wild onions, candied pecans, and venison," Amaryllis stated proudly.

"You didn't...you know, dress it yourself, did you?" asked Camille.

"Of course not, darlin'. Stop looking for evidence," she said after swatting her daughter's hand away. "The butcher in town got it this season. It's an early Christmas present."

"This is the butcher who's widowed, right?" asked Camille with a sly grin. "He's been flirting with you for years."

"Now, don't you talk like that. Not in front of the baby. I told that man I could bring down my own dinner thank you very much, but my daughter will be appreciative of y'all's generosity." Amaryllis took her long, reddish-gray braid, tied it in a knot at the base of her head then finished unwrapping the venison steaks. She plopped them onto the kitchen counter top. "Now, where is your flat iron?"

11

"I don't have cast iron Mom," stated Camille for the umpteenth time. "Or a spit. The BBQ has not been used in…at least year."

"Well now, we'll just have to improvise. Scoot, baby girl, go git yourself a drink and read a magazine. Lacey, you stay here and help your old granny," Amaryllis said with wide eyes then laughed until Camille turned to walk away.

"I don't drink, Mom," Camille said over her shoulder.

"Maybe you should start!" Amaryllis began searching through the cabinets for pots and pans while Lacey stood and watched. "Don't your momma feed you? You haven't grown a bit since the last time I was here. You're still only knee-high to a grasshopper."

"I grew two inches. Doctor said so," answered Lacey. She studied her grandmother carefully. The last time she had seen her was at her father's prayer service. Time before that was Christmas, and time before that was when they had moved to this house. Before that, she couldn't remember.

"Uh huh," answered Amaryllis, not really listening. She dropped a large frying pan onto the stove with a loud bang then began to pound the venison with a wooden rolling pin. "So, I see you waited until I got here to put up the Christmas decorations. I brought some left over from my last flea market trip. Sold most of them but saved a few for you and your Mommy. If you two had come to my house every year like I wanted then you'd have a whole box full."

"We were out of the country, Mom," called Camille from the living room.

"What for? How can you afford to travel on a teacher's salary Cami?" asked Amaryllis without looking up from her work.

"Michael was stationed in Japan for two years, remember? Germany before that, and Hawaii after we got married."

"I was born in Japan," stated Lacey proudly.

12

"Really?" Amaryllis stood up straight and folded her arms with the rolling pin in her hand. "You don't look Japanese. Not with that red hair!"

Lacey tried to read her grandmother's face to see if she was serious or not. On their drive home from school Lacey had done her best to remember what she looked like. Other than the skirt and the smell, her grandmother was not at all what she had pictured. She didn't look like the other grandmothers at church. This lady had long grey hair with red streaks tied in a loose braid that went all the way down her back and she talked weird. She had never seen grandmothers that wore old cowboy boots either.

"Now, all that travel is no excuse not to visit your mother. I get lonely out in the woods all by myself, you know."

"Willow is just down the street, Mom," said Camille. She poked her head in the kitchen to see what was going on.

"Now you go set yourself back down, Cami. Me and baby girl have things under control," Amaryllis said with a huff. "After dinner you and I are going to pull out the decorations and give this place a little cheer."

"I think so I don't want to," said Lacey in her usual turn of phrase when she wanted to make herself understood. She suddenly ran out of the kitchen towards her room but stopped just out of sight behind the large sofa.

"What?" asked Amaryllis. "No matter, she'll come around after she sees what I brought. The wildflowers were in abundance this year. And you," Amaryllis turned to her daughter. "What have you been doing with yourself? You both look so glum."

"It's only been a..." began Camille.

"You know, when I feel a little sad I go outside and commune with nature. Pick flowers, do some painting. Maybe you need to take up painting. Water colors to start."

"How's your health, Mom?" asked Camille. "When's the last time you had a check-up?"

"Now don't you start, Cami. I am healthier than a horse on race day. Hand me that bowl," Amaryllis stopped pounding the venison and began to make the salad without washing her hands.

"I'll do the salad, Mom. You focus on the meat."

After dinner, which Lacey ate very little of, Amaryllis walked around the house pointing out things that, in her opinion, needed to be done to liven things up. Lacey and her mother sat and watched for nearly an hour until finally the older woman came to rest in front of the fireplace.

"Well," she said, pointing to the two gifts on the mantle, "at least you got a few presents."

"Those are Daddy's," said Lacey. She ran up to the mantle, grabbed her grandmother by the hand before they were disturbed. "We're saving them."

Amaryllis looked over at Camille and stated, "That's not healthy."

"Mother, it's time for bed. Come on, I'll help you get settled."

"I can put myself to bed thank you very much." Amaryllis stomped off to the spare room.

"Can I sleep with you tonight?" Lacey asked her mother.

"No, I have some things to do before bed. Go brush your teeth then I'll come in for prayers."

"Okay, but I don't want to decorate tomorrow. Do we have to?"

"I...I don't know, we'll see. We do need to go Christmas present shopping. What would you like?"

"Nothing."

"A new doll, maybe a bike or some clothes?"

"No. I don't want anything. Not until Daddy gets home."

Lacey had not wanted any presents for her birthday, either. Her mother got her something anyway, a new book Lacey had admired at the bookstore. When she opened the present, Lacey retreated to her room, cried herself into another illness. She had been unable to celebrate anything knowing that her daddy was out there somewhere, lost. Birthdays and Christmases were for celebrating and Lacey just could not be happy until her daddy came home.

"Ready for prayer?" asked Camille from the doorway. She had a folder tucked under her arm. Lacey knew what that was for.

Lacey nodded, pulled out a picture from under her pillow, kissed it then said, "God, I know Daddy is alive. He said he would love us forever. But, God, if he is in heaven, please tell Mommy everything is going to be okay. Amen." The last part was said to get her mother to stop worrying about her. She desperately held on to the hope that her father would return. Lacey opened her eyes and put her arms around her mother. "I love you, Mommy," she whispered.

"I love you too. Good-night. Door open or closed?"

"Open."

Lacey waited until she heard her mother start talking to Gramma then snuck out of bed and sat just outside the open door to listen.

"See," Camille was saying, "these are all the documents."

"You called brass?" asked her Gramma.

"They don't call him that, but yes."

"What about your friend, the one who works on base?"

"She's not much of a friend. Every time I call her she says she will do anything for us, but it never pans out."

"Maybe she just doesn't have the power she claims."

"Do you remember, at the funeral, how she said she would organize everything? Well, it didn't happen. I thought we were friends, good friends. I guess I expected too much from her."

"What about your church?"

"We don't go much anymore. Lacey...well...anyway the elders and their families were great. At first. I couldn't have gotten through the hard stuff if it hadn't been for them."

"That's what church is for," stated Amaryllis enthusiastically. "So what do the papers say?"

"Basically that everything is on hold. No proof one way or the other. Because of Michael's mission, they can't tell me anything."

"What about hiring a private company to search?"

"On who's dime?"

"The military's."

"Not going to happen. Besides, I keep getting told that there is an active search going on."

"But in the meantime your benefits are in limbo."

"Exactly."

"What about the house? Can you keep living here?"

"I don't know, Mother. I won't be able to afford it on one salary. And with everything else...I don't want to rock the boat."

Lacey didn't understand what her mother and grandmother were talking about so she reluctantly went back to bed. Conversations like this between her mother and someone on the phone happened all the time and they all ended the same, with her mother upset and cranky the rest of the day. Limbo. That's the word her mother keep repeating. Lacey decided she would have to look that word up in the morning.

Chapter 2

The phone began ringing as soon as Lacey and her mother got home from school. Lacey drug her backpack behind her as she sniffed and wiped her nose on her sleeve.

"Hello?" Camille dropped her briefcase on the kitchen table, pointed at Lacey to go to her room, then plopped down onto a chair.

It was the last week of school before summer break and Lacey had woken up that morning with the sniffles. Her mother told her she absolutely could not miss anymore work and that she would be going to school sniffles or no sniffles. Between Christmas break during Gramma's visit and now, Lacey had been sick three times. Three more doctor's visits and zero answers to her chronic illness. The doctor had refused to give her anymore antibiotics. Her mother agreed, but was frustrated because they could not find anything to stop the sniffling. To make matters worse, Lacey had lost two pounds. This seemed to be of great concern to the doctor because he had asked to speak to her mother in private. The worry on Lacey's part ceased when the outcome was ice cream and homemade smoothies.

"Hello?" Camille said again into the phone. She pressed a button and set the phone on the armrest.

"Cami? It's Willow," said the voice on the other end through the speaker.

"Oh, hey. Can I call you back in a few minutes? I've got to give Lacey some medicine."

"No, but I'll hold," stated Willow her usual flat, uninterested tone.

"Fine." Camille slammed her hand down on the end table and made an ugly face at the phone. Lacey had only made it to the couch, so she pulled out one of the many cough and cold medicines in the kitchen cabinet. After dosing and wrapping Lacey in a blanket, Camille returned to the phone. "Still there?"

"Yes. Kid sick again?" Willow asked. Without waiting for a reply she began her reason for calling. "You have to go check on Mom. The church people called yesterday. Something about Mom not answering her door. I wouldn't either, by the way, if they came to my door. The man said they hadn't seen her in a while."

"You live down the road, Willow," answered Camille. "Call her and if she doesn't answer, go check on her."

"I did call her."

"So why are you calling me?"

"I told you why. You have to go check on Mom. I can't go over there. The place stinks. I'm allergic to cats. Every time I go over there we get into a fight and then I go home sick and smelling like a litter box," complained Willow.

"So pre-medicate, wear a mask, and go. You are less than an hour down the road."

"I can't."

"Willow," began Camille. "I'm a solid day's drive away. It's the last week of school, and Lacey is trying to be sick. On top of that, once school is out I start tutoring. There is absolutely no way…. Hello?" The phone let out a long monotone sound. Willow had hung up. Camille rubbed her temples then dialed her mother's number. "Busy. Willow must be talking to her. Good, problem solved."

"Aunt Willow doesn't like Gramma," Lacey said then let out a loud sneeze. "I don't remember her."

"Don't you worry about anything," Camille said in her usual soothing voice.

"But, Gramma," began Lacey. Knowing what was going on with everyone in her life made her feel safe and somewhat in control. Even though she was a very young girl, she knew that her life was different from her friends and classmates. Despite living near the base, she went to a public school with a good mix of military and non-military students. No one she knew had moved as many times and lived in as many places as she had. No one she knew had a daddy who was 'missing' and a mother who said her life was in 'limbo'.

"No buts, young lady. You close your eyes and get some rest. We both have to go to school tomorrow. A few more days and then…" Camille looked over towards the fireplace as if searching for the right words then continued with, "summer break. You can sleep late and watch TV every day. If you want, we can bake cookies Saturday."

Camille turned her phone to mute then returned her attention to Lacey. They read a book, ate dinner, said their prayers, and went to bed in their separate rooms. With coaxing, medication, and a little bribery they both made it through the last days of school. The following Monday, Camille began tutoring. Three students who were in danger of failing middle school came to their home, one at a time, beginning at 9 in the morning three days a week. While her mother worked, Lacey either played quietly in her room or read outside under the lone oak tree in the back yard. On days off, Lacey got to go to the park or the zoo or they both stayed home and spent the day on the couch reading. It was a very quiet existence. No play dates. No dates. No socialization except for the few times they went to Sunday morning church. Neither asked for more. Neither wanted more.

On the occasion that the weather was just right, Lacey sat under the tree and imagined where her daddy was and what it would be like when he finally came home. She imagined that it would happen early on a Saturday morning.

"The sun will be shining, but not too hot," Lacey told her favorite bear as they sat under the tree. "Daddy will bust through the door and say, 'I'm home. I'm finally home. Oh, how I've missed you.' Lacey, that's me, will jump into his arms and hug his neck ever so tight. He's wearing his dress uniform suit, the one with all the shiny medals on them. Plus one new big one for bravery. Daddy will tell Lacey again how much he missed her, kiss her on the cheek, hug her tight, and tell her that he will never, ever, ever leave her again. And that's how it's going to happen," Lacey said emphatically to her bear.

Every Saturday, she watched the door and every Saturday she was disappointed. By the end of the summer, Lacey had pretty much stopped dreaming of her father. Not because she believed any less, but more because of a particular phone call she overheard.

"Hi, Norma. It's Camille," she said with less enthusiasm than usual. "I was just wondering… Yes, I called them yesterday. No. Nothing. Yes, well they said the same thing. But how can they keep saying 'if we have news'? Everyone keeps putting me off. Either he is or he isn't. Yes, you keep saying that. Limbo might as well be hell," Camille said angrily. She pushed a button on her phone and muffled a scream into her hands. "Some friend you are!"

"Can we pray for Mrs. Norma?" Lacey asked her mother that night. She pulled her bear close to her heart in preparation for prayer time.

"Why?" asked Camille.

"So she can find Daddy."

Camille looked away, sighed, then smiled a little. "Of course we can, honey." With her arms around her daughter she began, "Dear God. Please bless Lacey with bright smiles and happy days. Bless Daddy, wherever he is, and please bless Norma."

"And bring Daddy home. Amen," concluded Lacey. "Do we have to go to school next week?"

"Yes ma'am. In-service first, though. You like in-service."

"I do?"

"Don't you remember last year? You got to play in the empty classrooms and meet your new teacher before all the other kids. It's been such a quiet summer. I'm ready to get back to work," Camille said with a smile Lacey hadn't seen in a while. "It'll be great. Just think positive and think of it as an adventure."

Lacey, on the other hand, was reluctant to go back to school, meet new people, start a new schedule. She had been perfectly content sitting under the oak tree all summer. She didn't want it to end, but it did. During the dreaded teacher in-service, before the other students arrived, Lacey met her new 2nd grade teacher and, fortunately, liked her immediately. She was a returning teacher and knew Lacey's situation very well. Mrs. Simpson had been one of the few teachers to be sympathetic to both Lacey and her mother. The school year started off well giving both mother and daughter a much needed boost in outlook. Even the threatened budget cuts that did not transpire failed to bring down their spirits. The first few weeks went without any problems at all.

The colds began a mere month after school began. They lasted a day or two, subsided then resurfaced about every six weeks. The doctors did every test imaginable. Blood, x-ray, CT, viral load, allergy testing, and even a psychologist. No definite diagnosis could be determined. Camille canceled their plans to drive up to Wildwood to visit her mother for Christmas after Lacey came down with the flu.

"Mommy, Mommy," Lacey called out from her bedroom in between sneezing fits early that spring, just days before the start of Spring Semester. "I'm sick." This cold was severe and lasted a full week. The day before, her best friend had fallen in the playground and sprained her wrist so severely an ambulance had to take her to the emergency room. It had upset Lacey so much she vomited right in the playground in front of her classmates. She could hear the boys snickering behind her back as she was led to the nurse's office.

Several weeks after returning to school following her 'embarrassment cold', Camille was called down to the nurse's office where she found Lacey with a runny nose sitting next to the principal.

"Mrs. Andreas," Principal Holbrook began with solemn demeanor. "I want you to know that I am sympathetic to your situation. I am. I'm not a cold man. However, your absences greatly affect your teaching. Your substitutes know your curriculum as well as, if not better than, you do."

"Yes, sir," stated Camille.

Lacey's stomach tightened. She just knew her mommy was in trouble.

He motioned for Camille to step out into the hall. "Now, because I am sympathetic I did some research. Calvary Academy is an online, virtual Christian school. They have several campuses all over Texas. The Academy caters to homeschoolers and recently developed online programs to add elementary grades. I called the president and told her about your situation. If you're interested, they'd like to interview you."

"I could work from home?" asked Camille.

Lacey's ears perked up. She had heard the words, virtual school, but didn't know what it meant. Home interested her.

"Yes, and Lacey could enroll at the school as a student," answered Principal Holbrook.

"I can call it a lay-off due to budget constraints so you can get a severance package," continued the principal. "That way you won't have a salary gap."

"Mr. Holbrook, I apologize for the problems my daughter and I have caused," began Camille.

"There is no need to apologize, Mrs. Andreas. We have no control over our lives. No matter how hard we try. Things happen and we as mortal humans must learn to live with the cards we've been dealt. Lacey isn't coping well. You need to be with her. You haven't allowed yourself to grieve because you have faith, and hope in a different outcome. Hope is good, but it has made you stagnant. Go home, Mrs. Andreas. Take care of your daughter. Calvary will provide you the means to do it."

"Thank you sir. Yes, I will call them."

"Here's the number. You can use my phone."

"Now?"

"Yes, now. I've got to make rounds." Principal Holbrook poked his head into the clinic, waved at Lacey, then walked away.

Less than a month after that very strange day, Lacey began her new school in the combination home office and classroom. The first few days were spent learning the computer system and how to do video chats. It seemed to her like a fun game and not at all like school. She had not spent much time on the computer except for the occasional trips to the library at school and video calls with her father. Now, she had a new laptop of her very own to use every day for her education.

Her mother had fifty new students, third through fifth grade. She spent her work days teaching virtual lessons, grading assignments, and helping the students one on one with the aid of video chat. When not teaching her virtual students, Camille helped Lacey with assignments from her new teacher, one they would never meet in person.

"Mommy, I like computer school," exclaimed Lacey one day after a successful video session with her teacher. "I don't get sick anymore!"

"You noticed that, did you?" Camille said with a wink and a hug.

"Uh huh. Lookie, I got all my work done for the week and it's Tuesday. Can we go to the park?"

"Sure, as soon as I've finished my work. You know, I heard your

Sunday School class is having a picnic after class. Would you like to go?"

Lacey's bright and cheery expression melted. "No, I don't think so I'd like to. I might get sick."

"Well, if you do," began Camille, "you won't have to worry about missing school."

"I know, but I like not being sick. I don't think I wish to go." Lacey picked up her book and marched to her room, a sign the conversation was over. She shut the door behind her and flopped onto the bed. Staring at the ceiling, clinging tightly to her bear, she said, "Daddy, you're not coming back are you?" Tears began to trickle down her cheeks. This time, she did not begin to cough.

Camille took Lacey to church on Sunday despite much protest. The little girls in Lacey's class were happy to see them, however, were not able to persuade Lacey to join in on their outing. Not wanting to cause a scene or worse, make Lacey ill, Camille reluctantly decided to return home. Before leaving the building, several of the women cornered Camille in the foyer and began asking her question after question.

"I heard you got laid off, I'm so sorry."

"How is virtual school going?"

"Have you heard any news of Michael?" asked the same woman who asked the same question every week.

Lacey listened as they discussed her as if she weren't there.

"Don't you think taking Lacey out of school is negative reinforcement? The girl needs to be in a social environment."

Lacey was surprised by that question since it was from a woman who's own child had learning disabilities and needed special attention.

"I heard you got fired. I'm sorry to hear that. I'll be praying for you," stated a woman who really didn't care, just wanted to know the latest gossip.

"Are you ready to start dating again?" asked a young divorcee. "I know someone you might like. Don't you think it's time to move on? "

Date? Lacey wasn't really sure what that meant but by the look on her mother's face, she knew it had to be a rude question. Camille grabbed her daughter's hand and rushed out the door without answering.

"Mommy?"

"Yes?"

"What is dating?" Lacey asked from the back seat while looking out the window.

"Don't pay any attention to them, sweetheart," stated her mother.

The rest of the car ride home was done in silence. Lacey knew something was wrong, that her mother had been upset by the church ladies. Camille continued her silence through lunch. The answer came that night after prayer when she heard muffled sounds coming from her mother's bedroom. Lacey sat next to the partially opened door and listened.

"Oh, Michael," Lacey heard her mother say through sniffs. "If you could be, you would be here. I don't know how I'm going to live without you. I don't know why I can't get any answers. I…I guess I have no choice but to put one foot in front of the other, take care of Lacey as best as I can and keep your memory alive for her. I'll never stop loving you, Michael, no matter where life takes me."

Lacey scooted closer and peeked in. Her mother looked sad, like the day the two men came, as she kissed the picture of her husband, replaced it on their dresser, then began the arduous, heartbreaking task of packing Michael's clothes. Lacey wanted to rush in and stop her. Tears fell as she watched her mother pack. Each shirt, each dress suit, each and every item held a memory, happy memories. When carefully folding his dress blues Lacey's mind flooded with memories. Ceremonies with important men in uniform. Picnics with families on base. The two flowered shirts brought back memories of Japan and all the fun they had at the beach. She didn't remember a lot of Japan, just that it was very crowded, even by the ocean. A pair of medical scrubs brought many tears to her mother's eyes. On his shirt pocket was an ink footprint. Lacey's from the day she was born. Camille put the shirt in a box of keepsakes on her side of the closet then broke down in tears.

"I can't do this," she cried. "Why God, why?" she sobbed. "I need him." Camille picked up her phone and punched a few buttons. "I can't do this," she told the person on the other end. "I thought it was time to pack Michael's clothes, but I can't. I hurts. I need him."

"You still haven't done it?" said the voice through the speaker. "Maybe you need him too much. Time to stand on your own two feet."

Camille's face began to get hot with anger. She threw her phone onto the bed and huffed, "Gee, thanks. That was so not helpful."

Lacey quietly retreated to her room. The sadness in her heart was overwhelming and she knew it would hurt her mother to know she had listened. It bothered her to see her father's belonging being packed away as if he were not coming home. He was, she insisted, he would return to her one day. Perhaps, she concluded, her mother was only packing his old clothes because she was going to buy him new outfits. That's what she did when Lacey grew out of her clothes. They boxed them up and bought new ones. This satisfied her enough to allow for a peaceful night's sleep.

Over the next few weeks, Camille and Lacey slowly packed up Michael's belongings. It was not to make room for new clothes, her mother had said upon questioning. Lacey reacted to the change the same way she always coped with change. This cold lasted an entire week. Even though Lacey said she understood why her mother was packing her father's things, she didn't like it.

"It's okay, Mommy. Daddy doesn't need his clothes anymore because he's in heaven now," Lacey said only to make her mother feel better.

"I know you miss him," stated Camille. She picked up a stack of Michael's shirts and placed them in a box. "I don't want you to think I've given up."

"Do you miss him?" she asked.

"Of course," answered Camille. "I will always love your father. I know he would rather be here with us."

"Heaven's supposed to be nice," answered Lacey.

"I'm sure it is. One day, when you are really old, you will see him there."

"That's kinda neat," stated Lacey. She looked down at her feet then quizzically back up at her mother. "Mommy?"

"Yes?"

"Are you going to get married again?"

"No. I…I don't know," stated Camille. "I haven't thought about it. How would you feel if I did?"

"I guess it would be okay," she said, deep in thought. "He can't already have a wife. And he has to be nice."

"Well, of course," Camille said with a slight laugh. "Hand me those boots. They go in this box."

"If you get married, will I get a brother or a sister?" Lacey said with one boot in each hand.

"Maybe. Would you like brothers and sisters?"

"A sister. I don't like boys. Missy has a brother. He's mean. Kai has two brothers. They are a lot older, 5th grade. She says they pick on her a lot."

"Oh, really?"

"Uh huh. Jenny has three little sisters. Triplets. She says she has fun playing with them."

"Maybe you could invite them over to play," suggested Camille. "You haven't seen your friends in a while."

"I think so I don't like to," stated Lacey matter-of-factly. Lacey dropped the last pair of boots into the box and marched to her room.

Lacey had become even more unsocial since starting virtual school. She liked the school, the classwork, and talking to people on video calls. She insisted she was happy and the only reason she did not want to have play dates was the fear of getting sick. Her mother, however, insisted that her immune system was just fine. She didn't get sick from the other children, she was told. It was stress, pure and simple, nothing else. That statement, unfortunately, just made the girl more determined to stay away from people. Even church was becoming a chore.

"We are going to church today," stated Camille in a commanding voice after missing several weeks in a row. "No arguments. You can cough, sneeze, cry, and throw up all the way there and back but we are going!"

"But Mommy," Lacey whined. "We didn't go last week!"

"I said no arguments young lady. Now, go get dressed!"

Lacey stuck out her bottom lip, retreated to her room and re-emerged in the worst outfit she could find. She stood in the living, arms crossed, in a pair of too-short blue jean pants, a pink tutu, and an orange Halloween t-shirt. On her feet were red flip flops. "I'm ready."

"Thank you," stated Camille, stifling a laugh.

Lacey had been sure the outfit would work. It didn't.

"You know, your immune system weakens when you are not around people. So, if you don't want to get sick you need to go out more."

"What does that mean?" Lacey cut in. "I don't get it."

"Never mind. Come on, I don't want to be late."

Outings with Lacey to church and to the grocery store went smoothly that Sunday and over the next few weeks with less and less protest. She still refused play dates and participated only the minimum amount necessary in her Sunday School class. Her mother, on the other hand, was noticeably frustrated with the women at church. Lacey could tell by the expression on her mother's face when they walked to the car. Her eyebrows scrunched together when she was mad. Even though they lived in a military town and several families in their church were in the military, none seemed to be true friends. Time after time, the woman Camille had admired for so many years let her down.

"We should go to lunch on Monday," Norma offered after church one day.

"I'd like that," answered Camille.

Monday morning, Norma called. Lacey answered.

"Mom's talking to a student," stated Lacey. "Can you hold for a minute?

"No, no. Not necessary, honey. Tell your mommy something's come up and I can't make our luncheon. Tell her, if she ever needs to talk, call me. Any time," stated Norma.

Camille returned the call later that day. Norma didn't answer.

When Norma asked Camille to look in on her house and water her plants when she went out of town, Camille and Lacey did so, happily.

"Thank you so much, Camille," Norma said upon her return. "I bought you a present. I'll give it to you on Sunday.

She didn't. In fact, Norma didn't even say hello that Sunday or the next.

"Does Mrs. Norma not like you anymore Mommy?" asked Lacey. "Is that why she didn't invite us to the pool party?"

Camille looked out the window over the kitchen sink with a blank stare towards the sky. She turned on the water to wash up for lunch and began slowly, "Sweetheart, I don't know why…"

The phone rang, startling them both.

"Maybe that's her," stated Lacey with a broad smile. Lacey pressed the answer-to-speaker button.

"Hello?" answered Camille.

"May I speak to Mrs. Andreas?"

"Speaking."

"Oh, hi. This is Lucas Ridgeway. You probably don't remember me. We went to high school together."

"Lucas?" Camille said thoughtfully.

"No matter. The reason I'm calling is your mother."

"Mother? What's wrong?"

"Well, maybe nothing. I routinely check in on her from time to time. She's still a member of the church, you know. Well, it's been a month now and I can't reach her. I've been by the house many times. I've called Willow. Can't reach her either. Willow had given me your number a while back and said if there was ever an emergency to call you. I was hoping you had heard from Amaryllis."

"No, I haven't," stated Camille. She dried her hands and stepped closer to the phone. "Mom travels a lot. Are you sure she's not just on one of her jaunts?"

"I don't think so. She usually tells people when she's traveling. Your mom likes to talk about her travels and her travel plans so usually we all know when she's coming and going."

"Maybe she just forgot," stated Camille. "Did Willow call you and say anything to you about Mom's memory?"

"No, why?"

"Because Willow wanted me to go check on her and at the time I couldn't. She was a little off last time she was here. I never heard anything after that. Mom and I don't talk a lot and she's never kept me in the loop."

"I'm sorry to hear that. So, should I be worried?" he asked.

"Probably not. I'll give Willow a call. If I need to, I'll come up this week-end. School's out so the timing is good. Maybe this is Willow's way of getting me to come up. Thanks for calling."

"School's over?" asked Lacey when her mom hung up the phone.

"Yes. You know that. Why do you think you were taking all those tests?"

Lacey shrugged. "Do we hav'ta go see Gramma?"

"Maybe. Might do us good to have a change of scenery." Camille pressed a few buttons on her phone, listened, then hung up. "Willow's not answering. I'll try her again in the morning."

******

A knock on the front door was a welcome interruption to a long day of reading. Lacey had been assigned one last book to read before her summer could begin. Her teacher, during their end-of-semester conference call, told both Lacey and her mother that she needed to practice reading out loud to improve her comprehension. Lacey didn't exactly know what that meant and was less than thrilled to read "The Lion, the Witch, and the Wardrobe."

"I'll get it!" Lacey exclaimed. She jumped up and ran to the door before her mother could protest.

"Look to see who it is first," instructed Camille.

"It's a lady. She's wearing a suit," stated Lacey. "Hi," she said to the lady after opening the front door just enough to peek out.

"Good morning. Is Mrs. Andreas home?" asked the tall, stern-looking woman.

"Yes, I'm Mrs. Andreas," said Camille, pulling the door open wider.

"I'm sorry to do this, Mrs. Andreas. But, rules are rules." She thrust her hand that clutched a sealed white envelope towards Camille. "Our office was told you were no longer eligible for housing."

Camille opened the envelope and read the letter. She shook her head. "I don't understand. I've never been informed about this or benefits or…"

"I don't make the rules, ma'am. I was instructed to inform you of the information in the letter. You can call the number on the bottom of the letter for further explanation. Good day." The lady gave a brief nod and walked away.

"Who's that, mommy?" asked Lacey.

"Finish your reading in your room, sweetheart. I've got to make some calls."

"But…" Lacey began. She didn't understand what it was all about, however, the furrow on her mother's forehead indicated bad news.

Camille shut the front door, walked quickly towards her bedroom and closed the door without answering. Lacey followed and sat by the door, trying to listen. Several minutes passed without being able to hear anything. She sighed a very loud audible groan then drug herself to her desk to retrieve her book. Something was wrong, she just knew it.

"Mommy's sad," Lacey said to her bear. "Why didn't she tell me what the lady gave her?" Lacey did not like not knowing what was going on. "What does el-gi-ble mean, Bear?"

"Good news, sweetheart," called out Camille a short time later. She had a broader than normal smile on her face.

Lacey looked over at her mother. A sudden change in mood was curious. "Daddy's coming home and we're moving to Hawaii?" She didn't really think that was it but it was what she wanted.

"We are going to Gramma's house for the summer! I'm going to get the suitcases out of the garage, then we'll go get more boxes."

"Why?"

"To pack."

"In boxes?"

"Well, we'll be gone a long time so we need to take everything with us."

"Everything?"

"Except the furniture. Go on now, start emptying your dresser onto your bed."

Lacey tried to protest by purposefully getting distracted with the toys in her closet. By the time her mother came back with the suitcases she had made a mess all over the floor and her bed. Instead of getting upset, which is what usually happened, her mother simply took the remaining clothes from the dresser and packed them in the suitcases. This irritated Lacey.

"What if Daddy comes home and we aren't here?" asked Lacey with a sniff. She wiped her nose on the back of her hand.

"I will take care of that. Don't you worry," answered Camille.

"What if Gramma doesn't want us to stay the whole summer?" she asked. A nervous feeling began in the pit of her stomach.

"Of course she does."

"She never answered her phone."

"How do you know that?"

"Well," Lacey didn't want to answer. "What about the kids you teach in the summer?"

"You worry too much, sweetheart."

"Did that lady tell you to go to Gramma's?"

"Enough questions. We have lots of packing to do and I've got a few errands to run before we leave."

"When?"

"When what?"

"When are we leaving?" Lacey plopped down on her bed with her bear. She fought tears while worrying about leaving her home.

"As soon as we're all packed and ready. Come now. No sad face. Think of this as a grand adventure. When was the last time we did anything fun?" Camille sat on the bed and gave her daughter a gentle squeeze.

"Nothing is fun without Daddy," Lacey sniffed. She then sneezed, blew her nose, and tried to think how packing up everything and going away for the summer to her grandmother's house was going to be an adventure. She had never even been to her Gramma's house. Not that she could remember.

"What would he say if he knew you were moping around here every day? Your daddy loves you and wants you to be happy. You and I both know…" Camille paused then continued with, "we both know that we must do our best to be brave and happy for Daddy. Do the best we can. I love and miss your daddy just as much as you do and I know he would be very sad to see you like this."

"Like what?" Lacey looked up at her mother inquisitively.

"Sad, sick all the time." Camille handed her daughter a tissue. "Not playing and having fun with your friends."

"But I thought if he came home and saw I was happy he would think I didn't miss him."

"That's not true at all. No, my dear Lacey. Daddy wants you to be a happy, full of life little girl. He knows you love him."

Lacey liked hearing the words, but didn't quite believe them. She followed her mother around the house, from room to room, robotically placing objects in boxes, fetching towels and paper to wrap dishes. Every item packed was questioned to the point of exhausting her mother. Lacey had not gone on vacation in a long, long time, but it didn't seem right to pack dishes, pots and pans, towels, sheets, books, and the computers. From time to time she sneezed, followed by a single cough. When her mother drove to the U-Move-It store to pick up a small trailer, she had a nervous, nauseated feeling in the pit of her stomach.

"Why do we need that?" Lacey asked with one hand rubbing her belly.

"Because we have a small car," answered her mother. She signed the paperwork, pulled her hair back with a clip, then took Lacey by the hand.

"But that's for moving, not for a trip to Gramma's house." Lacey began to cough on their way outside. "Why do we have to take the dishes out of the kitchen to go on vacation?"

"Because we do and I don't have room for everything we need to take in my car," she said without further explanation.

There was no time for further discussion. Lacey began coughing violently and threw up in the parking lot. This was too much change too fast and it sent Lacey into a downward spiral. After vomiting, she coughed so violently she began to hyperventilate. The manager of the U-Move-It store called 911. The ambulance arrived in less than five minutes. Lacey and her mother knew the EMS paramedic well as they had seen her in the ER on several occasions. After a few minutes of oxygen, Lacey's pulse and respiratory rate returned to normal, however, she had spiked a fever.

"Do you want us to take her to the hospital?" asked the paramedic.

"No, that won't be necessary." Camille said with an apologetic shake of the head. She sighed and looked at her daughter's tear-streaked face. "I have her meds at home."

"If her fever spikes, call us or bring her in," the paramedic instructed while filling out paperwork.

"I know the drill," said Camille.

Chapter 3

Two days later, Lacey's temperature returned to normal, however, she still coughed and sneezed fitfully when sitting up. The medication her mother gave her kept the coughs and sneezes to a minimum only as long as she was calm or sleeping. While she slept, Camille had finished packing the house. It was now bare except for the furniture. That night after dinner of a delivered pizza, Lacey was told they would be leaving their home and taking the long road trip to her grandmother's house early the next morning. While laying in the middle of the living room floor on the pallet made up from her mother's comforter, Lacey looked up at the fireplace mantle. Her Daddy's precious gifts were no longer there. Packed away safely, her mother had said. The anxiety-riddled little girl eventually cried herself to sleep while clutching Bear. Her mother could do nothing to console Lacey no matter how many times she was sung to, read to, prayed over, or reasoned with. Before dawn, Lacey was awakened and led to the packed car where she sleepily buckled her seat belt then closed her eyes tight. She tried to remember the day she and her parents moved into their house. The memories would not come. She remembered playing in the back yard, riding her bike down the street, and being tucked into bed by her Daddy who knelt beside the bed for nighttime prayers. Lacey opened her backpack and pulled out a picture.

She touched the paper and said, "Come home, Daddy. I miss you." After pressing the photograph to her chest, Lacey fell fast asleep.

The drive was long and boring. Lacey woke up after a few hours, coughed and sneezed until re-medicated, read a book, drew in her sketchbook purchased for the purpose of the trip, picked at her hamburger during the lunch break, then stared out the window until she was lulled to sleep again by the hum of the engine.

"Lacey, wake up. We're almost at Gramma's."

"I'm hungry," Lacey said in her faint, weak voice in between coughs. This was not surprising since most meals the past few days had been turned away due to lack of appetite. She rubbed her eyes and sat up. "Where are we? It looks like a forest."

"This is Wildwood," stated Camille.

The long, 2-lane road was flanked on either side with tall pine and majestic oak trees. The leaves were bright green and lush. Dotted in between the tree line and the road were patches of wildflowers. Red, yellow, and orange flowers gleamed in the bright sunlight. Lacey's curiosity was piqued. She looked back and forth, left and right, as they drove. Ever so often she spotted a house deep in the woods, shaded by the trees. The car slowed when they approached a small hut in the middle of the road. No one was in the hut and the great wooden bar that probably should have been blocking their path was sticking up in the air like it had been left there for years to wave at cars as they drove through. Up ahead was a small gray building. When the car turned the corner, Lacey read the sign.

"Wildwood Pit Stop. What's that mean, Mommy?"

"It's a little grocery store and gas station."

"Oh. How much longer?"

"Beyond the lake, over the bridge, and around the corner."

Lacey looked out the front window and there it was, the cutest little lake she had ever seen. On one side was a beach with pure white sand that climbed up a small hill and ended at a grassy park where picnic tables sat under oak trees. One large pavilion stood alone and empty. Beyond the trees was a small playground and a little building. Flowers in summer bloom surrounded its perimeter. A wooden platform floated in the water half way to the center of the lake. The opposite side of the lake was grassy, tree lined, and bare except for two wooden piers. Several swans swam gracefully near the beach. No other activity in or around the lake.

"Can we go there sometime?" asked Lacey. She liked the lake immediately. Especially since there wasn't anyone nearby or in the lake. To her, the lake was peaceful and serene.

"I'm sure we can later, when you're feeling better. I used to swim in that lake when I was a little girl. My dad even took us on boat rides and fishing trips. There were lots of kids here in the summer. We came here quite often before your grampa died. My sister and I used to ride our bikes all over the neighborhood. There were only a few houses back then. And a horse farm way back in the back."

"No kids now." Lacey blew her nose and sat up a little with the blanket pulled up to her chin.

"No. That's odd, especially on such a pretty, sunny day."

"Why?"

"I haven't been here in a long time and it looks exactly the same. Except no people. The place looks abandoned."

"Is that bad?" Lacey studied every inch of the lake as they drove slowly by. It looked fine to her. Not shiny new like the park she used to go to, but pretty.

"It just looks run down. Like it hasn't been used," answered Camille. "Gramma's house is over the bridge and right around the corner. The side of her property is across from the bath house. See." She pointed to the fence covered in vines in front with a tall hedge on the other side. "If you go straight, if I remember correctly, you can drive all the way around the lake. We turn there, at Blythe Street."

"Hey that's Gramma's last name," Lacey said, surprised.

"That's right."

"What's the bridge for?" asked Lacey. "No river."

"If I remember correctly," began Camille as they drove slowly over the one-lane wooden bridge, "There is a stream that flows into the lake at the north end and this is the exit point, where the water flows south. Looks like it's been plugged, maybe to keep the lake from drying up."

Lacy shrugged, not really listening to the information. Her attention was focused on the landscape of her grandmother's home. She couldn't believe her eyes. The driveway that led to the large, old house was made of gravel. It made an odd crunching noise as they drove over it. The front yard wasn't a yard at all. It was full of wildflowers and tall grass. Red clay pots sat haphazardly on either side of the driveway as if they were put there on purpose but not exactly neatly. In them were large green plants of different kinds. Some had tomatoes hanging over the edge. Some contained flowers and others Lacey had no idea what they were. Many of the pots held cacti of various species. A lot of the plants looked like nothing more than weeds. Sitting in front of the garage was Gramma's old van. The garage door was open and inside there were boxes, crates, and rubber tubs from floor to ceiling lining the walls. On the right side of the front door was an enormous metal sculpture, an arch of some kind, with flowering vines weaving in and out of the metal frame. Under the arch was a bench made from drift wood.

"Gramma's house is creepy," said Lacey when the car came to a stop. She looked up at the house. The paint was faded, but not peeling. Brightly painted window boxes under both the downstairs and upstairs windows were overflowing with colorful flowers and flowering vines.

"Mom likes wild things, wild plants, wild animals, antiques. Not expensive antiques, just old stuff."

"Why don't she mow the grass?"

"She likes it to look natural."

"She likes weeds?"

"To her, they aren't weeds. It's nature. Ready to see your Gramma?"

Lacey shrugged. She'd rather be back in her own home and in her own room. Ready or not, she was about to start her summer adventure. Lacey was not an adventurous little girl. Why her mother had used that word to get her excited was confusing. Lacey's idea of adventure was reading a new book. She opened the car door and stared while contemplating whether or not to get out.

Camille got out of the car and walked around to her daughter. She felt her forehead and frowned. "You feel warm still, but I think it's more from the blanket. It's much too hot to be wrapped up. Come on." She loosened the blanket and lifted Lacey out of her seat. "Would you like to ring the doorbell?"

Lacey shook her head no and retreated to the protection of her mother's back. "My tummy hurts. I think I'm going to be sick."

"Well, looks like she's not here," stated Camille after pressing the button and knocking several times while ignoring Lacey's moanings. "Good thing I have a key."

Lacey didn't think that was so good. She pulled a tissue out of her pocket and blew her nose.

Camille fished the key out of her purse, inserted it into the lock, and carefully pushed the door open. "Whew. No alarm."

Lacey peeked around her mother's waist as they stepped inside the dark house. The curtains were drawn and there were no lights on. All Lacey could see were dark shadows and even darker shadows. She jumped when her mother flipped on a light. "Gramma lives here?" she exclaimed.

The living room was full of bookcases and cabinets and more stuff than Lacey had ever imagined could be in someone's house. Boxes covered haphazardly with old blankets crowded the hallways and walkways. Two cats, one black the other grey with stripes jumped out of baskets sitting on an old leather couch and ran towards a doorway on the left. An old Western saddle perched precariously on a tattered wooden post looked like it could have been tossed there by its owner after a long ride. A pair of well-worn cowboy boots accompanied it. Every inch of the walls was covered in paintings, drawings, tapestries, and hand-woven things that Lacey had never seen before. The staircase to the right of the front door was cluttered with baskets. Each basket was filled to the brim with all sorts of different things, a lot of which Lacey could not name. She wondered if her grandmother intentionally decorated her house like this or if it was just messy.

"Mother!" Camille called out. "Mother, it's Camille. Are you here?"

A dog suddenly began barking from behind a set of French doors. Their glass panes were painted with colorful designs. Lacey followed closely as her mother walked towards the doors. They both leaned forward and tried to look through the colored glass. Lacey's stomach began to churn with butterflies and she sneezed several times when her mother turned the handle and pushed open the door.

Just beyond the doors was a bricked-in patio garden. Various plants similar to the ones in the front yard surrounded the patio in a scattering of clay pots, old tin cans, large rusted watering cans, rubber boots, hollowed out tree trunks and a free-standing wooden fence section with tennis shoes sprouting purple flowers. A rustic, weather-worn shed just beyond the fence was adorned with metal and glass artwork. There were two paths, one straight ahead made of flat rocks and a second, narrow dirt path, on the far right side of the patio.

"Gramma's funny," giggled Lacey.

"Come on. I hear the dog down this path."

Down the rock path flanked by tall grass and around the corner, Lacey and her mother found Amaryllis standing over a large brick Bar-B-Que. She had her back to them, stirring a black kettle. The dog, a large collie, sat beside her with her tail wagging. The dog barked but Amaryllis didn't pay any attention.

"Mother," called out Camille. "Mother!" she said a little louder. "It's Camille."

"Well, well, well," said Amaryllis over her shoulder. "Look what the duck dragged in. Come closer. I'm making blackberry jam. If I stop stirring it'll stick."

"Hi Gramma," Lacey said with a shy wave.

"Hey there honeybunch. Come give your granny a hand." Amaryllis grabbed a cinder block and plopped it in front of the pot. "Here, stir."

Lacey looked over at her mother, who gave her a nod, then stepped up to the pot, sniffed loudly, then began to stir.

"It's blackberry season, you know," began Amaryllis. "If I don't go pickin' as soon as they're ripe the varmits'll get 'em. The woods up near Lufkin have the best berries and I got a whole cooler full this year. My jam sells out every year, you know. Hush now, Diaz," she said to the dog. "Go find Troy."

"Who's Troy, Mother?"

"Her brother. He likes to chase rabbits. Some days I don't see him from breakfast to dinner. Now, as soon as that's thickened we have to jar 'em. Good thing you're here. I could use a hand. I've got the jars all ready to go in the kitchen."

"Mommy, I hav'ta pee," said Lacey. "My tummy hurts."

"Oh mercy me. Are you sick? She looks dreadful pale, Cami. This way child." Amaryllis took the pot by the handles and headed toward the house. "Get the door, Cami and don't let Diaz in. This way girls," she said, leading Lacey and her mother into the kitchen. "The bathroom's right there." Amaryllis pointed to a door. "The one on the right. The other goes to the garage."

Lacey nodded and opened the door on the right. She was a bit scared of what she might find. Toilet, sink, and a big stick with three forks. On one the toilet paper, the other two towels. Peculiar, but not scary.

Gramma was busy telling her daughter how to put the jam in the jars when Lacey emerged. She sat on a stool and listened as her grandmother chatted on and on about jam making and how and where she was planning on selling. The large kitchen was decorated like the rest of the house, with lots of unusual stuff on the counters and walls. Old black pots, baskets, a picture frame with old spoons, hand painted tea-cups. Lacey felt like she was in a museum or an arts and crafts store or maybe even an art school for old people. The old people thought popped in her head when she realized how strange the house smelled. Musty like a farm mixed with the time she had visited the nursing home with her Sunday School class.

"Mother, don't you want to know why we're here?" asked Camille.

"Well, now that I think of it. Y'all should've called first."

"I did. Several times."

"Like I said. I just got back from Lufkin. Why are you traveling all the way up here with a sick child anyway?"

"Mr. Ridgeway was concerned. He called."

"Nosy young man. Nice but nosy. Why would he be concerned about me? Did that neighbor of mine complain again?"

"Not that I know of, Mother. Lacey's fine," she said with a knowing look to her daughter. "How's Willow?"

"Who? Oh, Willow," said Amaryllis busily pouring liquid into jars. "I don't know. You know how your sister is. She never calls. Lives right down the street and never visits. She only complains when she does, so no matter. Busy she says. 'I'm busy, Mom. I'm working the night shift.' The girl needs a husband. All she does is work."

"She called me, too. Was worried about you."

"Worried? Her? Why? If that girl was ever worried about her momma she would come see me. What's all this fuss about?"

"Beats me," stated Camille. "But, I thought we'd come up for a visit for the summer. Make sure you were okay and just get out of town for a little vacation. Lacey's not good with stress, makes her ill, and I thought a change of scenery, even if traumatic at first, might be good for her. You know, fresh air and all."

"You happen to be in luck that I'm here. You know I was planning on a trip up north to go to the art festival. Then I remembered the blackberries and decided to stay put and make jelly. The berries up near Lufkin are ripe this time of year. I got a whole cooler full of them. When we're done I'm going to have a little sale at the lake. Make a little money for a trip up north."

"Yes, you said that," stated Camille. "Did Lucas come by last week?"

"Who?"

"Lucas Ridgeway."

"Oh. No. Don't think so. I don't hear the door bell when I'm out back, you know."

"You should get an answering machine."

"For the doorbell?"

"No, Mother. For your phone. So when Lucas or Willow calls they can leave a message. That way people won't worry about you."

"I have one of those contraptions. It's over there under the pine cones, I think. I don't like it."

"Mommy, I'm hungry," stated Lacey. She was getting bored. Hungry, but mostly bored.

"I don't have a big dinner planned but I can make sandwiches," stated Amaryllis.

"Thanks, Mother. While you do that, I'm going to get a few things out of the car."

"I'll come with you." Lacey got up and started to follow her mother.

"No, you stay put and eat something. I'll be back in a jiffy."

***

"How long are you planning on staying?" Amaryllis asked after the last dish from dinner was put away and the groceries Camille brought in from the car had been organized in the cabinets.

"I'd like to stay for the summer, if that's alright with you," stated Camille. "I don't have any tutoring lined up and Lacey needed a change of scenery."

Lacey shook her head in protest. She really did not want to spend her entire summer at this strange place. In fact, she was ready to go home immediately.

"Well then. Let's find you a place to sleep. If you had called, your room would be ready. Since you didn't, we'll have to clean up a bit," stated Amaryllis.

"I told you I tried calling, Mother."

"No matter. I'm glad you girls are here. This way." Amaryllis took Lacey by the hand and led her up the stairs, pushing boxes out of the way as they went up. "Shoo, Memphis," she said to one of the cats who blocked their path.

Lacey sneezed several times. "What is all this stuff?" she asked when they entered the room.

"My art supplies. Paint brushes for oil painting," Amaryllis said, pointing at each box. "Feathers for later. Buttons. These are great for all sorts of things. Paint. Ribbons for weaving. Clay, broken pottery. Here, move this box. It has seashells in it," Amaryllis said. "I have clean sheets in the closet there," she pointed to a door covered in a

Mexican-style blanket. Picking up a cardboard box off the bed, Amaryllis stated, "This is my next project, paper making. I've been collecting magazines and newspapers for months."

Lacey looked around the bedroom. It was about the same size as her bedroom but seemed smaller filled with the boxes and baskets overflowing with odds and ends. A folding table underneath the window held canvases of unfinished paintings and several drawing pads. Tin cans held brushes, pencils, pens, and a few feathers. She sniffed at the peculiar odor in the air. Sour, like wet towels forgotten in the washing machine. She sneezed again.

Camille looked at her daughter with concern, felt her forehead, then turned on the ceiling fan and opened the window. "The room needs to be aired out, Mother. Do you have your AC on?"

"No, it hasn't been on all summer. I can turn it on for the night, I suppose. I sleep downstairs where it's cooler. I'll go check to make sure it works." Amaryllis dropped the sheets onto the bed and hurried downstairs.

"It smells and it's hot," whined Lacey. "I wanna go home."

"Once the air is on it'll cool off. I'll get the allergy meds out of the car in a minute. Help me make up the bed."

"Where are we going to put our suitcases?"

"In the closet. There's room. Mother hasn't had company in a long while and since she wasn't expecting us, we will just have to do a little cleaning ourselves."

"It's dusty." Lacey ran her finger over the night stand. "I think so I don't like it here. It's hot and scary. And the cats make me sneeze. What's that noise?" she asked when a boom and a clank made her jump.

"Air conditioner is on!" Amaryllis called from the bottom of the steps.

"This is a big place, sweetheart," said Camille. She knelt down, placed both of Lacey's hands in her own, and looked her daughter in the eyes.

"You can spend most of the day outside and once we get this room cleaned up, you'll feel a lot better. There are lots and lots of places to explore. Maybe Gramma can teach you some of her crafts. Now, I'm going to finish unloading the car and see about putting the rest of the boxes in the garage. Come with me and get your backpack and then we can get ready for bed."

Lacey groaned at the thought of sleeping in that big bed that was not her own. She wanted to be back in her own bed in her own house. It had been a very, very long time since she had been to a sleepover. The last time was with the girls from church, in the church building with sleeping bags, popcorn, and movies. Her mother was there along with several other mothers. Never had she slept in a hotel or someone else's bed. Summer at Gramma's house was going to be miserable, she determined, and feared she would be sick the entire time. Lacey looked around the cramped room, sniffed, wiped her nose on the back of her hand, coughed, then followed her mother to the car.

***

A dog barking off in the distance woke Lacey early the next morning. She opened her eyes and nearly let out a scream. A large cat sat next to her head, purring softly. In a state of panic, she froze. The cat sensed movement, turned its head and kissed Lacey on the nose.

"That tickles," she giggled softly. Lacey rolled over to see if her mother was awake. She wasn't. Ever so quietly, the curious and anxious little girl slipped out of bed. The cat jumped down and followed Lacey downstairs. The other cat slept quietly on a box next to the stairs until the first cat pounced and woke her up. Lacey smiled watching them play.

The rooms downstairs were nearly all dark. Faint morning light from an open French door helped Lacey to see and make her way towards the back patio. She looked up at the trees to find the birds that were chirping happily in the early dawn. A noise from down the path drew Lacey's eyes. Around the corner emerged Amaryllis carrying an empty tray.

"Hi," Lacy waved.

"Well now, good morning," stated Amaryllis. "Feeling better?"

Lacey shrugged. "What'cha doin'?"

"Feeding the deer and the other critters. You hungry?"

Lacey nodded. "What critters?" she asked mimicking her grandmother.

"You'll see after breakfast. Mommy sleeping? She looked tired yesterday. And you've both lost weight since I last saw you. Hungry?" Amaryllis asked again.

Lacey nodded again. There was no point in speaking because Amaryllis immediately started talking about her latest project, the jam she had just made, and her plans for future projects, including homemade paper. Lacey simply bobbed her head up and down while she ate. Occasionally, a cat or two jumped on the table or onto her lap. They were shooed away then ignored, which Lacey learned cats do not like. Diaz and Troy pushed open the back door to demand attention from Amaryllis and her guest. They chased the cats away then sat down by Lacey's feet. All was quiet for about two seconds until the dogs heard movement coming from the living room.

"Get down!" Camille ordered.

"Just give'em a little love, Cami," stated Amaryllis with a laugh.

"I'd rather not. Good morning sweetheart." Camille kissed Lacey gently on the forehead. "You look better today. No sniffles?"

"Mostly better. Can we go outside now and see the critters?" asked Lacey. Her nose was clear and she hadn't coughed all morning, however, her weak muscles were a little weary from all the activity the day before. She got up and put her bowl in the sink. The dogs followed her, trapping her against the counter until she scratched them, one at a time, behind the ears.

"What critters?" asked Camille. "You mean there's more?"

"Yes. So, tell me again why you're here," asked Amaryllis. She poured her daughter a bowl of cereal from a box she didn't recognize. "Where'd this come from?"

"I brought that with me," began Camille. "I told you, Mother, we came to visit because Willow and Lucas, the man from church, were worried about you. But, that's not the only reason. We needed a change."

"Well, then. As you can see, I am just fine. Y'all can stay for a bit. I was planning on going to Denton for the arts and crafts festival later in the summer."

"When was the last time you drove that far, Mother?"

"No matter. I was still going," she huffed. Amaryllis turned and opened the pantry door.

"Mother!" Camille exclaimed. "What are you doing with that thing?"

Lacey jumped at the sight of the rifle in her grandmother's hands. It was long and brown and looked kind of like the guns she had seen at the military museum.

"This here's my BB gun. I take it on walks sometimes. Especially early in the morning and evening. We have prowlers."

"You didn't take it this morning," stated Lacey.

"I forgot. I bring it out now because I want you two to know it's here. Sometimes at night I hear things in the woods and the dogs go crazy. I bought this for protection. It's only a BB gun but the bad guys don't know it."

"Is it loaded?" asked Camille.

"I think so. Haven't checked in a while. Never shot it since I bought it. The man at the gun store showed me how to use it, so it's safe," insisted Amaryllis.

"When was that, Mother?"

"Oh, a while back." Amaryllis returned the gun to the closet and headed towards the back French doors. "Come on. I'll give you the grand tour."

Lacey followed her grandmother down the rock path. They stopped for a moment at the Bar-B-Que. Amaryllis started talking about fire safety and making sure the coals were cold. She listened carefully to the story about how the pit was made. Apparently, the bricks were found in that exact spot by the man who built the house. He didn't know where they had come from or what they had been used for. When he asked Amaryllis and her husband about them, they suggested he leave them and build the Bar-B-Que. Lacey asked if that's when she started collecting and her Gramma just laughed. The two dogs rushed by them, distracting Amaryllis from her storytelling, seemingly anxious to explore. Lacey followed the dogs down the path and stopped in front of a large, old, faded red barn.

"I didn't see this before," Lacey stated.

"Well now, that's because it's hidden behind the trees," stated her grandmother.

"It smells funny." Lacey turned to her mother and held her nose.

"Manure," stated Camille.

"What's that?" asked Lacey.

"Poop," said Amaryllis. "Come on." She walked around to the far right side of the barn to two pens. "This here," she said pointing to a large brown and white pig, "is John. Never throw your dinner scraps away. He eats them."

Lacey's eyes grew wide. "Can I touch it?" she asked while moving cautiously up to the fence.

"No," blurted Camille before Lacey reached out her hand.

"Yes, you can," Amaryllis said with a laugh. "He doesn't bite. Come John. Meet Lacey." Amaryllis opened a small gate and motioned for Lacy to enter the pen.

"Be careful, honey," said Camille.

The timid little girl looked over at her mother, her grandmother, the pig then took two steps forward. The pig grunted and waddled over towards Amaryllis. Lacey stopped frozen in her tracks when she realized the pig was almost as big as she was. A noise from the other pen distracted both pig and Lacey.

"What's that?" Lacey pointed and moved away from the pig towards the sound. "Hey, Mommy, it's a tiny little horse!"

"That's Muffin," stated Amaryllis. "She's a miniature. I use her mane and tail hairs for weaving. The tapestry in the living room was made from her hair."

"Can I ride her?" asked Lacey, not really sure she wanted to.

"No," stated her mother.

"Your mother is right, this time," said Amaryllis. "Muffin is not for riding. You can brush her and lead her around the yard, but she's too small to ride, even by a tiny little thing such as yourself."

"Oh," stated Lacey with a frown.

"Well now, let me show you the barn." Amaryllis took Camille by the elbow and led her inside while talking nonstop about weaving with hair collected from her miniature horse.

Lacey remained at the pen to watch the miniature horse eat hay. She thought her Gramma's chatter was getting boring. "This is so weird," she said to the horse. "My Gramma lives in a zoo."

Just then, Troy, the black lab mix ran out of the barn, brushed the back of Lacey's legs, and ran off around the corner of the horse pen. Curious, Lacey followed. A small dog-trot path led down the side of the fence and through the woods. She walked slowly at first and then began to jog to catch up with the dog who seemed to be waiting for her. Together they made their way through the thicket of trees until they came to the road. Across the street was the lake. Lacey was about to turn and go back when Troy dashed across the street.

"Wait for me!" she called out. Lacey looked both ways then ran as fast as her underused legs could carry her across the narrow road. Once safely on the other side, she stopped to catch her breath. She inhaled deeply, waiting for a cough or a sneeze. When it didn't happen, she trotted after the dog who was now on the beach chasing the swans.

The lake was completely empty, exactly like it had been the day before. Lacey thought it odd since it was a warm, sunny day. She wondered where all the children were. Only the swans and the dog occupied the lake. As she stood at the edge of the beach, Lacey contemplated taking off her shoes. She knelt down and felt the sand. It was warm and didn't stick to her fingers like the sand at the ocean. Instead of taking off her shoes or walking in the sand, she sat on the picnic table and watched Troy run up and down by the water's edge. Giggles could hardly be contained when the dog jumped in the water sending the birds flying off in every direction.

"I like it here," Lacey said to herself. "At the lake anyway."

Troy ran up to Lacey then shook himself, spraying water all over her.

"Hey," she said, starting to get mad. "That kinda feels good. It's hot. Come on dog, I'm thirsty."

Lacey headed back towards the path in the woods. Troy followed as far as the far side of the road then darted off into the underbrush. Not liking being alone, she ran until she reached the edge of the horse pen then stopped to catch her breath. Muffin stood at the fence with his nose between two bottom rails trying to reach a patch of grass just out of reach.

"Here you go," she said. Lacey grabbed a handful of grass and held it out for the horse who grabbed the whole bunch. His nose tickled her hand causing her to jump. "Hey, no biting." Lacey watched for a few minutes longer then, remembering the heat and her thirst, strolled back to the house.

"Well now, there y'all are," stated Amaryllis from the porch. She was shredding newspapers into a plastic bin. "Your mommy was looking for you."

"Oh."

"She's upstairs. Scoot now."

Lacey stopped just short of the top step. Her mother had one box in her arms and another she was pushing with her foot out the bedroom door.

"There you are, Lacey," she said, looking for a place to set the box. "Give me a hand. Open that door." Camille nodded towards the room next to theirs.

"What's Gramma doing out there?" asked Lacey. She stood with her back against the door to hold it open.

"Don't know. I've been up here cleaning," she answered. "Oh, good grief. Not this room, too."

The room was filled to capacity with boxes and bags, buckets, jars, old picture frames, a loom, and a spinning wheel.

"What about the other one?" Lacey pointed across the hall.

"I haven't tried those rooms yet." Camille dropped the boxes in front of the door and pushed them in. "It's been so long since I've been here I don't remember. By the way, where were you?"

"Oh, I followed the dog to the lake."

"The lake? You shouldn't go over there by yourself. Don't do it again, please."

"Okay. There wasn't anyone there. And I looked before crossing the street. No cars anywhere. The dog was playing with the swans. I didn't go near the water or anything, I promise."

"Fine, just don't run off again. Wonder why Mother said she didn't come up here much. Well, she said she didn't sleep up here. Obviously, she's been here." Camille opened the door on the right to find pretty much the same thing as the other rooms.

"Is Gramma one of those people you see on TV that collected lots and lots of stuff and they have to hire a 'sa-chi-tris to clean?"

"You mean a psychiatrist. No, your grandmother is not a hoarder." Camille stepped into the room then said under her breath, "I don't think."

"She likes arts and crafts, huh?" asked Lacey. She poked through a box of leather purses then another box full of fabric.

"That she does," answered Camille. "One more room." Camille opened the door slowly.

"Hey that's a real bedroom," stated Lacey. There were no boxes in this room. The bed was made up with a blue-flowered bedspread. Two dressers sat with perfectly clean tops on either side of the window. "Why didn't Granma put us in this room?"

"I'm not sure…"

Chapter 4

"Girls, it's time for my walk. Come join me," Amaryllis called from the bottom of the stairs later that day when the clouds rolled in and hid the sun making the day a bit cooler.

Lacey took her mother by the hand and they walked down the stairs together. Neither had a chance to ask about the bedroom because Amaryllis immediately started talking about her neighbors and the community of Wildwood until they reached the front yard.

"Well now, what's this?" Amaryllis pointed at the trailer still attached to Camille's car. "Is there something you need to tell me?"

"Not now, Mother," said Camille then quickly changed the subject. "I have to return it tomorrow. Tell me about the neighborhood." She took Lacey by the hand and led them to the street, away from the distraction of the trailer.

"Not much has changed," said Amaryllis once they had turned out of the driveway. Her two dogs ran ahead of them, leading the way. "Well now, that house there is a summer house. The Munoz family will be here in a week or two." She pointed to a small cottage in the woods. "The two lots on either side of them never sold. I told you the developer went bankrupt. Right around the time I moved here, I think. That's why this side is empty and the golf side is full. The golf side is closer to town and the builders were different than this side. They had the big bucks."

"This area was supposed to be a resort, wasn't it?" asked Camille.

"Well, yes, I suppose. The town benefited from the golf course. So they partnered up. That's why I bought up the land around me. Did not want those golf people anywhere close to me."

Lacey tuned out her grandmother while she went on and on about the home builders and how she severely disliked the golf community. Business talk was boring so Lacey trailed behind a bit to stop and look at the flowers, trees, squirrels, birds, and whatever else the dogs seemed to be interested in. To this young girl, who had been living in the city most of her life, her grandmother's neighborhood seemed like an enchanted forest with wild things and neighbors far, far away from one another. She was a bit hesitant to enjoy herself, however. Part of her wanted to go home and sit and read in her room, be where she was comfortable and safe. Her curious side wanted to know all about the woods. What was in them, the names of all the trees and flowers, and who lived in the houses that seemed to be empty.

"Now that house," said Amaryllis a bit louder than necessary. She stood in the middle of the street and pointed. "Lamont and Beverly live there. I don't know if you ever met them."

"No, I don't believe I have," stated Camille.

Lacey looked up at the house her grandmother was talking about. It was a small, one-story brick house. The yard was vastly different from her grandmother's with neatly trimmed bushes and pristine flower beds. Bright pink little flowers were all lined up in neat rows. A lace curtain near the front door was drawn back as if a finger held it. Lacey thought she saw someone in the window so raised her hand to wave. The curtain immediately fell closed.

"Those two are not friendly at all. Now, I've done my best to be neighborly. You know me. I try to be as nice and Christianly as I can to everyone. They complain about my house, my yard, my animals. Everything. I know it's just because they are sad and lonely so I don't hold any ill feelings." Amaryllis smiled and waved at the drawn curtain then continued to walk.

"Why are they sad?" Lacey asked.

"Well, honey," began Amaryllis, "they're just lonely. Lonesome people get grumpy sometimes."

"You're not grumpy," said Lacey.

"I'm not lonely," answered Amaryllis. "Now, around the corner..." she continued without letting Lacey get another word in.

Lacey turned around and looked at the window. Even though it was closed, she knew they were being watched. She waved again at the house then turned and ran to catch up to her grandmother who had not stopped her narrative. The rest of the walk went by uneventfully. There were no other neighbors outside or at the window to say hello to. Not even children. The dogs ran in and out of the woods while Amaryllis told everything she knew about every parcel of land, every homeowner past and present, and which owner died and left their land to this relative or that. They walked past a half dozen or so for-sale signs. Most of them looked like they had been there for years because the letters were faded and the signs cracked and rusty.

The trek around the neighborhood had taken much longer than Lacey had imagined. She needed to stop and rest many times. Her tired little legs and the heat slowed everyone, even the dogs. Amaryllis led Lacey and her mother up and down Blythe Street. A left turn at the bottom of the hill took them around the perimeter of the lake towards a wooded, undeveloped area and an unfinished bridge. Her grandmother shortened her usual route with the promise to do the full course again soon.

"Can we go over there?" Lacey pointed towards the newer, more developed neighborhood once they had rounded a clump of trees which had hidden it from sight. Their walk had taken them up Blythe Street then back down, turned left to go part way around the lake, then stopped at an unfinished bridge on the far side which led to the back of the golf development.

"No!" Amaryllis said bluntly. "I do not go there."

"Ever?"

"They leave me alone and I leave them alone. That's the way it's always been. I can show y'all the old horse farm later, if you want," Amaryllis said pointing to the left fork in the road. The older woman then pivoted and marched back to her house in silence.

"Mother," began Camille as soon as they entered the front door. "Why didn't you put Lacey and I in the bedroom on the left of the stairs?"

"That's my room," stated Amaryllis.

"You said you don't sleep upstairs."

"I don't."

"So, why not let us use it? It's clean."

"Well, I don't know. It's my room. I put you in the guest room."

"Yes, I understand, Mother, but the other three rooms are filled with boxes and your craft stuff."

"Art supplies," corrected Amaryllis.

"My point, Mother, is that you have one room that is spotless and…"

"Are you saying my house is a mess?" asked Amaryllis with a huff. She turned and headed out the back door.

"No, Mother, that's not what I'm saying." Camille followed.

Lacey picked up a stack of paper, followed the conversation, and wondered if her grandmother was going to get mad and make them leave. "Gramma," she began. "Could I sleep in your room? Please? The other one makes me sneeze."

"Well, yes you can honeybunch," Amaryllis said as if she were speaking to a baby. "It wouldn't be any fun at all if you were sick on vacation, now would it? Cami, you should have put little Lacey in my room last night. I don't use it. And you wouldn't have had to spend all morning cleaning."

Camille shook her head and said, "Yes, Mother."

Lacey helped her mother move Lacey's suitcases into the room now referred to as the 'clean room'. They then emptied the contents of the trailer into the garage, which was difficult since it was nearly full to begin with. Camille did the majority of the work with Lacey being so tired from the walk and the garage so dirty. Once Lacey had exhausted the remainder of her energy, she spent the rest of the day reading by the barn while her mother took the trailer to town. The cluster of large oak trees between the house and the barn made for a perfect reading spot providing shade and just enough grass to sit on. From time to time she got up and watched the animals but did not quite get up the courage to pet them. Troy ran back and forth between the woods and the barn. He sat with Lacey while she read, then when she got up to stretch her legs he trotted off. Several minutes later, he returned and sat down again. Lacey was curious about where he went but not enough to make her want to follow him, especially since her mother told her not to.

The next morning, Lacey jumped out of bed as soon as she heard the back door open. She ran to her mother's room and looked out the window. Walking down the path, there was Amaryllis carrying a tray of what looked to be leftovers from dinner. A short time later, she returned with an empty tray.

"What's wrong honey?" Camille asked sleepily.

"Nothing. Just watching Gramma. She's feeding the pig."

"Maybe you could start helping her," suggested Camille.

Lacey shrugged. She didn't want to get that close to the animals or go in that smelly barn. The next morning, Lacey watched her grandmother again except this time she noticed a water bottle. Perhaps she took it with her because it was hot and she got thirsty feeding the animals, she thought. When her grandmother returned, the tray was empty. No water bottle. Ever so curious, Lacey decided she would follow her the next morning.

"Will you set the alarm clock, Mommy?" Lacey asked at bedtime.

"You've decided to help your Gramma?"

"Yes, I think so," answered Lacey. She didn't want to fib, nor did she want to tell her mother she was spying.

Shortly after dawn, Lacey raced down stairs only to find the backdoor open. She tiptoed out onto the patio and crept along the path, darting from bush to bush to BBQ pit until she came upon her grandmother near the barn. Instead of turning left to go towards the barn, Amaryllis turned right, off the path. Lacey hid behind a tall patch of grass to see what was going on without being seen. Amaryllis walked up to a large tree stump, the size of an end table, knelt down, and removed from the tray a paper plate with leftovers from dinner, a sandwich, and a water bottle. She then turned around and headed back to the barn.

Lacey, full of excitement at the possibility of seeing the deer eat her grandmother's cooking, sat down and waited. She had never heard of deer eating people food. Apples and carrots, sure, but not the items laid out on the stump. Lacey heard the barn door close. A moment later, footsteps from slightly beyond the stump and behind a group of pine trees rustled the fallen leaves. Her heart raced. She was about to see wild deer for the first time in her life. Lacey's heart almost stopped when a man suddenly appeared. She sat up straighter and craned her neck through the grass. A tall, old man wearing tattered clothes looked left, right, then took two giant steps towards the stump. He picked up the plate in his left hand, picked up the sandwich with his right, took a large bite, set it on the plate, then grabbed the water bottle and retreated into the shelter of the trees.

"Oh my gosh!" Lacey exclaimed to herself. She had no idea what to say or think or do.

A noise from the barn drew her attention away from the man. Lacey jumped up and ran towards the horse pen.

"Hi, can I help?" Lacey asked her grandmother.

"Well, now. I've just finished so you're a minute too late," stated Amaryllis with the empty tray in her hand. They walked together down the path to the house. "You can help me make breakfast and then you can help me with the paper. I've just about got everything ready to start dipping. Except the flowers. We need to pick and dry some wildflowers."

"Good morning, Mother, was Lacey a good helper?" Camille asked from the opened French doors.

"She will be," stated Amaryllis.

Lacey sat down at the kitchen table. She watched her grandmother and wondered what she should do. Did her grandmother know she wasn't feeding deer? "Gramma, why do you feed the deer leftovers?" the inquisitive little girl asked as casually as she could.

"Well now, isn't that a funny question." Amaryllis put her toast down in preparation for a story. "These deer happen to like my cooking. Well, you see, one afternoon I was having my lunch out there by the barn. I had been brushing Muffin all day and it was such a nice day that I didn't want to go in for lunch. So I brought my lunch out and sat it on a tree stump. Troy was younger and he hadn't gotten used to Muffin. I think he thought Muffin was a dog so he wanted to play. Well, Muffin wasn't too happy about being chased by a dog so I had to go and separate the two just like with little children. Reminded me of your mother and Willow when they were young. Well, wouldn't you know it, when I went back to my lunch, it was gone! I saw tracks on the ground and so I said to myself, 'that deer ate my lunch!' The next day I brought an extra lunch. One for me and one for the deer. That day I accidentally left my water bottle on the stump. When I went back to get it, it was gone and so was the extra lunch. I've been taking those deer breakfast ever since. Some mornings, when it's really foggy, I see them. Deer are shy creatures so don't expect to see them anytime soon."

"Are you sure it's not just the dogs, Mother?" asked Camille. "I've never known deer to eat pot roast."

"Well, now, I thought the same thing until this happened. I saw the tracks. I've seen the deer. They are all over Wildwood. Get up at dawn sometime and take a walk with me around the lake. Not all the way around, of course. You'll see them there in the woods."

"Can we tomorrow, Mommy?" asked Lacey. "Please? I want to see the deer."

"That'll be fun," stated Amaryllis. "We can get up early and walk the lake like the other day. It's a full moon tonight so we won't need a flashlight. You can help me feed the critters when we get back."

"Is it safe?" asked Camille.

"That's why I have my shotgun," Amaryllis said, patting her pantry door.

Camille groaned but consented to the outing.

Later that afternoon the doorbell rang. Lacey was the only one in the house, so she answered.

"Hello," said the man dressed in a suit. Not a suit like her daddy's but a casual, summer suit. "Is Amaryllis at home?"

"Yes," answered Lacey. She was curious at who this stranger was and her initial feeling was that she didn't like him.

"My name is Mr. Ridgeway," he said holding out his hand. "You must be Lacey."

"How'd you know that?" she asked. She looked at his hand but her hands stayed glued to the doorknob.

"I'm a friend of your mother's," he began. He pulled his hand back and put it in his pocket.

"I know. You told her to come check on Gramma. She was in the back yard the whole time. She said she doesn't hear the doorbell when she's in

63

the back yard."

"Oh, I see. Would you let her and your mother know I'm here?" he asked.

"Okay." Lacey closed the door and ran to the back yard. "Mommy! Gramma! Mr. Ridgeway is here."

Camille abruptly stood up from where she was reading in the Adirondack chair. "He is? Where?" She looked beyond Lacey and towards the side of the house.

"At the front door," answered Lacey.

"What's he want?" asked Amaryllis, sounding slightly annoyed.

"I dunno. He asked if you was home."

Camille walked towards the house. "I'll let him in." She, followed closely by Lacey, went through the house to the front door. "Hello, Lucas," she said to the man who was pacing in the driveway.

"Camille, how are you?" he said with outstretched hands and an almost too-friendly smile. He grasped her hand and stared. "Wow. You look just the same as you did in high school. Same auburn hair, same eyes, everything."

"Not hardly," stated Camille, only somewhat flattered. "Come on in. We're in the back." She led him quickly through the house and out the French doors. "Mother, Lucas is here."

"Well now," began Amaryllis without moving from her chair. "I hear you been tellin' everybody I'm dead."

"No, ma'am," replied Lucas with a shake of his head. "I was getting worried about you is all." He turned his attention to Camille. "I'm sure glad to see you. How've you been?"

"Doing alright. What have you been up to?"

"I'm really sorry to hear about your husband," he said, ignoring her question. "It must be real tough on you and the little girl. You know, we had a high school reunion a while back and everyone was asking about you, hoping you would come."

"I know. Willow told me."

"Speaking of Willow," began Lucas, "she's why I called you. She called me a few times asking if I had spoken to you, Amaryllis. Excuse me if I'm out of line here, but she seems to want to know but not enough to get her hands dirty."

"Well now," laughed Amaryllis, "that sounds just like your sister."

"She hasn't come to church in quite a while," stated Lucas. He turned his attention back to Camille. "You see, I'm the benevolence deacon in the church, the same one we grew up in. And, it's part of my duties to check in on the elderly, the invalid, and those who haven't attended in some time."

"He's the check-off man," stated Amaryllis.

"What's that?" asked Lacey.

"If you don't go and check-off your attendance card, he comes a callin'," said Amaryllis with a slight chuckle.

"It sounds awful when you put it like that, Mrs. Blythe," stated Lucas. "I care about our members and I check on people to see if they are in need of anything. With you living out here all by yourself, and especially since Willow doesn't keep tabs…I mean since she doesn't visit regularly, I feel it my responsibility to check in on you."

"Well, isn't that sweet." Amaryllis looked over at Lacey and made a silly face.

"How long are you in town for?" Lucas asked Camille.

"Mommy said we hav'ta stay all summer," stated Lacey. She didn't like how close the man was sitting to her mother so she squeezed in between and sat on her lap.

"All summer? Then we'll see you in church on Sunday."

"Most likely," stated Camille.

"Are you still teaching? I can't remember who told me you were a teacher, maybe it was Willow."

"Yes," answered Camille without further explanation.

"Mommy teaches 'vir-tul school," interrupted Lacey.

"Virtual school," corrected Lucas. "That's a good choice, Cami. I'm sure it gives you a little more freedom to take care of your daughter, and your mother."

"Yes, it has been a blessing," stated Camille.

"I don't get sick anymore. Well, much anyway," said Lacey.

"Really?" said Lucas. "I'm sorry to hear you've been ill."

Camille pushed Lacey off her lap and stood up. "Is there anything else you needed, Lucas?"

"No, no," he said, looking around the back yard. "I just stopped by to check in on your mother. You know," he said while being escorted to the front door, "if you need any help cleaning up, doing yard work, things like that we have a ministry at church that can help. We have a team that regularly goes out helping the widows and whoever needs assistance." Lucas stopped at the front door and motioned towards the living room. "Are you sure she's okay?" He tapped the side of his forehead.

"It's under control," stated Camille. "Thank you for stopping by."

"My pleasure," stated Lucas. "It was very nice to see you again. See you Sunday. We should have lunch and catch up."

"Do we hav'ta go to church Sunday?" Lacey asked after her mother closed the front door.

"Yes. I want to see how Mother is around people."

"Why?"

"It will do you good, too. Maybe meet some kids who live in the neighborhood."

"I don't think so that it will. Maybe tonight we can meet kids and the deer."

"We'll see," stated Camille.

That evening at dusk, instead of waiting until morning, the trio set out to see deer. It was well past Lacey's bedtime but she had begged to stay up and go deer hunting at night. She was much too excited to wait. Both Troy and Diaz came with them. Somehow, the dogs knew the mission and stayed close. Amaryllis carried her BB gun over her shoulder like a soldier, leading the way. Camille held tight to Lacey's hand and held a large flashlight in the other just in case. Lacey had insisted the light stay off. Amaryllis again led them on the walk where they circled her half of lake in silence, stopping at every noise, every flutter in the woods. Lights were on in several houses, however, no one was outside. Birds, squirrels, and the swans were the only living things encountered on their trek. The silence was a bit eerie but the bright moonlight made for a beautiful scene, especially at the lake where the moonlight glimmered on the still water lighting up the white, sandy beach. While standing at the water's edge, Lacey and Camille both tried to persuade Amaryllis to walk a little further, towards the golf community, however, she refused.

"The two of you can go, but not me," she insisted.

Disappointed, Lacey decided she would find the deer on her own. She was feeling a bit braver, more adventurous, especially now with the mystery man who her grandmother thought was a deer. She was curious about him and not at all afraid.

Early the next morning, Lacey got up and snuck out of the house before her grandmother left the kitchen. She found a hiding place behind the grass and waited. Minutes later, Amaryllis rounded the corner, set out the usual spread of leftovers, a sandwich, and a bottle of water. After looking around, the older woman turned and headed towards the barn. Lacey crept forward, still hidden but closer. She held her breath when the man stepped forward. When he got to the stump, Lacey parted the grass as slow and quiet as she could to keep from startling him. It was the same old man she had seen before. He had long white hair and dressed shabbily in dirty jeans and a worn, thread-bear jacket. His face was thin and wrinkled, tanned from too much sun exposure and covered partly by a sparse beard with long, white curly hairs like those on his head. The man looked up, froze when he saw the little girl, then when Lacey did not move or say anything he picked up his meal and retreated to where he had come from. Lacey repeated this for the next two days. Not a word was spoken. On the third day, eye contact was made for several seconds and Lacey smiled at the man. She knew she wanted to talk to him but what would she say? The possibility of him harming her did not once cross her mind. Teachers and her mother had taught 'stranger danger' over and over again, however, Lacey did not feel one bit unsafe.

While walking back to the house, the little girl wondered what to do next. Should she tell her mother about the man? Should she tell her grandmother? Should she talk to him or go look for him in the woods?

"I think so that I won't," Lacey said to herself. She stood at the kitchen entrance and watched her mother and grandmother for a moment.

"Good morning sweetheart," said Camille who was sitting at the table drinking coffee. "I didn't hear you come down. Sleep well?"

"Yes," Lacey answered. "Gramma, can I feed the deer tomorrow?"

"I don't think you are going to see the deer, honey," stated her mother. "The dogs probably chase them off."

"Now, Cami, don't go spoiling things. Give it time, you'll see them."

"Tomorrow is Sunday," stated Camille.

"Well, what does that have to do with the price of corn?" asked Amaryllis. "The animals still have to be fed. Church starts at 10. Takes only twenty-five minutes to get there."

"Twenty-five minutes?" asked Camille. "I thought the church was just on the other side of the golf course."

"It is. But I don't drive through there."

"Really Mother?" asked Camille, shaking her head in disbelief. "You drive fifteen minutes out of your way just because you have a problem with the golf course?"

"You betcha," stated Amaryllis with a look on her face that dared her daughter to argue the point further. "Come down early, Lacey, and you can feed the deer for me while I feed John and Muffin."

"Whee! Thanks Gramma," exclaimed Lacey. "I'll be careful, Mommy, and I can take my bath after."

Early Sunday morning, Lacey met her grandmother in the kitchen. She filled the tray herself with leftovers, a sandwich, fruit, a jar of jelly from the new batch, and a bottle of water.

"I don't think the deer will eat the jelly," stated Amaryllis once Lacey finished filling the tray.

"They might," she said with the hopes that her grandmother might ask her questions or tell her something about the man.

"Well now, there's only one way to find out." Amaryllis carried the tray down the path as far as the barn. "Now, little one, you think you can carry this the rest of the way?"

"Oh yes, I know I can," stated Lacey confidently. The tray was very heavy, but she managed to get it all the way to the stump without dropping anything. Lacey stopped in front of nature's table, looked around to figure out how to get the food from the tray to the stump, then sat down with the tray in her lap. She peered into the woods and waited. The man did not appear.

"Lacey," called Amaryllis a few minutes later. "Hurry up or you're mother will fuss at me."

"Coming!" Lacey took one item at a time off the tray and placed it carefully on the ground. She then stood up and moved the meal back to the stump, looked into the woods and said softly, "I know you're there. Hope you like what I brought. See you tomorrow."

Lacey walked briskly behind her grandmother back into the house to an impatiently waiting mother. Breakfast dishes and cereal boxes were on the table, telling Lacey that she had better hurry up. She sat down and waited for her grandmother to join her. Instead, her curiosity was piqued as Amaryllis opened the door to the garage and began rummaging through several boxes and the cooler by the door.

"Mother, what are you doing?" asked Camille. "Breakfast is on the table.

"I'm looking for my blackberries. I need to make jam before they spoil," said Amaryllis without looking up. "I went to Lufkin last week and picked berries. They are in abundance this year."

Lacey looked over at her mother, full of confusion.

"Mother," said Camille gently, "you made jam days ago." Camille led Amaryllis back into the kitchen. "See," she said, pointing to the jars lining a shelf in the pantry.

"Well, I'll be," Amaryllis said. "No wonder I couldn't find the berries. Must have slipped my mind. You two being here has set my schedule all a kilter. Now, what would y'all like to do today?" Amaryllis closed the pantry door then began to search through the refrigerator.

"We're going to church this morning, Mother," stated Camille.

"Maybe we shouldn't," stated Lacey hopefully.

"You go get your bath," Camille instructed with a point of her finger towards the staircase. "I'll get Mother ready."

Lacey took one last sip of juice then walked out of the kitchen. She paused on the other side of the wall to listen.

"Mother, are you feeling okay?" Camille asked.

"Why? You're looking at me like I'm, I'm…"

"I'm concerned about you losing your memory, that's all. I think we should go to the doctor tomorrow."

"Oh, don't be absurd. I'm as healthy as a turkey the day after Thanksgiving."

"Do you often forget things, Mother?"

"What's with this hullaballoo? I'm going to get ready for church."

Lacey ran up the stairs before she could get caught for listening. Fear of her grandmother being sick ran through her mind while getting dressed. Was she sick? How does someone lose memories? Do they die from it, she wondered. Was that why they came, because her grandmother was dying? Lacey coughed, then her nose began to drip.

"Are you feeling alright?" Camille asked her daughter as they turned into the church parking lot. She looked at Lacey from the rear-view mirror.

Lacey thought for a moment. If she got sick, her mother wouldn't let her go outside. If she couldn't go outside, she couldn't feed the 'deer'. "I'm fine," she said, stifling a cough.

Chapter 5

"Mother, the parking lot is full. Are you sure you got the time right?" Camille asked.

"Yes," answered Amaryllis with an annoyed shake of the head. "Sunday School started at 9."

The church was bigger and much different that the one Lacey was had gone to back home. She stared wide-eyed, and began to get butterflies in her stomach. The large, red-brick, square building looked more like a school than a church. She followed her mother and grandmother through the parking lot and into the foyer where they were greeted by an older couple who knew Amaryllis. Behind the double doors, the people were already singing. This comforted Lacey a bit because it sounded very similar to what she was used to. After settling into a back pew, because the room was already full, Lacey began doodling on the bulletin to calm her butterflies. When asked to stand up for songs, the shy, scared little girl shook her head and stayed seated. She felt like everyone was staring at her and that made her stomach churn more and her nose once again started to run.

Lacey turned to make a run for the bathroom. At the same time, the preacher walked down the steps to make his closing remarks. She stopped, took several deep breaths, and her stomach settled. Following the closing prayer, Lacey followed her grandmother who practically ran out of the building.

"What's the rush, Mother?" Camille asked at the car.

"Church is over."

"Yes, I know, but I'd like to talk to a few people."

"Why?"

"Because…"

"Let's go, Cami, it's lunch time," insisted Amaryllis.

Lacey studied her mother's face on the ride back to her grandmother's house. She looked worried, and aggravated. The little frown lines on her forehead gave it away. Lunch passed in silence. No one spoke at all, which bothered Lacey quite a bit. It was the first time since their arrival that her grandmother had been quiet. In the afternoon, they all piled back into the car for a trip to the grocery store. Once again, they had to go the long way. The arguing began in the canned food aisle. Amaryllis insisted on buying the off-label brands and only items that were on sale. At the meat counter, they argued over which cuts of meat to buy.

"I live on a budget, Cami, something you should learn to do. There is nothing wrong with how I eat. In fact, most of my food is free since I grow my own vegetables and the eggs come from the chickens in my yard."

"You have chickens?" asked Camille. "I've never seen or heard them."

"That's because they are free to roam around. They have nests hidden here and there. Sometimes I eat the hens," stated Amaryllis in a huff.

"Is that safe? Chickens aren't the cleanest animals and with the state of your house…"

"What's wrong with my house?" Amaryllis stopped mid isle and put her hands on her hips.

"It's, it…Mother, your house is kinda…"

"Messy," stated Lacey who was just trying to help.

"I'll have you know I keep a very clean house," Amaryllis said angrily. "I may have a lot of things in my house, but they are my things. I know where everything is. I use everything I collect. There is nothing wrong with my house!"

"You have to admit it's a bit cramped, Mother," stated Camille. "I'd be happy to help you organize and… make things a little safer."

"Well, then, who wants spaghetti for dinner?" Amaryllis asked, directing the question to Lacey.

"Can we have a picnic at the beach tomorrow?" Lacey asked her mother. She was happy to change the subject if it meant an end to the arguing. "And then maybe we can all go swimming."

"I suppose," answered Camille with a groan and a shake of the head. She replaced several of the items her mother had put in the cart with items of her choice.

"Cami, how is Willow these days? I haven't talked to her in ages." Amaryllis pushed the cart towards the baking isle.

Lacey looked over at her mother, waiting to hear the answer. There was none. The little girl tried to break the silence from time to time but gave up after her mother kept shaking her head, an indication to keep silent, and her grandmother refused to make eye contact with anyone. After a painfully quiet ride home and dinner, she retreated to her room to read.

"Mommy, is Gramma going to die?" Lacey asked at bedtime.

"What makes you ask that?"

Lacey took her bear and her father's picture off the nightstand and held them against her chest. "You said she needed to go to the doctor."

"You don't need to worry, sweetheart. How's your nose? It was running this morning." Camille pulled the sheet up and gave her daughter a kiss on the forehead.

"I'm fine. Is she sick? She forgets things sometimes."

"Yes, I know."

Lacey waited for her mother to elaborate. "She's sick isn't she?" she again asked.

"Not sick like a cold. She's just getting older and she needs to see the doctor to make sure. Sometimes, when a person ages, their mind slows down. This causes their memory to not be as good as it used to be."

"Oh." Lacey wasn't satisfied with the answer. "But…"

"But it's time to go to sleep. Goodnight." Camille placed the photograph back on the nightstand, gave her daughter one last hug and kiss, then closed the door behind her.

*****

Troy bounded out from behind the thicket of trees when Lacey approached with the tray. He sniffed her shoes, the tray, then circled the girl. Diaz ran out, sniffed Lacey, then continued on down the path. Both dogs were wet, as if they had just had a bath or had been playing in the lake.

"Shoo, dog," Lacey said, then sat on the stump with the tray in her lap and waited. "I know you're there and I know you're hungry," she said quietly. "I didn't tell anyone I saw you. Promise."

A shadow moved from behind a pine tree. A twig snapped then the man's face emerged from behind a leafy branch into the faint morning light.

"Hello," said Lacey timidly. She stared at the man with excitement and a little fear in the pit of her stomach. "Here." Lacey held out an apple. "I'm Lacey."

The man stepped forward a few feet out of the forest, looked down the path, then took the apple out of Lacey's hand. He took a bite all while keeping his eyes moving, darting back and forth down the path and back at Lacey. In two more bites, he finished the apple.

"Did you like the jam?"

The man nodded.

"Want me to bring you more tomorrow?"

He nodded again.

"Here." Lacey held out the tray with the remainder of the food.

The man looked around then took another step forward and took the tray. He moved back and started to retreat.

"Wait, I need the tray back," stated Lacey. She stood up and motioned for him to sit down.

He shook his head, put the sandwich and water bottle in his pockets, picked up the paper plate piled with leftovers and covered in foil, then handed Lacey the tray.

"See you tomorrow," stated Lacey. She waved then skipped off down the path towards her waiting mother.

"What took you so long?" Camille asked from the porch.

"I was hoping to see the deer," Lacey answered truthfully.

"And did you see any?"

"No. Can we go to the lake now?" Lacey asked, not wanting anymore questions.

"Yes, go put on your bathing suit then come help pack a picnic. See if

you can find the sunblock. I think it's in one of the boxes in your room."
Camille stood up and walked into the house with her daughter. "I'll get
Gramma to help me pack up."

The lake was empty as it had been since their arrival. The family of
swans floated near the diving platform, out of reach from the taunting
dogs. Lacey stood impatiently while her mother covered her in sun block
then ran to the water's edge. Her mother and grandmother sat under the
large beach umbrella in silence. Lacey played in the shallows, splashing
her feet and inching her way in as the temperature rose. It was quiet and
a little more boring than she had imagined.

"Come swim with me, Mommy," Lacey called out.

"How about we make sandcastles?" Amaryllis stood up, turned to pick
up a bucket behind her chair then said in a whisper, "Your friend is
here."

"Hey there, everyone," Lucas Ridgeway called out. "Beautiful day for
an outing."

Camille slipped her arms through her cover-up then stated, "Hello,
Lucas."

"Hi, Lacey," Lucas waved and smiled at the girl then sat at the picnic
table next to Camille. "I came out to apologize for not speaking to you
yesterday."

"No apologies necessary," stated Amaryllis a bit gruffly.

"Yes, well I thought I'd stop by and see how you were getting on," he
stated.

"Thank you," answered Camille with a polite nod of her head.

"We should have lunch one afternoon. In town," he suggested.

"We eat at home," stated Amaryllis.

"How is your family?" Camille asked Lucas after a glaring glance at her mother.

"Fine, fine," he stated. "Often, on Sunday, a group of us go to lunch together. Nothing fancy, just the diner down the road. We'd love for all of you to join us."

"I'll think about it," stated Camille.

"I'm going to make sandcastles with Lacey." Amaryllis grabbed her bucket and marched towards the lake.

Lacey watched her mother and tried to listen to the conversation. She noticed the man was wearing a wedding ring. "Do you have kids Mr. Ridgeway?" Lacey asked suddenly.

Lucas stopped mid sentence, looked over at Lacey, paused for a moment then ignored her question. He turned his back to her and continued his conversation with Camille.

"He's harmless," Amaryllis whispered to Lacey.

Lacey wasn't so sure, however, with her grandmother's distractions she relaxed and enjoyed her day at the lake building sandcastles and wading up to her knees in the cool water. It had been a few years since she had been swimming and never in a lake. The last time she had been in an open body of water was in Japan. She was very young then and didn't remember it except by the few photographs her mother had in an album on her laptop.

"Are there things in the water?" Lacey asked her grandmother. She looked down at her feet through the cool water and wiggled her toes in the sand.

"Fish, a few tadpoles, turtles, but nothing harmful," she answered. "I'll bet in a few weeks you'll be swimming all the way to the diving platform."

"I think I'd not like to do that," Lacey stated. Afraid her grandmother might make her try, she quickly got out of the lake and ran up to her mother. "Is it lunch time?"

Lucas stayed through lunch, much to Lacey's disapproval. He ignored Lacey and Amaryllis for the most part, talking on and on about days gone by in high school. Lucas helped pack up then began to say his goodbyes after Camille insisted he was not needed to carry their picnic back to the house.. "See you Sunday ladies. Oh, Cami, I meant to ask you if you had met any of the neighbors."

"There doesn't seem to be any," answered Camille.

"Have a good day, Mr. Ridgeway," stated Amaryllis before he could find another excuse to linger. She patted him on the back in an attempt to get him to leave.

Lucas nodded, waved goodbye, and slowly walked away.

"Does he like you, Mommy?" asked Lacey.

"He's an old friend," she replied. "We went to school together."

"They dated," added Amaryllis.

Lacey looked over at her mother in surprise.

"He's married now, you know," continued Amaryllis on their walk back home.

"Yes, I saw his ring. He never mentioned her. Have you met his wife?"

"No. Don't think so."

"Not even at church?" asked Camille.

"I don't pay attention to such things," said Amaryllis.

Lacey stopped at the bridge that crossed the dried-up stream. She picked up a rock and dropped it, watched it fall and bounce off a fallen log. The stream bed wound around towards the lake and disappeared behind brush and trees. On the other side of the bridge, the stream bed narrowed but deepened. "Can we go down there?" she asked.

"No, it's too dangerous," answered Camille.

"Hogwash." Amaryllis laughed. "When you were little, Cami, you and your sister played in that stream. There was water in it then. Up to your ears. Been dried up for years now. The lake and streams have been ignored for so long, I'm surprised the lake hasn't dried up along with it."

"So, can I?" repeated Lacey.

"Some other time." Camille took her daughter by the hand and led her up the slight incline towards their summer home.

"Lordy, here they come." Amaryllis nodded in the direction of the older couple walking down the hill towards them.

"Mrs. Blythe," called out the woman, "we need to speak to you." She waved her hand high in the air to make sure she was seen and heard.

"Here it comes," Amaryllis said under her breath. "It's hard to be a Christian around those two. Sometimes I hate being the good one and for once, I'd like to be the bad guy and wring her ever lovin' neck."

"Mother!" said a shocked Camille.

"You wait and see," she whispered. Amaryllis put on her best smile and said, "Afternoon Beverly."

"Mrs. Blythe," stated the woman who was out of breath from marching down the street. "I have asked you repeatedly to please keep your chickens out of my yard. Just this morning I ran off two hens out of my azalea bushes."

"I don't have chickens, Beverly," stated Amaryllis.

Remembering the conversation in the grocery store, both Lacey and her mother looked at each other then at Amaryllis. Lacey had seen the eggs in her grandmother's kitchen, but had never seen any chickens - even though Amaryllis said there were some. Lacey thought maybe her grandmother was lying. She studied the couple in the street. They seemed older than her grandmother. He was tall and frail with only a few strands of white hair on the top of his head. His face was wrinkled, especially at the eyes, which drooped making him look sad. Brown plaid pants, even though cinched in tight with a worn white belt, barely hung on to his waist. The yellow dress shirt appeared to have been brought out just for the occasion. It was stiff and starched. Lacey thought he looked uncomfortable. Beverly, although not fat, was a plump woman in a brightly patterned house dress, neatly ironed. Her jet black hair, much too dark for her age and neatly combed back in a bun, made her face seem unnaturally tight and stern.

"Yes you do, Amaryllis." The woman looked at Camille then stated, "She does so have chickens. I know because I keep running them off." Beverly looked at Amaryllis and then her husband who stood in silence next to her with his arms folded and a scowl on his face. "If I see them again, I will call Animal Control. They'll put a stop to it! And another thing, if you're going to be entertaining kids, you need to warn them to keep the noise down. We go to bed early and don't like kids throwing parties and running up and down the street making noise."

"Clean up," the man leaned over to the side and whispered to his wife. "Tell her to clean up."

"I'm getting to that, Lamont," she said with a huff. Beverly looked at Camille with a forced smile. "I do hope you are here to help your mother clean up her property."

"Excuse me?" asked Camille.

"We just know that it's been difficult for Amaryllis to take care of the house and yard all by herself. You came to help, right? Her daughter, the one that lives in town refuses to help her mother even though I've asked her as politely as I could many times. The other daughter never visits." Beverly forced a smile until Diaz and Troy ran up to them full of energy and wanting attention. "These dogs need to be leashed! They run around and dig up my yard and leave..." she put her hand over her mouth and whispered, "poop," uncovered her mouth then continued loudly, "all over the place. You will do something about it or I will have to file a complaint!"

"Who with?" asked Amaryllis who could barely control her amusement at her neighbor's threats. "We don't live in the city limits. There are no leash laws here."

Beverly continued her tirade without hesitation. "Now that you have a child in your house, Amaryllis, you have her safety to think about. All that clutter in your yard and I'm sure in your home is in the same state. It's a hazard."

Lacey listened to Mrs. Beverly Jackson and her husband complain about bugs and rodents and noise until she could take the arguing no more. She stepped forward and tugged on Mr. Jackson's arm, "Do you have any kids?" she asked.

"What?" he asked with wide eyes.

"There's nobody to play with here at my Gramma's house. Do you have kids?" Lacey used her grandmother's name on purpose since they didn't know who she and her mother were.

Lamont's chin dropped like he was about to say something to Lacey but then took his wife by the arm and said to her, "We need to go home now, Bev."

Mrs. Jackson shook off her husband, looked at Lacey and Amaryllis with a scowl on her face. "We are not finished here. I insist you…"

"Come dear," Lamont interrupted. He took his wife by the hand and led her back down the street. He continued to quietly shush her when she turned and pointed towards Amaryllis every few feet.

Lacey waved at the glaring woman thinking that she looked more sad and lonely than mean and angry like her grandmother had described her. "Do they have kids?" she asked her grandmother.

"That's a story for another day," answered Amaryllis. "I need a nap." She walked home in silence, opened the front door and dropped her beach chair in the middle of the living room floor.

"Mother, I made an appointment for you to see your doctor," stated Camille before her mother disappeared to her bedroom. "Tomorrow morning."

"I do not need to see a doctor!" Amaryllis stated angrily. She marched to her room and closed the door with a bang.

"Lacey, go get in the tub. I'll be up in a minute."

Not wanting to hear her mother and grandmother argue, she obeyed.

"Why don't those people like Gramma?" Lacey asked at bedtime.

Camille pulled the sheet up over her daughter, gave her a kiss on the cheek, then said with a slight shrug of the shoulders, "I really don't know."

"I think they are really saaad," she said drawing out the last syllable.

"Why?"

"Because when I asked if they had kids they ran away." Lacey suddenly sat up. "Maybe we can invite them to lunch tomorrow."

"I think that's rushing things a bit. Besides, we have to take Gramma to the doctor," stated Camille. "Another day, perhaps."

"How come that man keeps coming over? I think I don't like him. He sits too close to you. Like Daddy used to."

"We were...friends a long time ago. He's always been like that," stated Camille while looking at the floor.

"Oh." Lacey sensed her mother didn't want to talk about him. "Does he have kids?"

"I think so."

"Why didn't he answer me? I think he doesn't like me. Can we pray for them? The neighbors and him? And for Gramma. Add them to my prayer for Daddy." Lacey yawned a long, sleepy yawn after rambling off her prayer requests then flopped onto the pillow.

"Of course," answered Camille. She began her nighttime prayer with the usual, "God bless Gramma, please keep Lacey well. Lead us in your way, Lord. Guide us and show us your will. God bless Mr. Ridgeway and his family."

"And God bless the neighbors and bring home Daddy," Lacey interrupted.

****

Lacey sat on the stump and called out, "Hi, I'm here with breakfast."

The morning sky was cloudy with a threat of rain. Large puffy clouds hung low with a few dark clouds blocking out the sun. Everything was damp from the humidity and the dew that had not burned off. Sweat beaded up on her nose as Lacey wondered what the man did to stay dry.

"Hello, miss," the old man said in a hushed voice from behind a tree.

"Hi there. We went to the lake yesterday. Me, Mommy, and Gramma. The dogs came, too. They tried to catch birds. It was fun until Mr. Ridgeway showed up," said Lacey with nervous anticipation. She hoped he would stay a while and talk to her. "I brought you more jam."

"Thank you." The man sat on the ground in front of Lacey. "Lady makes good jam."

"What's that on your jacket?" asked Lacey, pointing at the tattered ribbons.

"They come with the jacket," he stated.

"They look like my daddy's war medals," she stated. "He's in the Marines."

The man nodded his head while he ate.

"How long have you lived here?" she asked.

The man shrugged his shoulders.

"What's your name?"

"You can call me whatever you like," he answered.

"Okay. Hmm. I think I'll call you Danny. You look like your name should be Danny."

"Sounds nice."

"Does my Gramma know you live here?"

"Who is your Gramma?" asked Danny.

"The lady who brought you food before I came."

"Oh. I don't think so." He cocked his head to the side, shrugged his shoulders, then said, "Maybe."

"Where do you go when it rains?"

"I have a tent. It keeps me dry."

"Don't you get lonely?"

"Sometimes. The dog keeps me company."

"Troy? The one who likes to chase rabbits?"

Danny looked at Lacey for a moment with a blank stare then said, "Yes."

"My gramma's neighbor says chickens go in her yard. My gramma said she doesn't have chickens. Have you seen any?" asked Lacey.

"Yup. Them chickens used to live in the barn. They got out. I put 'em back but they kept gettin' out. The coop door was left open a lot. I found some wood and made a new coop. She never come lookin' for 'em. So I put the eggs in the barn in the old nest. Sometimes they gets out. The chickens, I mean."

"When?"

"When what?"

"When did you make the coop?"

"A while back," answered Danny.

Lacey was confused. Her grandmother changed her story about the chickens and didn't know there was a man living on her property. She found it very peculiar. "I have to go now. Mommy worries if I stay too long. See you tomorrow."

Shortly after breakfast, while everyone was still in the kitchen cleaning up, the doorbell rang. Amaryllis and Camille looked at each other in surprise.

"Expecting someone, Mother?"

Amaryllis shook her head no.

"I'll get it." Lacey dropped the towel she was drying dishes with into the sink and skipped to the front door. She opened it just enough to peek out. There on the front sidewalk stood a small, balding man with thick, black-rimmed glasses. He held a clipboard in one hand and a business card in the other.

"Hello, young lady. Is Mrs. Blythe home?" asked the man in a shaky voice. He held out the card and said, "My name is Mr. Pollock from the Greater Hardin Health Services."

Lacey took the card and turned around. Her grandmother was marching towards the door with her mother close behind. "He's from something health place." She handed Amaryllis the card.

"Well, I'll be a monkey's..." Amaryllis began.

"Mother," Camille said, stopping her mid sentence.

"She's gone and done it. Lookey here." Amaryllis handed Camille the card. She pulled Lacey away from the door to confront the man. "Well now, they sent the likes of you, did they?" Amaryllis scoffed. "What did the old bat say this time?"

"Good morning, ma'am," said Mr. Pollock. He took a step back, forced a smile and said, "I was sent by the department to check on the health and welfare of a child. We were informed, anonymously, that the living conditions in this home were…um… unsatisfactory."

"Anonymously, my a…" Amaryllis looked at Lacey then finished with, "Aunt Martha."

"May I come in and do a quick inspection, ma'am? If you don't give me permission, I must inform you that I will have to call the Sheriff." Mr. Pollock shifted his slight weight from side to side nervously.

"I've got nothing to hide," Amaryllis said, throwing open the door. "Should I call Beverly so she can inspect for herself?"

"Who?" the man asked with a slight quiver in his voice.

"Mother, let the man do his job," Camille said with a shake of her head. "Please, Mr. Pollock, come in."

Lacey watched with great trepidation the interaction between the three adults. The poor little man looked terrified with her grandmother hovering and yelling at him. She had never seen her grandmother get mad before, grouchy yes, ornery and confusing with the words she said all the time, but never really mad. Lacey thought her mother looked like the school principal trying to break up a fight. Amaryllis followed the man from the living room to the kitchen. When he wrote something down she started to say something and with one look from Camille she backed down but attempted to read over his shoulder. The two women continued to shadow the man when he went upstairs, watching him closely as he took notes. Amaryllis, with a forced reserve, questioned him and demanded he tell her what he was writing down. He refused. After every room had been thoroughly inspected, Mr. Pollock sat at the kitchen table and wrote in his notebook. Lacey stood behind him and read every word.

"Cluttered but clean. No insect in-fes-ta-tion. Child's bedroom is neat and tidy. Bathroom free of de-bris. Many boxes and personal items in the home, however, nothing o-vert-ly dangerous." Lacey read out loud much to Mr. Pollock's disapproval.

"Mrs. Blythe," began Mr. Pollock. He stood up as tall as he was able and stated, "Your home is very cramped with many belongings. I would suggest you clear out some things if the child intends to stay for a prolonged period of time. Your home is not a danger to her at this time. I apologize for the inconvenience."

"Ha!" exclaimed Amaryllis. "That'll teach her! That woman is wound up tighter than the girdle of a Baptist minister at an all night buffet."

"Yes ma'am," said Mr. Pollack. "Have a good day."

Amaryllis Blythe had a good laugh as she watched the timid little man drive away in his beat-up sedan. The trio then piled into Camille's car and headed off towards town for Amaryllis' appointment. They were in good spirits for all of two minutes. When Camille started to drive straight, towards the golf community, Amaryllis barked orders for her to turn right, immediately. After a brief argument, Camille turned in the direction her mother had insisted, drove all the way around the golf community to the doctor's office. Once there, Camille pointed to the sign a block down the street.

"Mother, there is the entrance to your neighborhood. We just wasted time and money to go the long way around."

"Money well spent," answered Amaryllis with a defiant smile.

Lacey sat quietly during the doctor's examination. He looked in her grandmother's ears, down her throat, listened to her heart and lungs, took some blood, then began a series of strange questions.

"Mrs. Blythe," began the doctor, "how long have you lived alone?"

"Since my husband died," she answered.

"What year was that?"

"What difference does it make? You were his doctor, you have his records."

"Do you have company frequently?"

"No. I like to travel."

"Alone?"

"No. Troy and Diaz come with me."

"Friends or grandchildren?"

"Dogs."

"Who is the president?"

"I didn't vote," Amaryllis stated. "All politicians are crooks."

"I see. What did you eat for breakfast?"

"You're a nosy one, aren't you." Amaryllis glared at Camille. "My daughter has been complaining about my cooking, has she?"

"When was your last trip to Lufkin?"

"I didn't go this year. Would have, if my daughter hadn't shown up. I told her she should have called first."

The doctor wrote in the chart then stated to Camille. "Your mother shows early signs of dementia. I do not believe it to be Alzheimer's but we can do gene testing if you'd like. Most likely, because your mother has lived alone for such a long period of time…"

"I'm right here, Doc," stated Amaryllis. "There is nothing wrong with my hearing or my memory."

"Actually, there is," he argued. "You seem to have memory lapses. Nothing severe, however." The doctor turned to Camille. "Your presence should help. Get her out of the house more often and around people. Maybe church activities."

"Oh for Pete's sake," groaned Amaryllis. "I'm not a child."

"Mother, there have been several occasions since we've been here that you've forgotten things. I'm concerned it could get worse, and maybe it could. I mean, if you are alone and…"

"Forget to turn off the stove and burn down the house?" stated Amaryllis. She grabbed her purse and stood up to leave. "I'm just fine!"

Lacey listened as her mother and the doctor tried to reassure her grandmother. The arguing continued all the way to the car then escalated when Camille turned left and began driving towards the golf community.

"I'm not going to waste money," argued Camille.

"It's only a dollar, you can afford a dollar," Amaryllis said with a wave of the arms.

"Gas is more than a dollar a gallon, Mother. Has been for years. If you don't like this road, close your eyes and count to 20."

Lacey started to giggle but covered her mouth. She remembered her mother saying something like that to her when she was younger. The statement did not sit well with her grandmother as she began to complain again about the doctor. Having heard enough, Lacey put her fingers in her ears and began to sing softly to herself. She was not used to arguing. Could not remember hearing her mother argue with anyone, not her, not her father, and not the kids at school. The very moment the car was put into park in the driveway, Lacey jumped out and ran.

Chapter 6

Not wanting to wait for the front door to be opened and needing solitude, Lacey ran around to the right side of the house. She had no idea where she was going because she had not explored this part of the property. Her only objective was to get away from the noise and find solace in the quiet of the wilderness that was her grandmother's back yard. Rounding the corner, Lacey dove into the tall grass.

"Wow!" she exclaimed, coming to a halt on a small dirt and gravel path. Hidden under years of neglect was what appeared to be a pond. Lacey slowly walked along the overgrown path until she came upon a little wooden bridge. Weaving under the bridge, through the weeds, was a dry, stone-lined stream bed. To Lacey's right, the stream bed led to the pond. It was lined all around with flat stones and filled intermittently in the lowest spots with mud and weeds. On the opposite side of the bridge was a small wooden bench made from intertwined vines. Tall weeds grew in the cracks of the large, flat paving stones that encircled the pond.

Lacey carefully walked over the bridge. She nudged the bench with her foot then sat down in a deliberate, slow manner. "I wonder if Gramma forgot this was here? I'll bet it was pretty once, a long, long time ago," she said to herself. Looking around at the pond and its surroundings, Lacey remembered a book she read about a hidden garden. "I'll bet Danny knows."

Behind the bench, Lacey thought she saw another path so she got up to go explore. It led deeper into the tall, thick weeds. Instead of exploring the path, she sat on the edge of the pond and stared up at the bright blue sky. It was slightly cooler in this spot, shaded by the trees and weeds. A faint breeze kicked up the smell of rot in the muddy pond.

"Lacey! Lacey where are you?" cried a familiar worried voice.

"Ugh," Lacey grunted, annoyed at being disturbed. She turned around, went back to the path, and made her way towards the brick patio where her mother stood with her hands on her hips, a sure sign of frustration and possible punishment.

"I really wish you wouldn't run off like that," said Camille. She bent down and gave her daughter a gentle hug. "I'm sorry if we upset you."

"You and Gramma were yelling. Are we going home now?" asked Lacey. She was relieved that her mother wasn't angry.

"No, sweetheart. Where did you go? We were looking for you."

"Just exploring." Lacey shrugged. She liked having a secret place where she could tune out the world, a place all to herself.

"I see. Just be careful and don't go too far, okay?"

"Okay, Mommy."

That night after dinner, it started to rain. Gentle at first, then the thunder rolled in bringing heavier rain and wind. Lacey immediately began worrying about the man in the woods.

"What do the animals do when it rains?" she asked her grandmother.

"They go in the barn."

"What about the deer?"

"Deer are wild animals. They are used to the rain."

"Troy and Diaz are outside. Where do they go?"

"Well now, aren't y'all full of questions tonight," Amaryllis said. She put down the wad of yarn she was untangling then said. "Well, I leave the barn doors unlocked. They can get in and out when they want too."

"They open the doors by themselves?" asked Camille.

"Yes. Smart dogs. I've gone out to feed the critters in the morning after a hard rain like today and will find the dogs in the barn with the door pulled closed. Don't know how they did it, but there they were."

"The wind probably locked them in," suggested Camille.

"Can we go now and see if the dogs are in the barn?" asked Lacey.

"Not in the rain," answered her mother.

"Is there a blanket in the barn?" Lacey asked, thinking that the man would need it.

"I don't think so." Amaryllis looked at Lacey with concern. "Don't worry, they can take care of themselves honey bunch. If it will make you feel better, you can look in the garage for an old blanket and take it to the barn in the morning."

"Can I really?" Lacey jumped up and did a twirl in the middle of the room.

Early the next morning, Lacey ran down the stairs to the kitchen. In the garage on a shelf, she found an old blanket with a tarp folded inside. She tied a piece of rope around the blanket then began making breakfast for her new friend while Amaryllis supervised.

"Need some help?" asked Camille.

"No."

"She's a big girl," stated Amaryllis. "She likes to do it all by herself."

"I can see that. I think I'll join you two today," stated Camille.

"The deer are shy, Mommy." Lacey panicked. She was sure the man wouldn't come out of the woods if her mother and grandmother were with her. "They won't eat if there are people watching."

"Oh, really. So you've seen them?"

"Almost."

"Then I suppose I could stay at the barn. How's that?"

That seemed to satisfy Lacey. She stood at the barn door and waited until her mother and grandmother went inside with the blanket. After carefully placing the tray on the stump, she whispered, "Hello" towards the trees.

"Good mornin' miss," said the man. He emerged from the shadows and sat on the grass across from Lacey.

"Morning Danny," said Lacey. She studied his clothes for a minute then said, "Did you stay dry last night?"

"Yes, miss," he said, looking down at the food placed before him.

"Did you go in the barn?"

The man, jerked his head up and looked at Lacey. "You saw me?"

"No."

"Does she know?" he asked, pointing towards the barn with a long, frail finger.

"No. Gramma said the dogs go in there. So, I figured you did, too. I brought you a blanket and a plastic sheet thing. It's in the barn."

"That's nice."

"My gramma doesn't know you live in the woods."

"She doesn't? She brings me food every day."

"She, well, Gramma has lots of animals. She calls them critters." The sun bouncing off something on the man's jacket caught Lacey's eye. "What's that?"

Danny looked down, touched the ribbons on his jacket and said, "War medals."

Lacey was astonished. "Were you in the Marines, too?"

"No."

"My daddy is a Marine. But he's lost. What are the medals for?"

"I don't remember. I've worn this jacket for a long, long time. Can't remember not having them. I was in the Air Force when I was young."

"Really? Did you fly a heli-copter? My daddy flies a 'copter. Well, he did until it crashed. Did you know my daddy?"

"No," stated Danny. He wrapped the sandwich in the napkin, put it in his pocket and shook his head.

"What's wrong?" asked Lacey. She studied the man's suddenly changed expression on his face.

"Lacey!"

Lacey jumped up and saw her mother and grandmother standing frozen in step on the path. She turned around towards Danny who was running into the woods.

"Lacey, who was that man?" asked Camille with a shaky voice.

"Mommy, you scared him." She turned towards the woods and called out, "Danny, come back!"

"Lacey, who was that?" Camille repeated with a more forceful tone.

"Um, Mommy…Gramma wasn't feeding deer."

Camille grabbed her daughter by the hand and walked briskly to the house, dragging Lacey behind her. Amaryllis retrieved the tray and followed. "Mother, do you know that man?"

"No."

"Lacey," began Camille calmly once safely indoors, "when did you first see him?"

"Um, one day when Gramma went to feed the animals. I followed her and hid in the bushes. I wanted to see the deer."

"Why didn't you tell me?" asked Camille.

"I dunno."

"I think we should call the police." Camille took her phone out of her pocket.

"No, Mommy, no!" cried Lacey. "You can't.

"Mother, how long has he been in the woods?"

"I don't know," said Amaryllis. She sat on the couch and shook her head. "I've never seen him."

"You didn't for a minute think that it wasn't a deer? Deer don't eat most of the things you take out, drink from water bottles, or eat jam!"

"But I did see deer. I saw tracks," insisted Amaryllis.

"I'm calling the police," stated Camille. "They'll know what to do."

Lacey let out a loud cry. "No, Mommy, no!" She ran out of the house and down the path towards the abandoned pond. Sobbing, with her nose running, Lacey threw herself down onto the ground in front of the bench. "No, no, don't send him away," she cried. Lacey began to cough. One little cough led to two little coughs, which turned into nonstop coughing and gasping for air. Lacey felt dizzy, doubled over with stomach pain while the coughing continued. After a very fitful cough, Lacey vomited into the stream then curled up into a fetal position.

"There she is. Lacey, take a deep breath," said Camille in her soothing, mommy tone. "Try to sit up." Camille put her arms around her daughter and pulled her onto her lap. "There's a good girl. Breathe in."

"You…" began Lacey.

"Shh. Hush now," said Camille in as calm a voice as she could. "Don't talk. Take a slow, deep breath." Camille stroked her daughter's head and rocked her back and forth.

"You…you can't call the police," Lacey said in between coughs.

"He might be a criminal," Camille said, continuing to rock her daughter.

"No, Mommy, no. He's a hero." Lacey hiccupped in a deep breath as tears ran down her face.

"What do you mean?"

"He was in the Air Force and has lots and lots of medals," she gasped. "Maybe he's lost, like Daddy."

"He told you this?" asked Camille. She looked over at her mother who shrugged.

"He wears a jacket like Daddy's, but really, really old. And he has medals pinned to it."

"That doesn't mean anything," said Camille. "He might have bought it. Or stolen it."

"No, Mommy, he's not a bad man." Lacey sat up. She looked back and forth from mother to grandmother, trying to read their expressions.

"How long have you been feeding him?" Camille asked her mother.

"I don't remember. A while. A few years maybe." Amaryllis suddenly looked around at the pond. She put her hands on her hips, turned around, walked a bit down to the bridge and said, "Where did all this come from?"

"What?" asked Camille, confused by her mother's question.

"This." Amaryllis pointed to the pond and the stream. "I don't remember it."

"Didn't you build it?" asked Camille.

"I…I…well, maybe." Amaryllis drew in the air with her finger as if she were remembering something.

"Come on. Let's get back to the house," said Camille. "I'm going to call Lucas."

"Why?" asked Amaryllis.

"It's either him or the police."

Lacey started to cry even more loudly. "Mommy," she begged. "Please, please don't send him away."

"For all of our safety," began Camille, "we need to find out who he is. Get him some help." She looked at her daughter's sad eyes then added, "If he's lost, then his family has probably been looking for him."

"Can the church man find his family?" asked Lacey. Her coughs began to subside and she felt a little better having convinced her mother not to call the police.

"I have to call him to ask," replied Camille.

"Okay," Lacey said, realizing what her mother meant about him being lost. He had a family somewhere who loved him and missed him.

"You two go on," Amaryllis said without looking at her daughter. "I'm going to sit here for a minute." She sat on the bench, slowly and carefully, with a faraway gaze in her eye.

"Are you alright Mother?" asked Camille.

"Fine as rain," she answered.

Camille paused for a minute to watch her mother, then turned her attention to her daughter. Once in the house, she closed the back door with her foot, laid Lacey on the couch, pulled her phone out of her pocket, and dialed. "Lucas, it's Camille. Do you have a minute? It's, well…that's really not necessary. Oh, okay, thank you."

"What he say?" asked Lacey.

"He's at the golf course and will be here in a few minutes."

"Mommy?"

"Yes Lacey."

"Who did you think Gramma was feeding?"

Camille looked at her daughter, put her finger to her lip and tapped it for a few seconds. "You know, sweetheart, I really hadn't thought about it. Certainly didn't think it was a person. A raccoon, maybe?"

"How could Gramma forget about that pond?" she asked in between mild coughs. "I'll bet she made it a really a long, long time ago."

"She probably let the grass grow when she went on several trips and when she returned it eventually was completely hidden. Out of sight, out of mind as they say." Camille sat down next to her daughter and felt her forehead.

"Is that when she lost her memories?"

"I'm not sure."

A few minutes later, the doorbell rang.

"Thank you for coming by, Lucas," Camille said. She walked Lucas into the kitchen and they sat at the table. "Mom is outside."

"Whatever the problem is," Lucas began. He patted Camille on the hand and continued, "I will do all I can to help. Is your mother ill?"

"We went to the doctor and he says she has early dementia," answered

Camille. She pulled her hands away and put them in her lap.

"Yes, that's what we all thought," he stated. "Is it Alzheimer's?"

"No, he doesn't think so. Mother isn't why I need to talk to you." Camille looked at Lacey, gave her a reassuring smile, then stated, "A homeless man has been living in the woods behind the barn."

"Oh?" Lucas sat up straight.

"Apparently for years. Mother told us she had been feeding the deer. Lacey discovered him."

"You did?" Lucas turned and looked at Lacey. "You've seen the man?"

"Yes, his name is Danny and he's a war hero," stated Lacey. She sneezed, coughed, and blew her nose, suddenly anxious again about Danny's discovery.

"Really? He told you all this?"

"Well... he didn't tell me his name. I call him Danny and he said he liked the name. He wears a uniform jacket like my Daddy's and he has war medals on it. He told me he was in the Air Force."

"Lacey has spoken to him several times over the past few days," Camille said to Lucas while wiping her daughter's nose. "We, Mother and I, caught them talking this morning. Mother had no idea."

"How long has this been going on?" Lucas asked Camille.

"Danny said he's been here for a long, long time, but he doesn't know exactly," answered Lacey.

"Same with Mother. It could be many years," reiterated Camille.

"I may be able to help," stated Lucas. "I oversee a homeless ministry at the church. It's not a shelter. It actually started after a hurricane several years ago. There was a lot of flooding. Since we knew there were homeless camps in several wooded areas, a group of us went around looking for the people who lived there to see if we could help. All of their camps had been flooded and they had nowhere to go. The elders and church members all got together and decided to open our doors and let them stay until things dried up. Everyone got involved. I volunteered to oversee the ministry. One thing led to another and, basically, we never closed. They don't spend the night any longer, except on really bad weather days, freezes, things like that. What we do now is give them a hand up." Lucas paused for a moment. He looked out the back door and stated, "I wonder if he was one of the men we served."

"What's that mean?" asked Lacey.

"We assist those who are willing with whatever they need to get out of the woods. We help them find jobs, get them their documents- birth certificate, SS card, help with transportation, connect them with family, and most importantly, we minister to their spiritual needs."

"Can you find Danny's family?" Lacey asked. "He's really shy. Danny's not his real name, you know."

"We can try," stated Lucas with a pastoral smile. "I'd like to show you the offices," he turned and said to Camille. "We provide meals twice a week and tomorrow would be a perfect day for all of you to come in. Lacey can give us a description of the man to put in our data base of missing persons."

"We can do that," stated Camille. "What should we do in the meantime?"

"Stay calm. Try to make contact with him again. He's been found out so it's possible he's gone."

"No, he can't leave," cried Lacey. She jumped up and ran to the door. "I have to go find him, Mommy."

"Lacey, stop," ordered Camille. "I will go with you in just a minute. Thank you, Lucas. We'll go in the morning. Where is the office?"

"The King's Hero is the name of the ministry. Our offices are on the church property. You'll see the signs when you drive in. Come at nine."

"We will, thank you."

"Is there anything else I can do for you?" asked Lucas while being escorted to the front door. "Does Amaryllis need anything? Does Lacey need a doctor with that cold? Do you need anything?"

"One thing at a time," stated Camille. "See you tomorrow." Camille closed the front door before Lucas could offer any other service, turned and headed out the back with Lacey.

"Don't scare him," Lacey said as she followed her mother.

"I'm not. I need to talk to your grandmother." Camille stood on the patio for a minute, searching for her mother, then headed down the dirt path. "Mother!" she called out.

"I'm right where you left me," answered Amaryllis.

Lacey ran down the path towards the pond. She stopped when she got to the little bridge. There was her grandmother on her hands and knees, pulling weeds out of the pond. Amaryllis had mud up to her elbows and a smear across her cheek. The prior night's rain had filled the pond but the weeds prevented the water from flowing to the stream.

"Mother, what on earth!" exclaimed Camille.

"Go get me a shovel and a bucket out of the garage, Cami," stated Amaryllis without stopping or looking up. "If you two will stop staring and help me, we can get this pond cleaned up by lunch time."

"Mother, stop," insisted Camille. "We need to talk."

"Talk while you work, Cami," stated Amaryllis. "The rain made a mess of my pond. Look at all these weeds. Last summer it was full of flowers, now weeds." Amaryllis looked up at her daughter. "What? Why are you just standing there?"

Camille knelt down in front of her mother. "You said, just a few minutes ago, that you didn't know this existed."

"I did not."

"Mother, when did you start taking food out to the tree stump?"

"For the deer?" asked Amaryllis with a puzzled look on her face. "Oh my goodness, I don't remember exactly. It was sometime after the last hurricane. Maybe before that."

"Is that the same time you saw a prowler and bought the BB gun?"

"Could be."

"Mother, the man we saw Lacey talking to this morning, remember him?"

"Yes, the old hobo." Amaryllis put down the clump of weeds, looked at her daughter with a sudden realization and said, "I've been feeding a hobo man, not deer. Dear Lord, I had no idea."

"Homeless," she corrected. "It never crossed your mind?"

"No. Is that why you took me to the doctor?" Amaryllis asked. She stood up, looked from daughter to granddaughter, then around the pond. "My memory is going, isn't it?"

"The doctor said it's because you are alone too much, Mother. I'm not sure if that's accurate, but…"

"Did he give me medication? I'm not taking drugs."

"No. He suggested you get out more and be around people," said Camille. "Tomorrow morning we are going to The King's Hero to try to find the man's family. Maybe you can volunteer there."

"Did you call the police?" asked Amaryllis.

"No, Mother."

"Good."

"Can I take a jar of jam to Mrs. Beverly?" asked Lacey to try to change the subject. She was fearful of what might happen to Danny and the conversation about her grandmother's memory was making her anxious.

"You should probably take a nap," suggested Camille. "I don't know any doctors here to take you to if your cough gets worse."

"I'm not sick," insisted Lacey.

"I thought you and I could go find Danny after you rest a bit," stated Camille.

"Maybe tomorrow." Lacey was fairly certain the man was not going to allow himself to be found. "Can I go? Take the jam? I'll be careful."

"They won't answer the door," Amaryllis said with her hands elbow deep in the mud.

"Then I'll make them a card and leave a note," said Lacey.

"Why do you want to take them jam?" Camille asked.

"Well," began Lacey. "If Gramma is loosing her memories because she's alone, maybe they are mean because they are lonely."

"Ha!" snorted Amaryllis. "It's not loneliness that makes them they way they are, dear. It's all bubble gum and roses until something happens then your bubble pops and the thorns prick you in your behind. Thorns make them mean."

"What's that mean?" asked Lacey.

"Never you mind." Amaryllis said with a wink. She pulled another handful of gunk from the pond and said, "You take them some jam, honey. Cami, you stay here and help me pull weeds."

"What about the homeless man? Shouldn't we try to find him?" Camille stood between mother and child, looking from one to the other.

"Leave it alone, Cami," stated Amaryllis. "Help me with the pond and let Lacey work this out for herself."

Lacey wasn't sure what her grandmother meant, but took the opportunity to make an exit. She ran to the house, found a piece of paper and markers. She then made a card, emptied a small basket and put the card and two jars of jam in it. Once at the front door of her grandmother's cranky neighbor's house, Lacey stared at the window contemplating whether or not to ring the doorbell. What to say, she wondered? Invite them over for lunch? Maybe ask about their garden? What if they didn't answer? Leave the basket or come back? Lacey slowly reached out her quivering hand and held it over the doorbell.

"What do you want?" asked a deep, gruff voice from the other side of the door.

"I brought you a present," Lacey said with a shaky voice. "It's scrumptious jam."

"Go away. We don't have visitors," he said.

"Can I look at your pretty flowers?" asked Lacey, looking for a reason to stay a while.

"On your way out. Don't touch anything!" he huffed.

"Okay, bye-bye," said Lacey. She sat the basket down and skipped towards the flower garden. In the hope of someone opening the door, she walked slowly around the yard pretending to be interested in the flower beds. When no one did after several minutes, she turned, waved at the window, then skipped back to her grandmother's house.

Chapter 7

At 9 am precisely, Lacey's mother drove into the church parking lot. On the far side of the building was an older office building with several cars parked in front. A half dozen or so bicycles were propped up against a tree and a light pole. To the left of the tree several people were working in a tiny garden. Lacey pointed to a man near the garden.

"There's Mr. Ridgeway," she said.

"Did you know this was here, Mother?" asked Camille.

"No." Amaryllis shook her head and sat up higher in her seat.

After parking in the regular church parking area, the trio walked towards the garden where Lucas Ridgeway was working. Lacey trailed behind, watching the men and a few women go in and out of the building. They went in empty handed and returned with a full bag or backpack. Most were dressed very shabbily in dirty jeans and t-shirts. Some wore shoes. Others did not. Lacey stopped and stared when a woman and a little girl came out of the building. The girl was younger than Lacey and wore a dress that was too small and no shoes on her feet. In her hand, the little girl carried a new pair of sandals.

"Does she live in the woods like Danny?" Lacey asked her mother.

"Shh, not so loud," Camille said in a hushed voice.

"Camille!" Lucas called out upon hearing voices behind him. "I'm so glad you could come. I was just helping the guys with our new garden. It's not much. We don't really have the space, but it gives them something useful to do." Lucas strode over and took Camille by the hand and shook it gently.

"So, how can you help us find out who this man is?" asked Camille, prying her hand away.

"Come inside and let's get to work on that." Lucas led Camille into the building.

Lacey and her grandmother followed close behind. She stared in awe at all the people as he introduced Camille to several women with 'King's Hero' t-shirts on as volunteers. There was a room the size of a large closet filled with food - a food pantry, they were told. Adjacent was a room lined with shelves of clothing, tents, and what looked to Lacey like camping supplies. The last room was an area with several desks and computers. A volunteer sat at each desk with a homeless man or woman sitting beside them.

"My office is in here," said Lucas Ridgeway. He opened a door and motioned the trio to enter the small office. "Please take a seat."

Lacey stood by the door watching the homeless people as they were escorted by the volunteers from room to room gathering supplies. A very large Hispanic man with tattoos over every visible part of his body looked at Lacey then quickly looked away and turned his back to her.

"Lacey," said Mr. Ridgeway, "come tell me what you know about this man."

From the doorway, with her eyes glued to the Hispanic man until he exited the building, Lacey described Danny as best she could and told everything she could remember about how long he had been living in her grandmother's backyard. "You're not going to call the police, are you?" she asked. Lacey stared intently at Mr. Ridgeway's face.

"No," he assured her. "If he's been living there for that long, like you said, and not causing any problems, I'm sure he poses no danger to anyone. Our mission here," he said more to Camille than Lacey, "is to help get him out of the woods. Reunite him with his family, if possible. Now, what I'll do is search the missing persons report I get every week. I will also e-mail the VA and see if they having a missing person who matches his description. Mrs. Blythe, you said you've been feeding him since the last hurricane, is that right?"

"At least. How long ago was that?" answered Amaryllis.

"Three years, Mother," stated Camille.

"Well, let me think. It was before the last time I went to your house. Before Michael's...you know. Before the art festival in Tyler. I did not evacuate during the hurricane. We didn't have any damage here. A few trees went down across the lake and it flooded by the old horse stables. I hire a young man, the butcher's grandson, to feed the critters when I'm traveling. Well, now I do remember telling him to feed the deer. I think that was before the hurricane."

"So, it could be longer than three?" asked Camille. "You didn't tell me you hired someone to help out. I thought Willow did that."

"No. Willow doesn't go near the barn. She says she's allergic."

"No matter," stated Lucas. "I can go back as far as ten years for missing persons. If he's a veteran it should be fairly simple."

"Is there anything we should do in the meantime?" asked Camille.

"No. Continue doing what you have been. Talk to him. See if he can tell you about his family. Reassure him he's not in any danger. We don't want him to run."

Camille stood up. "Thank you, Lucas. Please call if you find out anything."

"I will. See you at church Sunday? Maybe we can have lunch."

"We should be there," answered Camille.

"Can I see the garden?" Lacey asked on their way out. She was curious about what they were growing and who was gardening. Lacey had never had a garden before, not even a flower bed. She didn't think getting her hands dirty was any fun.

"No, let the men work. We don't want to bother them," stated Camille.

Early the next morning, Lacey began preparing Danny's meal. This time, Amaryllis made several sandwiches and put them in a plastic container.

"No leftovers today," Amaryllis stated. "Now that I know what, or who, I'm feeding."

Lacey sat on the tree stump and waited. She called out to the trees but received no answer. "Where are you?" she called out with tears in her eyes after waiting for what seemed like an eternity. Lacey feared the worst, that he had run away. With Troy by her side, Lacey picked up the basket of food and stepped into the woods. She contemplated which way to go while looking for a path. The dog, at home in the woods, took off deep into the thicket of trees leaving Lacey alone. With much trepidation, the small girl wiped her nose which began to run the moment she stepped foot off the safety of the grassy area then began making her way through the trees in the direction Troy had run.

A patch of sunlit fallen pine needles caught Lacey's eye after several minutes of walking. Lacey dropped to the ground to catch her breath. It was a hot and humid day without a hint of a breeze even at this early hour. All around there were trees, trees, and more trees. Looking up, tiny slivers of blue sky peeked through the green canopy. Lacey had never been in the middle of a forest before. The sounds of a few chirping birds and an overhead airplane broke the silence of the otherwise still woodland.

"Danny!" Lacey called out. "Danny where are you?"

Several minutes passed with no answer. Lacey got up to continue her search. She sneezed, coughed, and felt a tightening in her stomach because of the growing anxiety of possibly being lost and because of Danny's disappearance. A noise to her right made her jump with fright. She froze until she saw a squirrel run across the forest floor. Lacey began to sing to herself to calm her nerves. From time to time, she stopped to pick wild flowers that grew in patches in the sparse sunlight and put them in her basket with the intentions of making a bouquet for Mrs. Jackson. Prickly underbrush caught Lacey's shoelace causing her to trip and fall. "Owie," she cried. Using a napkin, she wiped the dirt and blood from her knees then got up and continued her quest. A large, fallen tree was a good place to rest, Lacey decided after a full hour of wandering. Her stomach growled.

"I can't eat Danny's breakfast," Lacey said to herself. "Well, maybe it'll be okay if I eat the apple."

Straddling the large tree, Lacey examined her surroundings while nibbling on the fruit. The forest continued to be quiet and still with the exception of an occasional scurrying squirrel and chirp of a bird in the highest branches. Tall pine trees stood at attention towering in the sky. Majestic oaks surrounded her with thick underbrush showing no sign of a path. Sweat ran down her back while her nose continued to run. The heat, combined with the exhaustion from her trek through the woods made Lacey groggy. She pulled the dishtowel out of her basket, placed it on the tree, then laid down face first onto the towel to rest. In a matter of minutes, she was fast asleep.

Something wet and scratchy against her cheek awoke the sleeping girl with a jolt. She jumped up to find Troy sitting next to her in the dim light.

"Good boy, Troy," stated a familiar voice.

Lacey jumped and turned toward the voice.

"It's just me, missy," stated the old man. "What you doin' out here all by your lonesome? You are far from the lady's house."

"You didn't come for breakfast," Lacey sniffed. She sneezed three times in a row.

"You sick?"

"No. Where were you?"

"Out there," he pointed. "Troy came and got me. Does your momma know where you are?"

Lacey sneezed and shook her head. She swung her leg around and started to stand up but felt dizzy and sat back down on the tree. "I brought you this," she said, pointing to the basket. "I ate the apple. Sorry."

Danny stepped forward, gently lifted the little girl into his arms and said, "Let's get you home."

Lacey put her head against Danny's shoulder. She felt so safe in his arms that her body relaxed. She knew the old man would take good care of her. Lacey coughed then took a deep breath, closed her eyes, and fell back to sleep.

A bright light and loud voices brought Lacey out of the shadows of sleep.

"There she is! She's with a man!"

"Lacey! Oh, God. Is she hurt?"

"No ma'am. I found her in the woods."

"Mommy?" Lacey said weakly. The bright light blinded her.

"Okay boys, she's home safe," barked Amaryllis. "You can go home now. Lucas, thank you for coming. We'll take it from here."

"You sure you don't want me to stay?" asked Lucas.

"Positive."

"Cami?" he asked again.

"We're fine, Lucas."

Lacey closed her eyes tight against the glaring lights until she felt herself being lowered onto the couch. "Mommy, I got lost," she said with a weak exhale.

"Why on earth did you go into the woods, sweetheart?" asked Camille. She knelt down beside her daughter and stroked her sweaty forehead. "Mother, I think she has a fever. Will you get me a cool cloth? And a glass of water."

"I'm sorry," stated Danny. "I…I didn't mean it."

"What do you mean?" asked Camille. "Please, have a seat."

Danny sat on the edge of a hard-backed chair. He looked around the room, quite uncomfortable, and said, "Little girl said she came to look for me. I didn't come 'cause I was scared."

"It's not your fault," Camille said to assure him. "She was told not to wander into the woods."

"Yes'm," said Danny.

"Why didn't you come?" asked Lacey with tears welling up in her eyes. "Why would you leave me?"

"Hush now, Lacey," said Camille.

"Danny, come in the kitchen and eat your supper," ordered Amaryllis. She gave Camille the damp cloth then motioned for the man to follow her.

"Don't make him leave, Mommy," cried Lacey. "Don't let him leave me…again" she saint with a faint whisper.

"No worries, sweetheart." Camille placed the cloth on Lacey's forehead, stripped her of her dirty clothes, then covered her with a light blanket. "Take a drink. Good girl. Now, get some rest."

"So, Lacey tells me you've been living in my backyard," Lacey heard her grandmother say. "How long have you been here?"

"I don't know," answered Danny.

"What is your real name?" asked Camille from the living room.

"I...Uh...Danny is fine. I like it."

"Yes, but it's not your name," said Camille.

"That's okay."

"You can say if you don't remember," stated Amaryllis. "Apparently, I forget things, too."

"Yes'm," he answered after swallowing a large forkful of mashed potatoes.

"We only want to help you find your family," stated Camille. She kissed Lacey on the forehead and joined her mother in the kitchen. "I'm sure they are worried about you."

"You know," said Amaryllis after a long silence, "I thought you was a deer. I told everybody I was feeding deer all these years. Never crossed my mind it wasn't. You can tell us. We're not going to call the police."

"Nobody cares. Nobody is looking for me," stated Danny with a sorrowful glance towards Lacey.

"Honey, don't you talk like that. I don't like to hear that kind of talk. Of course somebody cares. If you're somebody's daddy, they care. If you have a momma or a wife or a sister out there, they care. Even if they are all gone, there is still someone who cares."

"Who?" he asked.

"Jesus. Jesus and don't you ever forget it!" exclaimed Amaryllis.

"Yes'm," he said.

"We care, too. Can you remember anyone's name?" asked Camille. "A friend, family member, maybe a city or place where you lived?"

"No."

The inflection in the man's voice made Lacey turn around and look. She thought he was going to cry which made Lacey cry and her nose run even more than before. Thinking of her father, Lacey wondered if he was out there somewhere lost and not remembering her. Would he forget her? Maybe he would be lost forever if no one helped him. The same feelings she had when first learning of her father's disappearance welled up in her heart and her stomach. Lacey began to shake, then cough. She began to wretch but since she hadn't eaten since morning, nothing came up. Her mother ran over with a trash can. Lacey was pulled into her mother's lap and rocked and soothed until the shaking stopped, her breathing slowed, and she was able to drink a few sips of water.

"Lucas can help," Lacey declared with as much energy as she could muster.

"Yes, yes he can," echoed Camille. "Feeling better?" she asked her daughter. When Lacey nodded, Camille returned her daughter to the couch and covered her with the blanket. She pulled her phone out of her pocket and said to Danny, "I want to take your picture."

"No," he said with a shake of his head.

"It's okay. You see, a friend of mine helps people like you. People who have lost their homes, lost their way in life, lost contact with family for whatever reason. He knows how to find people." Camille spoke in her teacher's voice. The one that usually calmed the frightened and angry children.

"He a cop?" asked Danny.

"No, a Christian. He serves at a shelter at his church."

"Preacher?"

"Not exactly."

"He a good guy?"

"I knew him a long time ago. He was then."

"He still is a good guy," added Amaryllis. "He is why Camille and Lacey are here."

Lacey looked up to see her grandmother put her arm around her mother and give her a hug. She had never seen that before. Amaryllis usually didn't hug anyone except Lacey, at least that she had seen. The smile on her grandmother's face told Lacey that Amaryllis was softening. Just then the doorbell rang.

"I'll get it," stated Amaryllis. "Don't know who that could be. Maybe Lucas found something." Amaryllis stopped to pat Lacey on the head then opened the door. "Beverly. What now?" she said, obviously annoyed. Softness gone for the moment.

"Oh. You're fine, I see," stated Beverly Jackson.

"I told you," stated her husband.

"We saw all the cars and thought..."

"What, that my house fell down on me and you'd be right all along?" said Amaryllis.

"Well, it could happen." Beverly stuck her head through the door and looked around. "I mean, goodness look at all that stuff. You have a child in the house now, Amaryllis. What did you say to that poor man to frighten him into passing inspection?"

"So, what was all the commotion about?" asked Lamont, butting in. "Glad that you aren't hurt and all that of course."

"Not that it's any of your business," began Amaryllis, "but Lacey wandered off and got herself lost."

"Lost? The poor child," gasped Beverly. "Now, I told you, didn't I tell her Lamont? I told you something would happen if you didn't clean up your property.

Lacey wrapped the blanket around her and went to the door "Hi," she said from behind her grandmother. "It's not her fault. Mommy told me not to go into the woods."

"Oh, dear," stated Beverly. She crossed her arms and looked at Lacey with a very stern, tight-lipped face. "Poor child looks…ill. You need to learn to obey your mother, young lady."

"Yes ma'am."

Lamont leaned down and said to Lacey, "We're glad you are home safe now." Straightening up and tightening his expression, he said to Amaryllis, "I'm sure you will now get serious about your living conditions and consider what we've been telling you. This," he waved his hand towards the living room, "needs to stop before someone gets hurt."

"Goodnight and thank you for stopping by," Amaryllis said then shut the front door before her neighbors could say anything else.

"They were worried about you," Lacey said while her grandmother led her back to the couch.

"No, they only want to be right."

"They are right, Mother," Camille said from the kitchen. "Yes, they may be nosy and grumpy people, but they are right. We need to clean up inside and out."

"Balderdash," Amaryllis said with a huff then stomped off to her room.

"Now, about that picture," Camille said to Danny after a sigh and a shake of her head.

"Danny," Lacey said from the couch, "I bet your family misses you. I know I would if you were my grampa."

"Well," began Danny. He looked from Lacey to Camille then nodded his head in agreement.

"Tell me about how you've been living," stated Camille while taking pictures. She made sure to get close ups of the jacket and the military medals on it.

"I camp out in the woods," he said.

"What about water and bathing?"

"I use the lake and the bathroom at night sometimes."

"Lacey said you go in the barn in bad weather. Is that right?"

"Sometimes."

"Then you are the prowler Mother thinks she saw. She bought a BB gun a while back. Did you know that?"

"Yes'm. I seen her shoot it."

"Really? She said she hadn't used it. No matter. Something else she forgot about, I suppose. Mother's dogs like to roam the woods. Are they friendly towards you?"

"Yes'm."

"Before Mother started feeding you, how did you eat?"

"Trash, gardens, chickens and the eggs, whatever I could find around," he said with a wave of his hand.

"What about in the winter?"

"I keep warm enough." Danny looked over at Lacey who was watching and listening closely. "I should go now."

"Don't let him go back to the woods, Mommy," said Lacey. "Call Mr. Ridgeway and see if he can find him a place to live."

Danny looked over at Camille. He wasn't sure what Lacey was talking about. "I won't go to a shelter."

"It's not a shelter," said Camille.

"Could he sleep here?" asked Lacey.

"I'm okay in my camp," Danny answered before Camille had a chance to answer.

"What about the barn?" Lacey got up, wrapped herself in the blanket, and walked to the kitchen. "He can use the blanket. The one we put in there."

"Is that why you wanted it?" asked Camille.

"Yes. I'm sorry I lied."

Camille scowled at her daughter, shook her head, then looked at Danny. "You may sleep in the barn tonight, if you'd like. I'm sure mother won't mind."

"Yes'm."

"Come in for breakfast tomorrow," Lacey said with a happy smile. "Please."

"Just there," he said, pointing to the porch.

"A picnic breakfast, yippee," exclaimed Lacey with a sudden burst of energy.

"Goodnight, Danny," Camille said from the French doors. "Thank you for finding Lacey and bringing her home safely." She reached out her hand towards the man.

Danny looked at Camille's hand, then her face, then Lacey's smile. He took Camille's hand briefly before turning and disappearing into the night.

"You, young lady," began Camille.

"I'm tired and itchy," said Lacey. She forced a cough, sniffed, then reached down and rubbed her knees. "I think I'll take a bath now."

Lacey was quiet all during her bath while her mother scrubbed every inch of her, toweled her dry, then dressed her wounds. She studied her mother's face. The worry and sadness was gone that had been there before coming to Wildwood and the quiet of her grandmother's house. Lacey wondered if it was because she wasn't getting sick quite so often or if it was because they were on vacation. Getting lost in the woods had brought some of the worry back, but it was gone now.

"What are you thinking about?" Camille asked. She tucked Lacey in and sat on the end of the bed.

"How long are we going to stay?"

"You keep asking that. Ready to leave already?"

"No. I was just worrying about Gramma. And Danny. You gonna yell at me now?"

"I think I will let you think about it for a while first." She kissed her daughter on the cheek then said, "I'm concerned about your grandmother as well. I think we may need to stay a while longer." Camille handed Lacey the bear and the picture, said the nighttime prayer, then turned out the light. "Sleep well. I love you."

"Love you, too, Mommy."

After breakfast, once Danny had eaten and excused himself, Lacey got a thorough scolding. She took it in stride, having prepared herself for the worst all night. She had not been spanked in many, many years and knew if she had ever deserved it, this was that time.

"I'm very, very sorry, Mommy," Lacey said after her mother and grandmother had their say. "I promise to be careful from now own." No tears this time. No coughing and no sneezing. Lacey woke up that morning feeling very brave. Never had she disobeyed her mother, at least never with anything so dangerous. "Last night I had this amazing dream, Mommy. I dreamed that there was a little girl and she was taking care of Daddy, just like I am helping Danny. She found him and fed him and took care of him until he got to go home."

"Is that why you call him Danny?" Camille asked.

"Danny rhymes with Daddy," stated Amaryllis with a shrug and a nod of her head. "Makes sense."

"That is a beautiful dream, Lacey." Camille pulled her daughter onto her lap and held her tight. "It is just a dream, sweetheart. As much as you and I both would like it to be real, we need to remember to not get our hopes up, in case it doesn't come true."

"I know, Mommy," stated Lacey. She was certain it would come true. "Mommy, can Danny move in here?"

"No, I told you that last night."

"But why not?"

"Well, for one thing, he would say no. For another thing, he's still a stranger."

"I don't want any man living in this house," said Amaryllis with a determined slap on the counter. "No man has lived here since your grandfather. I wouldn't even let Lucas live here."

"But, he found me and brought me home," argued Lacey.

"That's not reason enough to bring him into my home, darlin'," stated Amaryllis.

"What about the barn, Mother?" Camille said. She tapped the table with her fingers like she always did when she was thinking.

"Well, what about it?"

"I was thinking we could clean it up a bit. Fix him a room. That would get him out of the woods until we find his family." Camille paused for a moment then added, "He's apparently slept in the barn during storms."

"Well now, that's an idea. But what if we don't find his family?" asked Amaryllis.

"We can cross that bridge later. Let's go talk to Lucas." Camille stood up, indicating she was ready for action.

***

"We can put the man to work," Lucas said later that morning. "If he's willing to come here, that is. The guests earn points, which are equal to dollars. They save them up to earn things they need. We do this to get them back into the habit of working, instead of us just handing them everything. Some of these guys have been homeless for so long, they've forgotten how to work, how to provide for themselves. You see, the problem with being homeless is they get used to it. No bills, nowhere to be at any given time, no responsibilities. Once they start working, they give it their all. They are grateful for the opportunity, the hand up. Most, not all, anyway. Those guys at the garden earn points for planting, pulling weeds, harvesting. They get to take some of the produce for themselves and also sell it at a farmer's market. I know, it's a really small garden, but it's a start. If we had room to do a bigger one, we would. Several church members have hired, by hire I mean with points, guests to do work around their homes and others have worked at a shelter serving meals."

"Could they help us fix up the barn?" Camille asked.

"I haven't decided if I want it fixed up," stated Amaryllis.

"You said Danny could live there," Lacey said, hoping her grandmother wouldn't change her mind. "He already sleeps there sometimes."

"Yes, well I know." Amaryllis folded her arms and let out a sigh. "I don't want y'all messing with my stuff."

"Tell me about your barn, Mrs. Blythe," said Lucas. He pulled his chair around from behind his desk closer to Camille. "Is the roof leaking? Is there water and electricity?"

"The roof is fine as far as I know. My late husband built it. I had a horse and other critters and he built it real nice. I had plans to use it as an art studio after I sold the horse."

"So, it just needs to be cleaned up and maybe remodel a section for a bedroom and a bathroom?" asked Lucas.

Lacey watched her grandmother's face. It seemed to Lacey that her grandmother was warming up to the idea because she smiled, nodded, tilted her head from side to side and patted Camille on the knee. "Please say yes, Gramma," Lacey pleaded. "Please, please, please."

"Well now, looks like I'm outnumbered," Amaryllis said with a sly grin. "I will concede on one condition," she said with a wave of her finger in Lucas' face. "Nobody messes with my stuff. I use everything I have. Took me years to round up some of my collections. Everything has a purpose. You don't see it, but I do."

"We promise not to throw anything away," Camille said with an assuring squeeze of her mother's hand. "Without your permission."

Lacey leapt up out of her chair and clapped her hands together while jumping up and down. "Yippee!"

"Camille," Lucas said leaning in close to get her attention, "I will send out those pictures to the VA and other agencies I work with immediately. Monday, I will bring a crew over to start the clean up." He smiled at Camille and then said to Lacey, "We will get that barn fixed up for your friend in no time."

Lacey suddenly became very still. "What if Danny gets scared and runs away?"

"He won't if you explain to him what we are doing," answered Lucas. "It seems to me that he trusts you. Keep talking to him. Ask him more questions about his family and let him know you are his friend. However," he stopped and looked sternly into Lacey's eyes. "Remember he is a stranger. So, don't go anywhere with him alone. Veterans like him sometimes have short fuses."

Lacey didn't understand the last part, but understood his general meaning.

"That's right," continued Camille. "When we get home, if he's in the barn talk to him. Outside. If he isn't, go to the stump and call for him. One way or another, we will make sure he knows before anyone comes over."

Contemplating how Danny might react and how she should talk to him, Lacey stared out the window at the men wandering around in the parking area. "Do you really think you can find his family?" she asked. What she was really thinking was, 'if you find them soon he will leave me and I won't see him anymore.'

"There is no way to say for sure," answered Lucas. "But I will do my best."

Chapter 8

Danny was not in the barn when Lacey ran in to talk to him. Fighting tears and the fear of not finding him again, she slowly made her way to the stump. "Danny!" she called out in the loudest voice she could. "Danny!" Lacey sat on the stump and waited.

"Hello, Miss." Danny emerged from the dark of the forest. He stopped at the edge of the shadows and leaned against a large pine tree.

Lacey's face brightened. "I was afraid you ran away again."

"No, miss."

"We just come back from the church. Mr. Ridgeway is going to fix up the barn for you. He says he is going to bring some people like you and they are going to fix it up real nice." Lacey quickly rattled off the details. She was so excited about building a room for her friend that the words spilled out without her thinking about how he might react. "Mr. Ridgeway says he's going to try to find your family. He says the homeless people work for him and he pays them. Not in real money. He says they will be here soon on Monday morning and start cleaning up the barn for you. Just for you, isn't that nice! He says you can help, too. He says to tell you not to be scared. He kept saying that, 'tell Danny not to be scared.' He says…"

"Do I hav'ta?" Danny interrupted. He started to pace back and forth, in and out of the trees.

"Hav'ta what?"

"Go to the homeless shelter."

"No. Mr. Ridgeway says you don't have to help if you don't want to. You know, because you've been alone for a long, long, long time. He does want to meet you. He says he and the homeless men are going to fix up the barn real nice. Make you a real bedroom and a real bathroom. You won't have to live outside in the woods anymore. Until…"

Danny slumped down onto the ground. He looked away and said, "I like my solitude."

"Mr. Ridgeway says it's because you're used to it." Lacey's thoughts again went back to her father. "My daddy said he would love us forever. Even when he's not here. You think your family loves you forever? I think they do."

"Don't know."

"Mommy still loves my daddy. She said so."

"How long he been gone?"

"I was 6."

"That why you help me?"

"No. Well, maybe, I guess." Lacey looked at him then told him about her dream. This time she embellished it a bit. "Then at the very end, my Daddy walked into town holding the little girl's hand. A big heli-copter landed on the street and picked him up and flew him all the way home. The 'copter landed on the beach by the lake over there. Me and Mommy were having a picnic and he jumped out of the 'copter and ran over to us."

Danny smiled. "That's a nice story."

Lacey and Danny sat in silence for several minutes. She didn't want to walk away, didn't want him to either. The reasons she was helping him hadn't really occurred to her. She only knew he was alone in the woods and that was someplace wet and cold and lonely. People shouldn't live alone in the woods with no food or family. She knew that now especially after getting lost.

"Maybe I can help with something on my own," Danny said, breaking the silence.

"Do you know about the pond?" asked Lacey.

Danny shook his head.

"Come on, I'll show you." Lacey took Danny by the hand and led him down the path towards the house.

"Where are you two going?" asked Amaryllis. She was dressed in jean shorts - a little too short for a woman her age, an old tank top, and her usual boots, sitting on the patio weaving pine needles into a wreath.

"I'm going to show Danny the pond." Lacey forced back a laugh at the sight of her grandmother, thinking she looked funny.

"What pond?"

"The one down that path behind all the weeds," stated Lacey a little surprised her grandmother had forgotten so quickly.

"Really? Well now, I want to see that myself," Amaryllis said. She put down her handful of pine needles and followed.

"Where's Mommy?" asked Lacey.

"On the phone inside. She's busy so lead the way."

Lacey skipped ahead through the weeds and tall grasses on the faint path until they reached the pond. The mud from just a short time ago was now all dried up. Disappointed that it looked exactly like she had first found it, she frowned, shook her head and said, "See. Can't you imagine how lovely it used to be? I bet there were flowers here and there, maybe a fountain, and I'll bet the bench used to be the perfect spot to read."

Amaryllis walked around the pond pointing at different plants and features of the stream while Lacey and Danny watched. "I remember this place. My father laid the stones and my mother planted a breathtaking assortment of flowers. I used to keep it real pretty."

"What happened?" asked Lacey. She had no idea her parents had been on the property. Lacey thought her grandmother was remembering wrong.

"Well now, I guess I just forgot."

"Them chickens used to come here," stated Danny. His face suddenly changed as if he were remembering something. "One time, the coop door was left open. They all got out and came here."

"When was that and where was I?" asked Amaryllis.

"I...I..." Danny sauntered around to the far side of the pond where the stream made its way back and connected again at the high side. He scratched his head and said, "I don't recall. Memory just came about them silly chickens."

"Well then, I do have chickens. Beverly said that my chickens got into her yard. I haven't seen any in a while."

"I made a coop for 'em," answered Danny. "In the woods by my camp. I didn't steal 'em."

"No, of course not." Amaryllis walked over to Danny and put her hand on his arm. "You probably saved them from a forgetful old woman who didn't close the coop door."

"Yes'm. I suppose."

"Gramma," began Lacey, "you told Mommy that you hired a boy to take care of the animals when you traveled. Did you really, or was Danny doing it all along?"

"Did I say that?"

Lacey nodded her head.

Amaryllis walked over and sat on the bench. She folded her arms and looked up into the sky.

"Hey there," Camille said intruding on the moment as she rounded a clump of weeds. "What's going on?"

"Mommy!" Lacey ran over and gave her mother a hug.

"Hey sweet girl, you look very chipper," said Camille.

"Cami, did I say I hired someone to look after the place when I traveled?" asked Amaryllis, still in a bit of a daze, staring at the clouds.

"You did, Mother. Why?"

"I can't remember doing that. Maybe I did once. I just was thinking about the time when I went blackberry picking in Lufkin. I packed up the dogs and left. Last time I came to see you, I left the dogs here. I think Danny's the one who's been taking care of things."

"Is that right, Danny?" Camille asked.

"Yes'm."

"How did you know when she was traveling?"

"When she didn't bring breakfast." Danny shuffled his feet and looked down. "I don't remember the first time. Just, whenever she don't come, I know she gone."

"What did you do for food when she was gone?" asked Lacey.

"I make do. There's a garden yonder," Danny turned around, looked from side to side as if he was thinking and finally pointed beyond the pond.

"How did you feed the animals?" Camille asked.

"The garage door is always unlocked, and the barn."

"Did you think she knew you were here?" asked Camille.

"I…"

Lacey began to feel uncomfortable with all the questions. She sensed Danny's discomfort as well. "Mommy, can Danny fix up the pond while Mr. Ridgeway does the barn?"

"Oh, that's what I came out here to tell you. Mother, Lucas and his crew will be here Monday morning at 9. Danny, he would very much like to meet you."

Danny nodded. "Missy say the men he bring are homeless."

"Yes, that's right," said Camille. "He can tell you about it then."

"Where will Danny sleep while the barn is being built?" asked Lacey.

"I sleep in my camp," answered Danny.

"Can we see it?" Lacey was curious about where Danny lived and what the chicken coop looked like.

"No, sweetheart, we don't want to intrude on his privacy." Camille took Lacey by the hand and pulled her close.

"I can start now," Danny said. He motioned to the weeds blocking the stream.

"I'll help!" Lacey offered.

"No, I need your help inside. We have to get ready for Lucas and his crew." Camille led a sad Lacey by the hand away from Danny and the pond.

"You know where the tools are," Amaryllis said to Danny over her shoulder as they walked away.

"Can I make cookies?" Lacey asked once her mother had her safely inside the house.

"Yes, let's make cookies," agreed Amaryllis.

Both Lacey and Amaryllis were anxious about the changes Monday morning would bring. Amaryllis' anxiety was simple – she didn't want her stuff messed with. Lacey had a lot more on her mind. Change was something she had not been able to handle well. As much as she wanted to help Danny get out of the woods, into a dry home, and find his family, she had become comfortable with the way things were, even after such a short period of time. Danny had been Lacey's secret friend and she liked that. Now that everyone knew about him, the excitement was no longer there. If his family was found, that meant he would leave and she would be all alone yet again. Repairing the barn meant people, lots of people, grown-ups. That meant staying out of the way and playing by herself. What if Danny didn't want her to help with the pond or if her mother didn't want her to be outside when all the people were there? What if her mother decided Gramma no longer needed their help and they had to go back home? Lacey shook her head while scooping out the dough and putting it on the cookie sheets. Too much change, she thought. She took a deep breath, anticipating the usual, but it did not come. No coughing, sneezing, or running nose.

"Can I make a card and take some cookies to the neighbors?" Lacey asked.

"Why on earth would you want to do that?" asked Amaryllis.

"Mother! Yes, of course you can," Camille said to her daughter. "Why don't you draw something pretty, maybe your vision of the pond, while the cookies cool?"

"Oh, yes. I think I like to do that!" Lacey exclaimed.

Amaryllis huffed, then reluctantly gave Lacey a piece of watercolor paper and paints. A table by the back window was set up for Lacey to paint on. "Use this. They won't appreciate it, but if that's what you want to do, go right ahead."

"Maybe you could invite them to church," suggested Camille.

Amaryllis turned and shot her daughter a shocked look, opened her mouth to say something, then turned and went back into the kitchen without saying a word.

The sun was high and hot by the time Lacey reached the Jackson's front porch. She reached up with greater courage than the last time and rang the doorbell. No answer. Lacey leaned over the porch railing and looked in the window. The curtains were closed tight. Lacey rang the doorbell again then sat on the porch swing. She wasn't planning on waiting for them for very long because her mother told her to go straight there and straight back. It was just too hot to walk home right away. Lacey swung back and forth a few times, creating her own breeze. Several minutes later, she gave up. The simple water color picture of the pond was propped up between the basket of cookies and the back of the swing so the Jackson's could see it as soon as the door was opened or someone came onto the porch.

"Bye. See ya later," Lacey called out to the front door then skipped back to her grandmother's house.

Sunday morning, the household awoke to the crack of thunder. Amaryllis refused to go to church arguing that she never drove in thunderstorms. Much to Lacey's relief, her grandmother did take Danny a day's worth of meals in a cooler out to the barn. Camille refused to let Lacey help or even step foot outside as long as it was raining. The day passed quietly while Camille read and Lacey paced the house or watched her grandmother bounce from one craft project to the next. After lunch, Camille tried to rearrange some of the boxes in the living room, but Amaryllis would have none of it. Lacey, not wanting to hear an argument, found a book and retreated to her room. The previous summer, reading in her room was all Lacey wanted to do. This summer, after being able to run and play outside every day, being inside was torture. Amaryllis did not have cable or even a TV to watch videos on so her only options were to read or join in on the crafts.

The thunderstorm stopped shortly after midnight and by morning there was little trace of it having ever rained. Dry, dusty ground had soaked up the rains quickly and the rest evaporated in the heat of the morning sun. East Texas summer was upon them in full force. It was hot and humid with steam rising from the pavement and patio as if the ground were on fire.

Even with the air conditioner on, Lacey woke up in a sweat with the sheets on the floor. She jumped up and pulled on a pair of old overalls and a tank top. Today was barn day, as she was calling it. First one down the stairs, Lacey made breakfast for Danny and ran out the door before anyone could stop her. Remembering her mother's orders, just in the nick of time, Lacey knocked on the barn door.

"Mornin' miss," Danny said after pushing open the door.

"You stay dry?" she asked.

"Yes, miss. I heard the thunder and came here fast. It's that time of year."

"What do you mean?"

"Storm season. Happens every summer." Danny took the tray out of Lacey's arms then asked, "Them men here yet?"

"No. Nobody's up yet."

"I'll eat then go to the pond and start my work. Scoot, yer momma will worry," Danny stated.

"Okay. See you later."

At 9:30, two trucks and a van pulled into the driveway. Lacey watched from the upstairs window. She counted four men and two women as they climbed out of the van. Lucas gathered them all together then walked by himself to the front door. Lacey ran downstairs as quick as she could. Her mother beat her to the door.

"Good morning, Lucas," Camille stated.

"Good morning. Missed you at church." Lucas smiled and reached out to pat Camille on the shoulder.

"Mother's afraid of driving in the storm." Camille looked over at Lacey then said, "Mother's in the back. Why don't you take them around the side of the garage to the barn. I'll meet you there." She shut the door then said to her daughter, "I'm going to be busy today so I need you to find something to do near the house."

"I told Danny I would help him with the pond," Lacey said sitting on the steps with her arms crossed. "He's probably waiting for me."

"That'll be fine as long as you don't go into the woods. Let me get some supplies for you from Mother. I think she has rubber gloves in the garage."

Lacey followed her mother while she gathered supplies and then out the back door. She and her mother stopped in their tracks on the patio. Amaryllis was barking orders to the group.

"Don't anyone think about throwing anything out," she was saying. "Put everything on these tarps and I will sort through them." Amaryllis pointed to the blue tarps she had spread out in front of the pig pen. "No smoking and no alcohol on my property either. Show me your plans, Mr. Ridgeway."

Camille picked up a rake and shovel that was leaning against the little wall and led Lacey to the pond. "I think Mother has things under control for the moment."

Lacey watched for a few seconds. Her grandmother barking orders reminded her of a drill sergeant she had seen once at the base. A strangely dressed drill sergeant with her wide-brimmed straw hat, jean shorts, and cowboy boots. Mr. Ridgeway kept nodding as if he were listening very carefully to every word. She wondered what the two women in the group were going to do. They were dressed for work in well-worn jeans and t-shirts. One lady looked about her mother's age and the other much younger. Were they here to clean or to build?

"Good morning, Danny," said Camille once at the pond. She sat the tools down and looked from side to side. "Rain's got it all muddy again."

"Yes'm."

"Lucas and his men are here. Would you like to come meet them?"

Danny shook his head. He kept his head low while pulling weeds out of the stream.

"That's fine. Do you mind if he comes over in a little while?"

"Okay."

"Lacey wants to help. I'd rather she not get muddy. Are there snakes in there?" asked Camille. She peered into the murky waters.

"No."

"Good. She can hand you tools and be your assistant. Lacey," she said turning her daughter by the shoulders to face her, "stay out of the water."

"Yes, Mommy."

"I'll be back in a little bit." Camille patted her daughter on the shoulder then walked away, looking behind her every few steps.

"You don't like dirt?" asked Danny.

"Mommy doesn't," stated Lacey. "I've never…done that," she said pointing to Danny with his hands elbow deep in the mud.

"Mud don't hurt. But she say 'no', then 'no'." Danny pulled out a handful of weeds. "Hand me that bag."

Lacey worked with Danny, him pulling weeds and her holding open the trash bag or picking up the weeds he dropped until she got extremely hot and tired. Cleaning up the pond was going to be a long, dirty, hot process, she decided. She talked to Danny briefly about plants and flowers and tried to get him to remember what the pond looked like the first time he saw it. He shook his head and insisted he didn't know.

"I'm gonna get a drink. Be right back. I'll bring you one, too," Lacey said, tired of the heat.

Inside was not much cooler, even with the air conditioner on. Lacey drank her fill, found a water bottle for Danny, filled it up, then when she headed back outside, the phone rang. Her mother's phone was sitting on the end table next to a cat. Lacey hesitated, then grabbed the phone and answered it.

"Hello?"

"Camille?" said the voice on the other end.

"No."

"Oh, Lacey," said the slightly annoyed-sounding voice. "Hello, dear, this is Mrs. Norma. Is your mother at home?"

"She's outside with Gramma," stated Lacey. "I'll go get her."

"That's not necessary, dear. Please give her a message. I'm going out of town on Thursday and I would so very much appreciate it if you and your mommy would come by and take care of things like she always does," stated Norma in a sickly sweet voice.

"Okay, I'll tell her but we probably can't."

"Whatever do you mean?" she asked. "Camille always takes care of things when I'm away."

"We're on vacation," stated Lacey.

"Oh, I see." There was silence for several seconds then, "Well, when will she be back?"

"I dunno."

"She didn't tell me she was leaving town," Norma huffed.

Lacey shrugged. She didn't know what to say. "You want me to get her?"

"No," Norma said bluntly with an audible sigh. She then hung up.

Lacey shrugged, put the phone down, picked up the water then started to go back outside. The doorbell rang. Lacey put the water down, shrugged again, and went to the door.

"Young lady, is your grandmother at home?" asked Beverly Jackson the second the door opened.

"Hi," said Lacey. "Did you get the basket?" She looked from Mrs. Jackson to her husband and back.

"What basket?" Beverly looked cross. Folded her arms and stared at Lacey.

"The one I left on the porch. I drew a picture of the pond for you."

"Lamont got it," she answered without a tone of appreciation, a thank you, or a smile.

Lacey waited for her to say more. Instead they stared at each other for several seconds, which seemed like much longer.

"Well?" Beverly finally said with her arms crossed over her chest and even more of a scowl on her face.

"She's in the back yard," said Lacey.

"Well don't just stand there," snapped Mr. Jackson. "Go and get her."

"I don't think so that I should. She's kinda busy. You wanna come in and go out back with me?"

Lamont and Beverly looked at each other then she said, "Go in there? I think not."

Lacey shrugged. "You can go around." She pointed in the direction the workers had gone.

"Who's at the door?" Amaryllis called out from inside the house.

Lacey turned around. Her grandmother was standing in the opening of the back French doors. "The neighbors," she answered.

"Good Lord, what do they want?" Amaryllis said half to herself. She stomped the dirt off her boots then made her way to the front door. "What?" she asked the couple at the door.

"We were just checking on you," said Beverly with a forced smile. "With the storm last night and all these trucks this morning, we just came by to see if everything was alright."

"Sure you did," stated Amaryllis. She folded her arms and planted her feet, ready for a fight.

"The barn's getting re-modeled," stated Lacey hoping to stop an argument.

"Oh?" Beverly looked shocked. "You are going to remodel the barn but leave this?" She pointed towards the living room. "I hope you pulled permits."

"What permits?" asked Amaryllis. "We don't live in the city."

"I thought you didn't have the money to remodel," said Lamont.

"The homeless men are doing it for free," said Lacey with a huge smile, thinking that would please the neighbors.

"What?" they both gasped.

"You have…homeless…," Beverly whispered, "people here? On your property? With a little girl. That's just not right, Amaryllis. You've gone and put all of us in danger."

"Should I call the police?" Lamont asked his wife.

"Don't be absurd," laughed Amaryllis. "Would you like to talk to the preacher? He's here too."

"The preacher? What's the preacher doing hanging around homeless people?" asked Beverly. She was quite shocked at the idea.

"I guess for the same reason Jesus preferred to hang out with sinners," stated Amaryllis.

"Well…I…," began Beverly.

"Good-bye. Unless you want to help, don't bother coming again." Amaryllis pulled Lacey back and slammed the door shut. "The nerve of those people," she shouted. "Come on, baby girl, we've got work to do."

For the third time, Lacey once again headed out the back door. Amaryllis picked up the water bottle and led the way towards the pond. Lacey stopped abruptly at the entrance. Danny was working side by side with the two women.

Amaryllis handed Danny the water bottle then said, "Lacey, this is Rona and Susan. They are going to help with the pond. Ladies, this is my granddaughter, Lacey."

The women and Lacey nodded at one another. Lacey looked up at her grandmother as if to say, what am I supposed to do? The woman named Rona motioned for Lacey to help her rake up the debris pulled out of the pond and put it in the trash. They smiled and worked silently pulling weeds, cutting down grass, and washing slime off the rocks Danny pulled out of the stream bed.

During their lunch break, Lacey and the other women prepared sandwiches on the patio. Camille took lunch first to Danny, and then Lucas came and helped her take lunch to the men in the barn. It was even hotter than the day before and Lacey wanted very much to go inside, take a cool bath and get a nap, however, the activity and her curiosity about the people who had invaded her quiet existence kept her from doing so.

"What is that, Mrs. Blythe?" the woman called Susan asked. She pointed to the boxes on the side of the patio containing twigs, horse hair, pine needles, dried flowers, and the three old wicker-bottom chairs.

"Those are two different projects," began Amaryllis. "That one, I'm making wreaths out of the twigs and dried flowers. With the chairs, I'm going to build planters."

"What will you do with them?" asked Rona.

"Sell them at the flea market and craft fairs."

"Can you teach us?" asked Susan. "Where I live this stuff is all over the place."

Well, I suppose I could," stated Amaryllis. She stood up a little taller and smiled. "Rona, would you like to learn, too?"

"Yes'm."

"Mother," interrupted Camille. "Can we finish one project at a time, please."

"Yes," Lucas said, jumping in, "I'd like Susan and Rona to help Danny finish the pond first. We have plenty of time for crafts."

"If we had a weed-whacker we could get the pond cleared a lot faster," stated Rona. She picked up a half finished wreath and traced her finger around the vines.

Lucas looked over at Camille who was nodding in agreement. "Let me make a call," he stated. "I'm sure I can round up all the supplies you need." Lucas stood up a little straighter after getting an approving nod from Camille, pulled his phone out of his pocket and dialed.

Chapter 9

Lacey wandered back to the pond after eating her PB&J sandwich. There, she found Danny already hard at work raking weeds out of the stream. Picking up where she left off, Lacey began putting the discarded plants into the trash bags. An hour or so later she heard a loud whirring noise. The weed-whacker had arrived. The dust it kicked up made Lacey's eyes water and her nose run so she had to leave the pond area. Instead of going indoors like her mother suggested, the little girl sat under a large oak tree and watched the men who were working on the barn. Two tarps were piled high with boxes, crates and plastic bins, old bicycles, and saddles. Muffin, the miniature horse was running around the pen, neighing. Concerned that all the activity was upsetting her, Lacey picked up a grooming brush from the tarp, climbed inside the pen, and began to brush the horse. Muffin pranced around a bit, agitated at all the commotion, then finally settled down to let Lacey brush her. From the corner of her eye, she saw her mother watching.

"I'm surprised you hadn't befriended Muffin sooner," Camille stated. "Most little girls love ponies." She walked up and leaned against the wooden railings.

"She's soft," stated Lacey. "Kinda like a big dog."

"Remember what your gramma said." Camille ducked under a rail and joined her daughter in the corral. "No riding her."

"I know." Lacey stroked Muffin's nose then said, "Oh, Mommy! I forgot."

"Forgot what?"

"Mrs. Norma called."

"She did?" Camille squatted down to be eye to eye with her daughter.

"Yeah. She said she wanted you to watch her house. I told her we were on vacation and she sounded kinda mad."

"Seriously?" Camille straightened up and shook her head. "We've been gone two weeks and she just noticed? I suppose shouldn't be surprised. Did she say anything else?"

"No. She hung up. Then, the neighbors came to the door," Lacey said, continuing to brush Muffin down her shoulders and across her back.

"Oh?"

"Yeah Gramma came in and told 'em to go away. They didn't say thank you," Lacey said with a sad shake of her head.

"They probably had other things on their mind."

"Uh-huh. Mrs. Jackson almost fainted when I told her homeless people were here."

"Hmm." Camille was about to say more when Lucas waved and walked over to join them.

"We are done for today, Cami," he said. Lucas smiled at Lacey then stated, "We've got a lot of work to do on that barn. We can handle it, though. The weather should hold for at least a week, if we're lucky." He looked up at the sky as if to study it.

"How long do you think it'll take?" asked Camille.

"Hopefully not that long. A few days…a week. I met with Danny briefly. He wouldn't, or couldn't, tell me his real name. Nice guy. Total memory loss from what I can tell. He and your mom are in the same boat. She's a hoot by the way."

"Yes, well we all knew that. What do you think of Rona's idea of learning crafts and selling them?"

"I think that's a great idea. Of course, after we get our initial projects near completion. Will be good for the women and for your mom as well. I know of a few other women who might enjoy learning. I'll bring them tomorrow if I can. Let them get a feel for the place."

"That's good. I'd like for them to use up some of this stuff and get rid of it." Camille pointed to the growing piles on the tarps. "She wasn't in the way too much was she?"

"Who? Your mother?" Lucas placed a hand on Camille's shoulder and laughed. "No, she gave us orders and stayed out of the way for the most part. Helped where we could let her. I noticed her memory isn't so good. From time to time she forgot things we had just talked about."

"The doctor said stress makes it worse," answered Camille.

"I can see that." Lucas stood and smiled at Camille, looked around as if thinking of something else to say, then said with a reluctant sigh, "I guess it's time for us to head out. See you tomorrow, Cami. Bye Lacey." Lucas waved then headed towards the group who had huddled up under the oak tree.

For the next two days, Lucas and his crew arrived in the morning and worked diligently throughout the day cleaning and remodeling the barn. Rotten wood was removed and replaced, new beams installed, and Danny's new rooms began to take shape. Rona and Susan were joined by two other women who worked on the pond until all the weeds were gone and the path, bridge, and bench could be seen from the house. They then discovered the barely used garden. Amaryllis was still using about an 8-foot square section of it, however, the original size was three times bigger. Danny told them he often kept it weeded and watered whenever

Amaryllis forgot about it or was traveling.

Late in the afternoon the women gathered on the patio to learn how to make twig wreaths. Lacey sat and watched as Amaryllis took on a new role as their teacher. The sweet grandmotherly voice became more authoritative much like her mother's when in front of a classroom. Lacey liked this change and tried her best to join in but she had a hard time bending the twigs. Most of them, she broke at first attempt. After several valiant efforts she gave up, deciding instead to move a stool close to Rona who got the hang of it quite quickly. Rona's first attempt, Lacey thought, was flawless. Perfectly round and looked like a starburst. Red and yellow dried flowers attached to the ends made the wreath look like it was on fire. The little girl began to follow her grandmother around in amazement. The older woman seemed happier and completely at ease as she patiently taught the women the fine art of wreath making.

"How come you can do that?" Lacey asked Rona. She was curious about this woman who was such a hard worker and learned new tasks much faster than everyone else.

Rona shrugged, "It's not hard."

"Yours is almost better than Gramma's," Lacey whispered.

"Thanks." Rona smiled, darted her eyes towards Amaryllis then down to the ground.

"How come you're homeless?" asked Lacey. "I don't think so you should be. You're smart."

"Life happens, little one," stated Rona.

"Like what?"

"Like grown-up stuff."

"What kind of grown-up stuff?" Lacey could tell Rona didn't want to talk about her life, however, she wanted to know if her life was similar to Danny's. "Were you in the Air Force?"

"No," Rona said. She put the wreath down, looked Lacey in the eyes, then said, "You really want to know?"

"Uh-huh," she said to Rona then looked over at her grandmother for approval. Lacey had been curious ever since the first day Lucas brought the 'homeless' people to her grandmother's house. They all worked hard. No one complained. Sure, some of them smelled funny and their clothes were old and worn. It didn't make sense to her that such hard-working and nice people did not have homes or families who cared for them.

Rona moved a stool to a shady spot at the edge of the patio. "I moved to Texas with my husband," she began after sitting and staring at the pond for a moment. "I grew up in Colorado. A couple of years after, our kids went back to Colorado to go to college. My husband, well he did some bad stuff and lost his job. I was working but it didn't pay all the bills. We lost one car then two, went from a nice house to an apartment to a trailer. One day, he didn't come home."

"He died?" asked Lacey.

"No. He, uh, he moved on."

"Oh." Lacey wasn't real sure what that meant. She guessed he moved back to Colorado.

"Anyway, I got real depressed – sad. I didn't go to work for a while then when I did go back I was fired. I went to a shelter for women, but didn't like it there."

"Did you call your children?"

"No." Rona reached out, touched Lacey gently on the arm, then retracted and looked away. "They were doing so well. Making good grades in school. I didn't want to upset them. Both kids were on scholarship and living in dorms. I didn't want to burden them."

"What about your parents or brothers or sisters?" asked Lacey.

"My parents were angry when I moved away. They didn't like my husband. I knew they would just say, 'I told you so.' I wasn't about to call them. I was too embarrassed to call my brother. He would probably be embarrassed to know he had a homeless sister. He's a successful businessman now. I don't want to embarrass him.'"

Lacey looked at Rona. She didn't understand how someone who had family couldn't reach out to them for help. It wasn't her fault. She didn't do anything wrong. Wanting more answers, Lacey spoke her mind. "If your family loved you, they would understand you didn't do anything wrong. You're not a bum. It's…it's what you said. Life happened. I don't know what that means, but I don't think so that your family won't help. You should tell them exactly what happened to you."

"I can't," stated Rona. She stood and looked over towards Amaryllis who was working with Susan and the others who were packing up and getting ready to leave for the day.

"But why?" asked Lacey.

"What can you teach us tomorrow, Mrs. Blythe?" asked Rona, ignoring Lacey's question.

Lacey sat in Rona's chair. She was sad as well as confused by Rona's refusal to contact her family. She wondered if Mr. Ridgeway knew about the woman's family and if he could call them. "I'll ask him, myself," Lacey whispered to no one.

"How about planters, like those?" suggested the youngest woman. She pointed to the wall of eclectic planters. "We can maybe use some of the things that came out of the barn."

"Oh that's a great idea," chimed in Susan.

"Well, now," Amaryllis said. She smiled as she admired her students' work. "That's a scrumptious idea."

"You ladies ready to go?" Lucas asked as he strolled up to the patio. He wiped his face with a rag while looking straight at Camille.

"Mr. Lucas, can we sell these at the farmer's market?" asked Rona.

"I don't know…"

"Of course they can," stated Amaryllis. "You said yourself you wanted to teach them a trade. Teach them how to make a living. I've done it for years and so can they."

"We'll talk about it in the morning," stated Lucas. "I need to talk to you about the garden tomorrow as well. Good night Camille, see you tomorrow."

"That man should be ashamed of himself," Amaryllis said after Lucas rounded the corner of the house. "He flirts with you shamelessly."

"He's just being nice, Mother," stated Camille with a shake of the head.

"There's nice and then there's nice," she said with a wag of her finger.

"You're not going to marry him are you, Mommy?" Lacey asked. She had noticed how friendly Mr. Ridgeway was, how he was always touching her mother, and she didn't really like it.

"Of course not, honey," assured Camille. "He already has a wife."

"Oh," she said with great relief. "Did you know Ms Rona has a family in Colorado?"

"No," answered her mother.

"Maybe you can tell Mr. Ridgeway and maybe he can find them. She told me she didn't want to…uh…burden…yeah, burden them."

"She didn't say anything to me," stated Amaryllis. "Are you sure she's telling the truth?"

"Mother, of course she is. Why would she lie to a little girl?" Camille shook her head at her mother then said, "I'll talk to Lucas tomorrow, sweetheart."

"Okay, Mommy. Can I stay outside until dinner?"

"For an hour," answered Camille. "Don't go far. I'll call you when dinner is ready."

"Can Danny eat with us?" Lacey asked. She pointed towards the pond where Danny was sitting on the bench.

"Well...I..." began Camille.

"Yes, he can," Amaryllis finished. "He's been working very hard. Go invite him, baby girl."

Lacey skipped off towards the pond. She loved how much better it looked and admired Danny and the others for their work. They had not planted any new flowers yet, but the weeds were all gone, the grass cut down, and the water now flowed freely through the pond, down the stream and back thanks to a pump that one of the workers found and repaired. The tall, grassy weeds around the garden had also been cut back. The garden itself still needed work, a lot of work. Lacey stood on the little wooden bridge and marveled at all the work that had been done. Her grandmother's back yard was looking less and less like a forgotten secret garden and more and more like a nature preserve or an old-fashioned farm.

"What'cha think?" Lacey asked Danny.

"Looks nice."

"Gramma says you can come to dinner."

"I'm real dirty," answered Danny.

Lacey shrugged. "So. I don't think so that it matters."

"I can't go inside dirty."

Lacey thought for a moment, then said, "Don't you have other clothes?"

"No."

"Really?" Lacey was shocked. She hadn't paid attention to his clothes before, but now that she looked him over, really looked, she noticed he was much dirtier than when they first met. "Be right back." Lacey ran to the house, flew through the back door and out of breath announced, "I need clothes for Danny. He doesn't have anything. Nothing at all. His clothes are all muddy from working and he has no clothes to change into. Gramma, do you have something for him to wear? Anything at all?"

"Slow down, Lacey," cooed Camille. "You mean he only has the clothes he is wearing?"

"That's what he said and he is really, really dirty," said Lacey. "He says he won't come to dinner because he's too dirty."

"I have a box in the garage." Amaryllis put down her big spoon and headed to the door.

Lacey followed. "I didn't know," she said almost in tears. "He wore the jacket all the time, but I...I...I didn't know."

"It's okay, Lacey," stated Amaryllis.

"No, it's not," she said with a sorrowful heart. "I should've asked. I change my clothes every day. Mommy gets mad if I wear the same underwear two days in a row. He's worn his...forever in a row."

Amaryllis made her way to the back of the dusty, cramped garage to a large plastic tub on a top shelf. She climbed a footstool and pulled the box out. It slid out of her hands, hit the floor, and cracked open. "Take out whatever you think might fit."

"Where'd these come from, Mother?" asked Camille, who had followed.

"They're your father's."

"You kept them?"

"Do you see me throwing anything away?" asked Amaryllis. "I told you. I keep everything because you never know when you might need something one day."

Lacey pulled out two pairs of pants and two shirts. "How will he get clean?"

"The shower has been roughed in," Camille stated. "He can clean up in the barn. Mother, I need soap and a towel."

Supplies in hand, Lacey returned to Danny who was touched by the gift. Lacey walked him to the barn and told him to come to the house as soon as he was dressed. She noticed his feet and ran back to the garage to find shoes. With the assistance of her grandmother, the little girl found what she was looking for, placed them on the patio and waited. Several minutes later, Danny arrived in his newer clothes.

"They're a little big," stated Lacey.

"Fit fine," said Danny.

"I found the shoes."

"Thanks miss."

"Come on, dinner's ready." Lacey took Danny by the hand and marched him proudly to the kitchen table.

The meal passed quietly. No one knew quite what to say or how to act with this man in the house. Even Amaryllis was uncharacteristically mute. After the meal, Danny took his plate to the sink, said his thank you, and excused himself for the evening with the promise to return in the morning to work in the garden. Lacey waved and watched him retreat to the barn. As soon as he was out of sight, the phone rang.

"Hello," stated Camille with a tone of voice that indicated she knew who was on the other end. "Yes, I've seen Mother. In fact, I'm at her house now. Improving. Remodeling the barn. Come down and see for yourself. No, not yet. No, the house does not stink." Camille looked at her mother and shook her head. "Willow, if you are so concerned I suggest you get in your car and drive yourself the 20 minutes it takes to get here. Bye Willow."

"Is she coming?" asked Amaryllis once Camille hung up.

"I don't know."

"She's just mad because today's her birthday and nobody called," stated Amaryllis.

"It is?" Camille gasped. She tapped on her phone a few times then said, "Oh, sure is. Oops. I've been so busy I forgot. How'd you manage to remember that?"

"It's on my calendar in my room. I keep an old-fashioned paper one with big numbers," answered Amaryllis with a wave of her hands to show the size. "I might not remember once I leave the room, but I do have it on my calendar. I guess her call just now brought my rememberies back," she said to Lacey with a wink.

"Can we make Aunt Willow a cake and invite her over?" asked Lacey.

"You would be okay with that?" Camille studied her daughter's face. "You ready to start celebrating your own birthday?"

Lacey shrugged.

"What do you mean? You don't celebrate your birthday?" Amaryllis was astonished.

"Not for the past two years," Camille answered for her daughter.

Amaryllis sat on the couch and pulled her granddaughter onto her lap. "I know you miss your daddy, honeybunch. You love him very much, so does your mother. Wherever he may be, whatever may have happened to him, you must continue to live."

Lacey nodded then leaned back against her grandmother's chest. She didn't like to think about her father not coming back, of growing up without him. Her mother's words came back to her, how her father might feel if he knew she was sad all the time and not happy, not playing with friends or going to birthday parties but moping all day every day. He knew she loved him. She told him on the last video call and he had told her he loved her and to 'have fun'. Doing what, she didn't remember.

"Well now, baby girl, do you remember your grampa?"

Lacey shook her head no.

"Your mother's father, my husband, died a very long time ago. He was sick. He was a very wise man. One day he said to me, Amy. That's what he sometimes called me. Amy, he said, I love you. Because I love you and I know that you love me, I want you to promise me that you will not be sad when I'm gone. I'll be home, in heaven with God, so be happy. Live your life. Tell our children and grandchildren to be happy. Think of me and smile. Keep the memories alive. I'll be watching from heaven and I want to see you smile. Life is short. Live it to the best of your ability. Get married again if you want to. I won't mind. Being sad and grumpy all the time will make your life seem much longer and that's no fun at all."

"He didn't really say that," said Camille. "The last part, I mean."

"Did so. Your momma don't tell no lies."

"Why didn't you get married again?" asked Lacey.

"Because I am perfectly content just the way things are. And, because no man has even come close to making me happy like your grampa." Amaryllis looked at her daughter and added, "But that doesn't mean that you can't remarry. You're younger than I was."

"But," Lacey sat up and looked at her grandmother, "but Daddy's just missing. He's coming back." When her mother and grandmother didn't say anything, Lacey jumped up and ran to her room. Tears filled her eyes and she forced back a cough. "I'll never give up hope," she said to the picture of her father on the nightstand.

The van and two trucks pulled into the driveway at 7 am, much earlier than expected. Lacey watched from the upstairs window as the men and women walked quietly around the side of the house to the barn. A couple of new people were with them this time. One man in particular stood out. He was tall and looked like a soldier the way he walked, tall and confident. The man also was dressed much nicer than the homeless and more like Mr. Ridgeway with clean jeans and a nice button-down, short-sleeved shirt. The man had reddish brown hair, long in the back that stuck out from under his baseball cap. Curious about the new people and why they were early, Lacey raced to the back door.

"Good morning," Camille greeted her daughter with a kiss. She was seated on the patio drinking coffee watching the procession of workers. "Morning Lucas." Camille waved for him to join her.

"Mommy, why are they here so early?" asked Lacey.

"Because of the heat and because Lucas wanted to talk to me and your grandmother," she answered. "Please go see if she's up and then get yourself some breakfast. Cereal and bowl are on the table."

Lacey nodded and slowly backed up towards the door while watching the activity. The workers were walking back and forth bringing in lumber, tools, and what looked like trays of plants. She reached back for the door knob and bumped into something soft.

"Eyes forward," laughed Amaryllis. "It works better that way." She lifted a tray up over Lacey's head and sat it down on a table near Camille. "You're here early," she said to Lucas.

"Yes ma'am," he answered. "I cleared it with Cami last night. We brought in breakfast so you don't need to take anything to Danny." Lucas took a chair and scooted it close to Camille. "I have a few things to discuss. First, about your garden."

"What about it?" asked Amaryllis.

"You know that we have a small garden at the church," he began.

"You do?" asked Amaryllis.

"Yes, I showed it to you. Doesn't matter. The point is, I would like your permission for our guests to come and work in your garden. Re-plow, put in irrigation, plant vegetables, maybe enlarge it. You have room for twice the current size, maybe more."

"I can't afford all that," stated Amaryllis.

"Won't cost you a thing. I was on the phone all night and lined up donations." Lucas looked at Camille with a proud smile then turned to Amaryllis. "Do you remember me telling you about the points system and the farmer's market?" He didn't wait for her answer before continuing. "What I propose is, bringing the workers here several times a week to tend the garden. Plant, harvest, maintain. You, of course, get first pickings of all that grows. After that, we take what is harvested to the farmer's market. We will share in the profits of course, seeing how it's your land and all."

"It would be like a co-op, Mother. They pay you for use of the land out of the crops and the money they make," stated Camille.

Amaryllis smiled a wry, mischievous smile. "Beverly will hate it! I'm in. Well, except for the fact that y'all be traipsing through my yard."

"We can fix that," stated Lucas. "There's a dirt path that leads from the road to behind your barn. We can widen it. I'll have to check to see if we need a permit but I think as long as we don't pave it, it'll be fine. I'm also going to see about using the pavilion at the lake for a semi-permanent farmer's market. It would bring in more traffic to this area, maybe get people to move this direction."

"Beverly will hate that even more!" exclaimed Amaryllis. She laughed heartily until Camille shot her a disapproving look.

"Will they be supervised?" asked Camille. "The workers, I mean."

"Yes. A staff member will have to drive the men, and the women. They will stay with them. I will come when I can. I'm sure we can get the church on board and more members involved. They want to, we just haven't had the opportunity to do more." Lucas stood up and looked out towards the garden. He was silent for a moment while he watched Danny raking away the weeds. "The other thing is," he said, sitting back down. "We believe we found his son."

Lacey suddenly straightened up and stared hard at Mr. Ridgeway's face. He was serious. If that was such good news, why did Lacey suddenly feel alarmed and want to run? "For real? Are you sure?" she asked.

"Yes," answered Lucas. "I'll be right back."

Camille took Lacey by the hand. She stroked her daughter's hair and said, "This is wonderful news, sweetheart. If it is the son, his search is now over. His father is no longer lost."

Lacey stared out towards the barn where the men were still bringing in supplies. Two women carried a large cooler and sat it by the oak tree. Lucas stopped to speak with them then went inside. He re-emerged with the man she had noticed earlier. When they stopped half way between the barn and the patio, Lucas spoke to him and pointed towards the garden. The man nodded and kept his face turned in that direction for as long as he could while walking to the patio.

"Ladies, this is Finn Ryan," introduced Lucas. "We believe this is the son of the man you have been calling Danny."

"Good morning," said Finn nervously in a distinct quiet southern drawl. He pulled an envelope out of his shirt pocket. "This is a picture of me and my father. It was taken at my mother's funeral." Finn handed the photo to Camille.

Lacey looked over her mother's shoulder. It was indeed her Danny. She looked up at the man and then back to the photograph. The men in the picture looked sad. She nodded her head, affirming his identity.

"My father's name is Barry. Barry Ryan. Here is another picture." He handed it to Camille but Lacey took it. "That was when he retired from the Air Force. The woman is my mother. Dad disappeared shortly after her funeral."

"When was that?" asked Amaryllis.

"Six years ago," he said so quietly everyone had to lean in to hear him.

"There's no way he's been here that long," stated Amaryllis with a severe shake of the head.

"Lucas told me about him living here," said Finn. "I appreciate all you've done for him. We were living in San Antonio when he disappeared. How he got here and for how long really isn't important." Finn turned and looked in the direction of the garden. He stood in silence, watching the man for several minutes. His chest rose and fell a number of times as if to hold in his emotions. "He's alive. That's what's important. Not knowing, wondering all these years. That's been the hardest part." Finn shoved his hands in his pockets and dropped his eyes to the ground.

Lacey suddenly broke down in tears as she listened to Finn tell his story. He spoke in a soft tone, one that spoke of a humble man, a retrospective and kind-hearted man. Shortly after his mother's funeral, Finn went to check on his father who was now living alone. He wasn't home. His phone, wallet, money, car, car keys were all in the house, but no Barry. Finn checked with the neighbors, knocked on every door. No one had seen him. Finn called the police and filed a missing person report. There was no sign of foul play, no money was missing from his bank account, nothing stolen in the house. Barry had vanished. Finn called the TV stations, the VA, everyone he knew. He put ads in the newspaper, posted on social media, and held prayer vigils in his church. Lacey watched the man's face, saw the tears in his eyes as he spoke. Unable to fight her emotions any longer, she ran as fast as she could and into the arms of Danny, now Barry.

"What's wrong, miss?" he asked. "Shh. Hush that crying now."

Lacey's heart was broken. She realized how selfish she had been, not wanting Barry's family to be found. Her world was changing at much too fast a pace. New people were entering and exiting her life just as she was getting used to them. At this moment she wanted to go home, be 5 again and in her father's arms. But now, this. Reality of life was difficult for her to deal with. Finn had been searching for his father much longer than her's had even been missing. She was happy for him, but sad at the same time. Lacey also felt like she was right all along to not give up on her father. If Finn could be reunited with his father, so could she.

"Danny," Camille called out softly.

Lacey looked up. Her mother, grandmother, Mr. Ridgeway, and Finn stood staring at them. "Danny," the little girl said, letting go and taking a step back. Without another word, Lacey looked up into her friend's eyes and pointed to Finn.

"Hello," Barry said dropping his head. He looked at the ground and shuffled his feet.

"Dad," Finn said, choking back tears. He took a small step forward, then stopped abruptly.

Barry didn't look up, not realizing the statement was directed to him.

"Dad, it's me, Finn."

"We found your family," Lacey said with tears streaming down her cheeks. She tugged at Barry's shirt.

Barry slowly looked up. He shook his head.

"It's okay, Dad." Finn took a step forward. "I've come to take you home."

Barry shook his head, dropped his rake and backed away. "I live here," he stated then turned and ran into the woods.

"Danny!" Lacey called out. She tried to run after him but her mother caught her and held her tight. "Danny, don't go!"

"Let him go," she whispered. "He needs time."

"He didn't recognize me," stated Finn. "I didn't expect that."

"Can you stay awhile?" asked Lucas. "Maybe, if you come back, he'll get used to you and the two of you can get to know each other again."

"What can I do to help?" asked Finn.

***

Lacey climbed out of bed before dawn and ran to the barn. Barry was not there. She ran to the stump and called out. He did not come. Lacey ran back to the house, made sandwiches and packed a basket. She took the food out to the stump and called again. No response. She sat and waited. Lucas, Finn, and the rest of the workers began filing in several minutes later. When she wandered, with a heavy heart, back to the barn, Finn asked Lacey to show him around. She took him to the stump. They sat there together for a few minutes in silence and then she took him to the pond while explaining all that had happened since she discovered Barry. Camille joined them at the little bridge.

"Don't take it personally, Finn," said Camille. "When I first met your father he disappeared for a few days. Things have been moving pretty quickly since we arrived. It's a lot for him to take in."

"I understand. It...it's difficult for me to see him like that," said Finn.

"Are you in the Air Force?" asked Lacey.

"No," he answered.

"Why not?"

"Because I wanted to be a doctor," he answered.

"Are you?"

"Yes, I am."

"Do you work in a hospital?" Lacey asked, full of curiosity.

"Most of the time."

"Lacey, don't be so nosey," Camille said. "Sorry, she's always curious about people."

"That's alright. I'm sure she wants to know about the man who wants to take away her friend." Finn looked into Lacey's eyes and said in his soft, calming voice, "When I'm not being a doctor in a hospital, I work with Physicians on a Mission."

"What's that?" asked Lacey.

"It's a group of doctors who go to poor countries and do our best to take care of people who cannot afford a doctor. We give immunizations, take food and medicine."

"Like a missionary?"

"Exactly," stated Finn. His eyes gravitated out towards the forest. "Do you know where he went?"

"Lacey tried to find his camp once," stated Camille. "Unfortunately, she got lost. Most likely he's back at his camp site."

"How far back does this go?" asked Finn. He pointed at the line of trees.

"Not sure. Mother said she had ten acres, but with her memory, it could be more, or less. I've never seen the property line in that direction."

"I went way back there," stated Lacey, "the day I got lost. Danny will come back. We talked about his family some the other day. He doesn't remember you. Anybody. He thought nobody cared and nobody was looking for him."

"I don't understand why..." Finn began.

"Excuse me," Lucas interrupted.

Lacey rolled her eyes. Lucas Ridgeway was always interrupting. She stepped in front of her mother before he could get any closer.

"We've got a few issues with the barn. Your mother doesn't seem to understand," he stated.

"What's wrong?" asked Camille.

Lacey sat on the bench and listened while the adults discussed the repairs of the barn. Apparently, it was not in as good a condition as her grandmother had thought. The barn was going to need a lot of work, which was going to take more time and more money. Lucas believed he would be able to get much of the supplies donated, especially since repairing the barn would benefit King's Hero. They also needed to build an additional structure to house all of the crafts and boxes of supplies Amaryllis had stored in the barn and refused to throw away. Amaryllis, Lucas told them, was immersing herself in teaching the women her crafts and had sent him to consult with Camille regarding the building projects. Lacey laughed to herself. She had learned that Amaryllis got involved in the projects she liked, became totally engrossed with them, and shut everything else out.

Chapter 10

Bored with the building conversation and curious about what her grandmother was up to, Lacey got up and skipped towards the patio. The two women, Rona and Susan, were now joined by two new women. They were all busy doing something with hair. Lacey quietly watched her grandmother take charge of her students like an experienced teacher. The hair, she told them, was horsehair harvested from her pony, Muffin. The hair was combed, washed and hung to dry before use. The students were at first a little surprised but when they were shown the finished product became excited and eager to learn. Lacey was encouraged to join in, however, she had more fun watching. Besides, her thoughts kept wandering back to the woods.

At lunchtime, everyone gathered on the patio. Except Lacey. She took her lunch and one for Barry along with a book and a beach towel to the stump.

"Danny! Danny!" she called out from just inside the tree line. Lacey knew not to go too far in. Getting lost once was enough. "Danny, I have your lunch!" she called out once more then returned to the stump.

The sun, high in the sky, radiated a fierce heat over the land. There were no clouds nor breezes to cool people or animals. Sweat dripped down her back. Lacey spread her towel down in the shade of the oak trees on the small path that had been worn down a few feet inside the tree line. It warded off the fiercest rays but the temperature remained the same. Diaz and Troy ran over and sat next to her begging for food. Even the dogs were too hot to be much of a pest. They gave up begging after only a minute, plopped down on the ground next to Lacey and went to sleep. Lacey ate her sandwich then picked up her book. From time to time she heard a noise deep inside the forest. When she and the dogs looked, all was quiet again and she didn't see Danny. He was there, she could feel it.

"Sweetheart, it's time for dinner."

Lacey looked up. Her mother stood next to the stump with the fading sun to her back. Something about her mother looked different. Maybe it was the dirt on her pants or the sweat frizzing her hair. No, it was the face. Her face seemed softer, peaceful.

"Mommy," said Lacey without getting up. "Are you glad that man is here?"

"Do you mean Mr. Ryan?" Camille stepped closer to Lacey and began to pick up her picnic.

"Uh huh."

"I'm glad we were able to help reunite him with his father," she answered.

"He's nice. Maybe he can stay here and Danny won't have to leave."

"His name is Barry and that is not up to us," stated Camille.

The next two days were spent with Lacey bouncing between watching the construction projects, the garden being tilled, and her grandmother teaching arts and crafts to the women. Plants for the pond and the garden arrived with another set of men who began planting under the watchful eye of Amaryllis. Finn came every day. He worked alongside Camille in the garden. Lacey took breakfast and lunch to the stump in the hopes that Barry would appear. He took the food when no one was looking, but he did not show himself until Saturday afternoon.

Lacey was sitting in her spot in the shade drawing a picture to take to the Jacksons. They had not come over since the day the barn began getting remodeled. She was putting the finishing touches on drawing from memory of a picture of her and her father when Troy jumped up and began to wag his tail.

"Hello, Miss," stated Barry.

The little girl dropped her colored pencil and jumped up. "Oh, Danny!" she ran and dove into his arms. "I was so worried about you." Lacey held onto him tight and did not want to let go.

"I'm not going anywhere," stated Barry. "Just needed time to think is all."

"Are you going home now?"

"This is my home. Can't remember living anywhere else."

"But your son," Lacey said, pointing towards the garden. "He's been looking for you for years and years. Don't you want to go with him?"

"Is he mad at me?"

"No." Lacey looked up at the man. She was confused. "Why would he be mad?"

"Because I left him."

"Not on purpose. You didn't leave and lose your memories on purpose," she insisted. "If he was mad, why would he still be here?"

"He is?"

Lacey nodded. "You want to go talk to him?"

"I don't know."

"They brought the plants for the pond," Lacey stated in hopes that would draw him out.

"Maybe tomorrow."

"Tomorrow's Sunday. Nobody is coming tomorrow. Maybe me and you can make the pond pretty together."

"Maybe. What're you drawing?"

"A picture for the neighbors."

"It's nice."

"I have to go now. I don't want to. I'd rather stay and talk to you, but Mommy said if I wanted to take it I had to go before dinner." Lacey picked up the basket and held it out, "Here. I made you a sandwich and cookies." She smiled and waved good-bye then ran all the way to the neighbor's house.

"Who is it?" asked a gruff voice.

"It's me, Lacey," she answered.

"What do you want?"

"I brought you something."

Lamont Jackson opened the front door just enough for one eye and peeked out.

"Hi," she said. Lacey smiled and waited, holding the picture behind her back.

"Come inside before you melt," he said with a scowl on his face.

"Thank you." Lacey stepped inside the cool living room and looked around. She felt like she was in an old-timey museum. Lace doilies and trinkets and nick-nacks filled every shelf and end table. Too afraid to sit down, she held out her hand. "Here. I made you this."

"What is it?" Mr. Jackson asked.

"It's a picture of me and my daddy," answered Lacey.

"Who are you talking too?" called out a voice from down the hall.

"The neighbor girl," Lamont yelled back.

"Amaryllis send you over here?" asked Mrs. Jackson. She marched into the living room and snatched the paper out of her husband's hand. "What's this?"

"She drew it for us," he answered.

Lacey shrugged. Now that she had gained entry into the 'mean neighbors" house she wanted to look at everything in it. Their house was the complete opposite of her grandmother's. Inside a glass case were several photographs. Lacey took one step forward, saw something unexpected and asked, "Who's the little boy?"

"None of your business." Mrs. Jackson stepped in between the case and Lacey.

"Is he your grandson?"

"I think it's time for you to go home," she answered. After a huff and as an afterthought, Mrs. Jackson added, "Thank you for the picture."

"How's the work coming?" Mr. Jackson asked once Lacey had been pushed to the porch.

"Oh, it's really, really good. Come over tomorrow and see."

"No. Goodnight." Mrs. Jackson closed the door quickly before her husband or Lacey could say another word.

Neither Lacey nor Amaryllis wanted to go to church Sunday morning. The dark skies could not hide the fact that it was summer, nor would the clouds empty themselves to relieve the ground of its dust. The long week of working outside had drained everyone's strength. Camille, however, insisted and since Lacey was a child, she didn't have a choice.

Amaryllis only agreed because she knew the church building was cooler than her house. The drive was quiet; no one had the energy to argue over the route. When the trio arrived, Lucas stood alone at the entryway handing out bulletins. Lacey was annoyed at how easily he brushed off her mother's questions about his wife. When he reached over to put his arm around Camille to walk her inside, Lacey stepped in and pulled her mother away.

"Have you met his wife?" Camille asked Amaryllis.

"I don't know. Probably."

After the church service concluded, the women meandered toward the auditorium's exit. Several women came up and introduced themselves. Lacey didn't pay any attention until a very petite woman stepped forward.

"Hello. I'm Morgan Ridgeway. It's very nice to meet you," she said.

Lacey noticed a slight shake in her voice.

"I'm so glad to finally meet you," stated Camille. "Lucas has been such a huge help. With Mother and all."

"Oh? Really?" Morgan asked. She adjusted her purse's shoulder strap and took a small step back.

"Yes. Of course, he's told you all about the work he and King's Hero has done at the house," Camille said.

Morgan shook her head. Not a hair on her neatly arranged head moved. "He doesn't talk much about his work. He talks a lot about you, though."

"Why don't you come over for lunch?" Camille's expression changed a bit. "We can talk and I'll show you around."

"I'm afraid I can't," stated Morgan.

"Well, then come over in the morning," suggested Amaryllis. "Lucas brings the homeless crew over at dawn now. To beat the heat, he says. I don't know what all's going on in the barn. That's Cami's department. Finn and Barry have the gardens in tip top shape. Do you paint?"

"He's doing all that?" Morgan asked with a wide-eyed expression. "I didn't know. I mean, I know he volunteers at King's Hero when he can get away from work but…"

"He has another job?" asked Amaryllis. "He never said."

"His father owns Ridgeway Oil and Gas. Lucas is VP."

Camille and Amaryllis looked at each other but didn't say anything. Lacey observed them and sensed something weird was going on, especially with her grandmother, but it bored her so she walked away. Just outside the front door of the church several girls her age stood in a huddle talking and giggling. Conflicting feelings stirred within her. Remembering scenes like this at school, Lacey was sure they were talking and laughing about her. She also remembered a time when she was in that huddle, many years ago, and it made her feel very alone. One of the girls looked up at Lacey and smiled. Thinking the girl was laughing at her, Lacey ran back inside to find her mother.

All was quiet back at the house. No workers, no sounds of hammering, sawing, or other clattering sounds of construction. Not even Barry or the dogs had ventured outside. A slight, muggy breeze kicked up the dry topsoil in the empty gardens. While Camille and Amaryllis napped, Lacey curled up on her bed with a book. After dinner, near sunset, the trio took a long stroll around the lake. Amaryllis carried her BB gun like a drill sergeant even though Camille had reminded her why it was no longer necessary. Other than the mosquitoes, everyone was indoors.

"Can we go swimming at the lake tomorrow?" Lacey asked when they stopped for a rest on the picnic benches.

"Maybe after the workers leave," answered Camille.

"I noticed there were a bunch of girls your age at church," stated Amaryllis. "You want to invite them over? Have a lake day?"

166

Lacey thought for a moment then said, "No, I don't think so I would like that. They didn't look nice."

"Why do you say that?" asked Amaryllis.

Lacey shrugged. She got up and began walking home. In her short life, she had learned a group of girls like that meant 'keep away, there's no room for you'. All of her former friends were back home and she had not spoken to her internet friends from virtual school since classes ended. Making friends had never been easy and she had determined it was better to be alone than put herself in a position to be teased.

"Mommy, can we video chat from Gramma's house?"

"I don't know. Mother, do you have internet?"

"Have what?"

"A computer? Internet access?"

"Nope. Don't use those fancy contraptions."

"Who were you wanting to call?" asked Camille.

Lacey shrugged. "Nobody." She stopped at the bridge and watched fireflies blinking their signals. "The creek is all dried up."

"There must be a clog up at the lake," said Camille. "I noticed the water line looked a little lower, too, so maybe there's a clog at the other end as well."

"Happens every summer," stated Amaryllis. "No rain and lots of heat evaporates the lake. Nothing to get your knickers in a bunch about."

***

The workers arrived wide awake and ready to get down to business before dawn. Lacey watched from the patio as her mother and grandmother supervised, taught, and dealt with the people at the construction sites and the gardens. Most of the time, Finn and Lucas were right by her mother's side. Lacey couldn't tell if the men were following her mother around or if she was following them. It made the little girl uncomfortable seeing her mother with men who were not her father. All morning long she watched. It made her want to get up and tell them to go away, but she stayed inside and kept watch instead. Shortly before lunch, the trio brought a wagon full of flowers to the pond where Barry was working alone. Father and son worked side by side for a while after Lucas and Camille returned to the barn. Neither spoke from what Lacey could tell. She was glad that Barry didn't run off. However, at lunch time, Barry retreated to the woods instead of joining the others on the patio. After lunch, Lacey was about to go to her room to read under the ceiling fan when the doorbell rang.

The petite woman from church stood on the front porch holding a girl's hand. It was the same girl who had waved at Lacey on Sunday.

"Hello. I hope it's okay that I dropped by," she said. "Your mother and grandmother invited me."

"Okay," stated Lacey. She leaned on the door and held the handle tight. Lacey and the girl stared blankly at each other. "You're Mr. Ridgeway's wife, right?"

"Yes. I'm sorry. I didn't introduce myself." The woman dressed in a light yellow dress and shoes not meant for walking stretched out her hand. "I'm Mrs. Morgan Ridgeway and this is my daughter, Fiona. Fiona, this is...Lacey."

"Hi," said Fiona with a wave and a forced smile.

"Hi," Lacey answered. "Everybody's out in the back. You can come through here." Lacey pushed the front door open wide with her back to let the visitors in. She shut the door then hurried to the back door. She stood on the patio and looked around. "I don't see anybody, 'cept Gramma. She's teaching. Come on, I'll show you around."

Walking slowly, happy to have something useful to do, Lacey escorted Mrs. Ridgeway and Fiona to the pond, purposefully bypassing her grandmother. She told the story about how she discovered it and what it looked like, who all had been working on it, and what she hoped the finished product would be like. From the pond, they made their way to the garden. Barry, Finn, and two other men were planting. Lacey didn't know what they were planting so she just said, 'food'.

"Is that the homeless man your grandmother told me about?" asked Mrs. Ridgeway. She pointed to Barry.

"Homeless? That's weird," stated Fiona.

"Uh-huh." Lacey motioned towards Finn. "That man is his son. Mr. Ridgeway found him last week."

"Oh," said Mrs. Ridgeway with a gasp.

Lacey turned to walk to the barn. "There they are," she said.

Camille, Lucas, and another man stepped out of the barn and stopped under the oak tree. Lucas pulled a bottle of water out of a cooler and handed it to Camille. Morgan lifted her hand to wave, but dropped it quickly when Lucas began to laugh at something that was said.

"Hi, Daddy!" called out Fiona. She nudged Lacey's arm and the two of them ran over to the barn.

Lucas looked up. He two took steps back away from Camille and called out to his wife who was making her way over, "What're you doing here?"

"I invited them," stated Camille. "Morgan, so glad you could come. This must be Fiona."

Morgan Ridgeway looked at her husband with a slight air of agitation. She nodded politely to Camille and the other man then glared at her husband while Lacey spoke.

"I showed them everything 'cept the barn," stated Lacey. "Mr. Finn and Barry are working together, can you believe it?"

"I know," said Camille. "Isn't that wonderful? Progress comes when we are patient."

"Why didn't you tell me you were doing all this?" Morgan asked her husband.

"I, uh," Lucas darted his eyes from his wife to Camille and back. "I didn't think you were interested."

"Want to see a pig?" Lacey asked Fiona.

"Sure." Fiona looked at her mother for permission then nodded to Lacey.

"Don't get your dress dirty," instructed Morgan.

Lacey took Fiona by the hand and led her to the pig's enclosure. "This is John. He lays in the water all day when it's hot."

"Can I touch him?" asked Fiona.

"Sure." Lacey crawled through the fence and walked right up to John.

"He doesn't stink," said Fiona. "I thought all pigs were stinky." She carefully followed Lacey's steps through the fence, desperately trying to stay clean, then reached over and barely touched his back. She squealed and pulled her arm back. "That's weird."

"Nope, he doesn't stink and he doesn't really do anything except eat and waller in the mud."

"What's over there?" Fiona asked. She pointed to the corral.

"Muffin. She's a miniature horse. Come on." Lacey led the girl into the corral. "You can't ride her or anything. Gramma uses her hair to make stuff."

"What kind of stuff?"

"I dunno. Arts and crafts stuff."

"That's weird."

"Kinda." Lacey stroked Muffin's nose while she watched Fiona. The girl with the shoulder-length brown hair and brown eyes seemed nice enough but Lacey didn't want to get her hopes up that she would become a friend. Besides, Lacey thought, they were only here for the summer.

"Fiona, time to go," Mrs. Ridgeway called out from where she was standing under the tree.

"Aww, Mom. Do we have to go?" whined Fiona. "I want to see what Mrs. Blythe is making."

"You can see it on the way out," she ordered with a wave of her finger.

"See ya." Fiona stuck out her bottom lip and waved to Lacey. "This place is weird, Mommy," Fiona whispered when she thought no one could hear her.

Lacey followed Fiona and her mother to the patio where Amaryllis was busy showing the women how to fasten a pot for planting onto the bottom of the chairs. "Hi Gramma. Watcha makin'?"

"Well, hey there," Amaryllis looked up at Lacey and the visitors. "I didn't see y'all come in. You're Ridgeway's wife, right?"

"Yes ma'am," answered Morgan Ridgeway.

"What's that?" Fiona pointed to the wall hanging.

"It's a tapestry made from horsehair," stated Amaryllis proudly.

"That's weird." Fiona made a face but then reached out to touch it. "That's neat," she said pointing to a finished chair.

"What will you do with all of this?" Mrs. Ridgeway asked.

Rona stood up and said, "Mrs. Blythe is teaching us and we are going to sell at the craft fair and farmer's market."

"I see."

"Mom, can we come back tomorrow?" asked Fiona. "I want to make one. I'll bet no one at school has a chair like that."

"That's rude, dear. We haven't been invited," Mrs. Ridgeway said through an embarrassed smile.

"Well now," began Amaryllis. "Y'all can come back anytime. I think Miss Lacey might like someone her own age to talk to for a change."

"I'll check my schedule," stated Mrs. Ridgeway.

"Maybe next time we can go swimming," Lacey said when they reached the front door. She watched as they walked to their car.

"In that lake?" Fiona asked. She grimaced at the thought.

Mrs. Ridgeway nodded and smiled a forced but friendly smile while her daughter waved goodbye. "I'll try to come again soon," she stated from her car.

At the end of the work day, Lacey stuck to her mother's side. She listened as the two men, Lucas and Finn, talked to Camille about this project and that. For some odd reason, Lacey felt like the men were competing for her mother's attention with the way they spoke, interrupting each other, trying to get in the last word.

"Your wife is very nice, Lucas," stated Camille. She sat with Lacey on the wooden bench by the pond. "I hope she comes back and brings your daughter."

"I doubt it. She's never been interested in King's Hero," he stated.

"She looked interested to me," said Finn.

"Habit," stated Lucas. "She's learned to look interested."

"A woman is always interested in what her husband does," Finn said, leaning in to Camille.

Lucas folded his arms and huffed, "It's time to go."

"I'm going to stick around a little longer," said Finn. "I want to try to talk to Dad."

"Oh. I guess we can hang out a half hour or so."

"No, you go on ahead."

"It's not a problem. We can wait a while," argued Lucas.

"Not necessary. I'm sure your group is tired and ready to leave," said Finn.

Lacey shook her head, got up and walked over to the garden. "Hi," she said to Barry.

"Hi, miss."

"Mr. Ridgeway has a daughter," said Lacey. She took a hoe that was on the ground and followed Barry down the row he was working on. "He never told me that before." Lacey watched in silence for a moment while he worked. "Coming to dinner tonight?" Barry didn't respond so she continued. "You don't have to be invited every night anymore, you know."

"Your grandmother say it's okay?"

"Sure."

"I'll go wash up." Barry took the tools and headed toward the barn.

"Dad, can we talk?" asked Finn as he crossed Barry's path.

"Hav'ta wash up for dinner," he answered.

Lacey tapped Finn on the arm as he was about to speak again. "Stay for dinner," she whispered. "I'll tell Mommy."

Dinnertime was awkward. Lacey set the table then showed Finn to his seat. Amaryllis and Camille noticed how many plates were set then made uncomfortable small talk with Finn until Barry arrived. Lacey led him by the hand and sat him across from his father. She took over the conversation by asking Finn questions about his life. With each answer, she watched Barry's face. Nothing registered, not even stories about Finn's childhood with his parents or his mother's illness.

"Dad," Finn finally said. His voice was soft, as if he were speaking with a child who had gotten their feelings hurt at school. "I know losing Mom was traumatic. I understand your pain. I want you to know I'm not angry with you. I love you. I've missed you. More than anything, I want to bring you home."

"This is my home," answered Barry after a long silence. "I don't know how long I've lived here, but it's home."

"I understand," stated Finn. He reached out and laid his hand gently on his father's. "I was told by a therapist to not to try to force you to do anything. As much as I want you to come home, I won't pressure you to do anything you're not comfortable with. Selfishly, I thought as soon as you saw me your memory would return. I should have known better, being a physician and all."

"Well now, that's a wise decision, young man," stated Amaryllis. "Barry can stay here as long as he wants."

"I'd like to… that is," began Finn. He looked at his father then Camille and said, "I've decided to move here. There's a small practice nearby. The doctor is elderly and needs someone to help with his patient load. It's part time. On my off days I can offer medical services at King's Hero. The details haven't been worked out yet, but I'm sure Lucas will let me on board."

"That's a great idea," stated Camille.

"What do you think, Dad?" Finn asked.

Lacey studied Barry's face. She thought he liked the idea by the way his eyebrows raised and lowered and he tilted his head from side to side. "Does that mean you won't be coming here as much?" asked Lacey.

"Unfortunately, yes," answered Finn. "At least not for long periods of time. I can stop by after work and maybe, Dad, you and I can have dinner together, just the two of us."

Barry didn't answer. He nodded again as if he liked the idea but kept his eyes focused on his dinner. From time to time he looked up at his son then to Lacey and grinned.

"So," said Camille to break the silence, "Mother, when is the craft sale?"

"Next Saturday," answered Amaryllis. "The ladies will each have several items ready by then. I still have all my jam to sell and leftover projects that are taking up room in the shed. They have a small crop to harvest at the church and will bring what they can. My garden is worth squat this year. Rona and the girls are making signs and fliers for advertisement and Susie called the newspaper."

"Can I help?" asked Lacey.

"What would you like to do?" asked Camille.

"I can take fliers to the neighbors," she answered.

"I guess we can do that," Camille nodded.

"She meant by herself, dear," said Amaryllis.

"No, I don't think that would be safe."

"Safe? Hogwash, of course she's safe. You rode your bike all around here when you were her age."

"Yes, but things are different now, Mother."

"Poppycock! You said yourself, nothing has changed. Same people, no traffic. Let the girl go, she'll be fine," argued Amaryllis.

"Please, Mommy," begged Lacey. "Please."

Early in the morning the day before the craft sale and farmer's market, Lacey set out with a bag full of fliers. One of the men who came from King's Hero fixed up a bicycle for her to ride and even put a basket on the front. She put a large water bottle in the basket with the fliers and set off, remembering her mother's words, "Keep your helmet on. Ride your bike facing traffic. Look both ways before crossing the street. Don't go inside anyone's house. Put the flier on the door, ring the bell, and leave."

Not a blade of the tall grass on either side of the street was moving. The trees and their leaves also stood motionless. Dark clouds blocked the sun's rays, but not its heat. Lacey could almost smell the air, not quite stale but like that of rotting leaves mixed with hot tar and manure. Sweat began to form on the bridge of her nose before she reached the Jackson's house. While getting off the bike, she began to regret her decision to deliver the fliers.

"What brings you our way?" called out Mr. Jackson from his driveway. He bent down and picked up his newspaper, tucked it under his arm and waited.

"I'm delivering these fliers," Lacey answered. She handed him one.

"Lamont, your breakfast is getting cold," cried out Mrs. Jackson from the front door.

"Good morning, Mrs. Jackson." Lacey waved, hoping for a greeting in return.

"What does she want?"

"There's going to be a flea market at the lake," shouted Mr. Jackson over his shoulder.

"What? Who gave that woman permission to turn the lake into a junk yard?" Mrs. Jackson stomped off the porch and snatched the flier out of her husband's hand. She read the flier, crumpled it up, and turned back towards the house. "We'll just see about that!"

Mr. Jackson and Lacey followed her into the house. By the time they got inside, she was on the phone and arguing with someone. Remembering the photograph, Lacey went and stood in front of it, studying the face. A second photo sat just behind the first, hidden from view at first glance.

"Who are they?" Lacey whispered to Mr. Jackson.

He walked over to Lacey and said in a low voice, "That boy is our son. The boy behind him is our adopted son. He was an orphan and we took him in."

"What happened to them?"

"They died," he said.

"Lamont!" exclaimed Mrs. Jackson. "How dare you discuss our personal business with this girl."

"I'm sorry about your children," stated Lacey. Tears began to well up in her eyes. "My daddy," she began, "they all think my daddy is dead."

Lamont and Beverly stood and stared at each other, at a loss for words.

"Mr. Ryan, he thought his daddy was dead. He wasn't. He was living in my Gramma's back yard this whole time. I think it was real nice of you to take care of the orphan boy. Even if he did die. Sometimes, sometimes when I hear the homeless people talking about not having families, sometimes I think that's what it's like to be an orphan. I knew an orphan at school once. She lived in a foster home. I think King's Hero is kinda like an orphanage for grown ups. They don't have families either. Except Rona. She's just too embarrassed to call hers."

"That's the most ridiculous thing I ever heard." Mrs. Jackson put her hands on her hips and stared at Lacey. "I think it's time you went home."

"Makes sense to me." Mr. Jackson shrugged sheepishly.

"Nobody asked you," she huffed. "You can tell your grandmother the police will be shutting her down. There will be no flea market in my neighborhood!"

"Yes, ma'am," stated Lacey. She didn't really believe her. Nothing she had threatened to do had happened so far.

Lacey returned to her bicycle and continued to pass out fliers until they were all gone. Riding was hot and hard work, however, it was much better than walking would have been. When she got up enough speed, Lacey created her own breeze. One small hill in the back of the neighborhood was shaded from the sun. After a difficult climb, she stopped to rest before coasting all the way down the other side. Upon reaching the bridge by the lake, Lacey got off her bike and took a few steps towards the creek bed. From that vantage point, she noticed her grandmother's property was higher up than the lake. She groaned at the thought of peddling uphill. Handing out fliers had turned out to be not any fun at all, except for the people she met. They were much friendlier than the Jacksons and not at all upset to have the craft fair. Their only concern was the heat and threat of rain.

"I hope it does rain," stated one man who was walking his dog. "This summer has gotten off to a fire-hot start. That doesn't bode well with me. Something's brewing. I can feel it in my bones."

Lacey didn't know what that meant so simply said, "Yes sir," and kept going.

Chapter 11

The picnic area at the lake was buzzing with activity early Saturday morning. Cars filled every available space in the parking lot and many were parked along the road. People of all ages milled about. Children ran barefoot in the sandy beach and splashed in the water while their parents stood in the shade of the pavilions. There were no police cars. The picnic tables were adorned with brightly colored sheets, found by Amaryllis the night before in the garage. Laid out expertly were the arts and crafts on two tables and the produce on the third. Several large pieces of art, made by Amaryllis, had been placed near the corners to draw people in. Rona, Susan, and Amaryllis stood behind the craft table and two other women stood behind the produce. All were busy talking to customers.

"Where's Mommy?" Lacey asked her grandmother.

"Well child, she's around here somewhere," stated Amaryllis. "Now, that one was done when I traveled to New Mexico," she said to a woman who was admiring a basket.

Lacey wandered around, watching all the people come and go. She recognized some of the faces as people she had seen at church. Several women wore tennis outfits as if they were either going to or coming from playing at the country club. In the distance, coming down the road,

Lacey saw it - a police car.

"Mommy, Mommy!" Lacey called out to her mother who she had just spotted near the playground. She ran over and pointed. "Mrs. Jackson called them. She said she was gonna but I didn't believe her. She really, really did it."

"What are you going on about?" asked Camille.

"She got real mad when I showed her the flier."

"And she called the police?"

Lacey nodded. She and her mother stood and watched. A second car turned towards the lake and was following the first. The first police car parked in the full lot behind a customer's car. The second parked right next to it. A tall, dark-skinned man in uniform got out. He adjusted his hat and looked around. A man and woman, both in uniform, got out of the second car. The back door on either side of the first car opened up and out stepped two very poorly-dressed men. Each had on dirty blue jeans, ill-fitting shirts, and flip flops. The front passenger door opened and out stepped Lucas. Lacey pointed, put her hand over her mouth and held her breath. The men and one woman walked up to the pavilion and disappeared into the shade and the crowd. Lacey and Camille watched and waited. Several minutes later, the officers emerged from the shade.

"Look, Mommy," said Lacey. "They bought stuff."

"It looks like Mrs. Jackson's plan backfired," stated Camille, half to herself. She looked at Lacey and they both giggled.

***

The wind began to blow on Sunday morning. It started as a gentle breeze. Lacey thought it would rain and then go back to being steaming hot. By Sunday afternoon, the wind was still blowing and the sky grew darker, but no rain. Monday, the sky was bright blue and the wind just a tiny bit stronger. It was a warm wind that came in waves. A period of wind, a few gusts, then perfect calm. Not only did it not cool anyone off, it had the opposite effect. The workers slowed their pace and took more frequent breaks for rest and water. Often, they stood and stared at the sky. Lacey spent all day looking intently at the clouds from the shade of her favorite oak tree.

"There's a hurricane in the Gulf," Camille stated at dinner.

"Figured as much," said Amaryllis. "Where's she going?"

"The newscasters are in disagreement," she answered. "One says due north, the other says east towards Florida."

"Is that bad?" asked Lacey. "Are we going home now?"

"And leave your old granny?" asked Amaryllis. "Most likely we will get a little wind and nothing more. This happens all the time. It's that time of year."

"Have I ever seen a hurricane?" asked Lacey. She was nervous and a little excited.

"No. We were further inland. Never had a storm when we were in Japan or Hawaii."

"Blessed is what you are," said Amaryllis. "You two have dodged storms your whole life."

"You talking literal or figurative?" Camille asked her mother.

"Mommy, how come Fiona and her mommy haven't come back?" asked Lacey, eager to avoid a debate between her mother and grandmother.

"I really don't know. Did you see them on Sunday?"

"Kinda. I saw Mrs. Ridgeway and I think Fiona was there with her friends. I thought they were going to come back and go swimming with me." Lacey suddenly felt her stomach tighten. She remembered catching a glimpse of the girls looking at her and giggling.

"Now, don't you worry about those two," said Amaryllis. "I think she only came to spy on her husband."

"Mother," stated Camille with a sharp, curt tone.

"Well, I'm just callin' it like I see it. I heard her talking at church. Like I always said, what's down the well comes up in the bucket." Amaryllis tapped herself on the chest and continued, "Those golf course people are all the same."

"Mother, you're just as judgmental as you accuse them as being."

"Well, at least I admit it."

"What does that mean?" asked Lacey.

"It's out of the Bible, sugar plum," said Amaryllis. "People like Morgan Ridgeway and all those golf community people are real nicey nicey to your face but then as soon as you turn your back, what's in their heart comes right out of their mouth."

"Mrs. Jackson isn't like that," stated Lacey. "She's mean right to my face."

"With her, you know where you stand," stated Amaryllis with a nod and a wink.

"Oh." Lacey thought about what her grandmother said for a moment then said, "So, you mean Fiona isn't my friend?"

"Maybe not now, baby girl," said Amaryllis, "but that doesn't mean you can't be her friend. Be kind to her no matter what."

Overnight, the winds picked up. Lacey slept fitfully. Every time the wind blew, it rattled the wind chimes in the back yard. By the time things quieted down and she fell asleep, the chimes sounded again. Near daybreak, Lacey gave up on sleep. Quietly, she slipped out of her bed and tiptoed down the stairs. The two cats nearly tripped her on the steps and followed her to the back door. They began mewing for food so she fed them before going out the door. A full moon lit up the sky and the entire landscape. A few brightly lit clouds sprinted across the sky, being blown by the wind high in the atmosphere. Lacey didn't expect the heat so late at night. She tread softly down the path to the pond, sat on the ledge, and put her feet in the tepid water. After splashing her legs and cooling off a bit, she leaned back on her elbows to watch the sky.

"I don't see a hurricane," she said to herself, watching the stars and the one cloud float across the sky. Short bursts of wind followed by calm repeated over and over again lulled Lacey to sleep.

"Mornin', miss," Barry said, waking Lacey just before dawn.

"Huh?" Lacey opened her eyes. Startled, she sat up quickly and almost fell into the pond.

"What're you doin' out here so early in the morning?" he asked.

"Couldn't sleep." Lacey rubbed her eyes and looked around. Workers were already parading in. "How come they're here so early?"

"I hear there's a storm comin'," he said. Barry sat on the bench and they watched together.

"I'm hungry," stated Lacey after a few minutes. "Wanna eat breakfast with me?"

"Sure."

"Well, well," stated Amaryllis from the kitchen. "I thought you were sleeping in for a change. Morning Barry."

"Nope. I've been up for hours," said Lacey with a glance towards Barry.

"Get your breakfast quick, there's work to be done," she instructed.

"What's going on?" asked Lacey.

"We've been told to secure the property," said Camille. She walked into the kitchen with her cell phone in one hand, holding it up to her ear. "Lacey, I need you to stay close to the house. I have some errands to run and there's going to be a lot going on at the barn."

"Can't I come?" asked Lacey.

"I'd rather you stayed here," answered Camille. She grabbed a muffin with her free hand and hurried out the door.

"Can she help me round up the chickens?" Barry asked Amaryllis. "They'd best be moved inside."

"I'll go with you," she answered.

With cat-carry crates in hand, Barry led the way into the dry thicket of trees towards his camp. A well-worn path led them through the underbrush. Mosquitoes and flies buzzed around their heads. The trail was not anywhere close to where Lacey had wandered and gotten lost. Barry made a sharp turn to the right, towards the Jackson's property, about 50 yards in. After about a five-minute walk, Lacey heard the distinct sound of chickens clucking. Sure enough, just like he had described to her, there was a crudely-made chicken coop. Discarded 2x4 boards, wire mesh, and sheet metal were attached to three trees in an almost circular formation. A platform with a wooden coop sat on one end. Inside were six hens and a rooster. Barry climbed in, retrieved several eggs, which he handed to Lacey, then one by one caught the chickens and put them in the crates.

"Is there a place for them in the barn?" Amaryllis asked.

"Yes'm," he answered. "Mr. Lucas has a place for everybody in the new barn. My room is upstairs. It's real nice."

"Can I see it?" asked Lacey.

"Not until after all the workers are gone," stated Amaryllis. "There are a whole bunch of guys over there today. Sounds like they want to try to get finished before the storm hits. If it hits. Which it probably won't."

"What's a hurricane like?" asked Lacey. From the way everyone was acting and talking, she didn't think it was a good thing. In fact, she was becoming distressed and worried. A tickle began in the back of her throat, one that she hadn't felt in weeks. Lacey cleared her throat with a little cough then asked, "If it probably won't, then why's everybody acting so weird?"

"It's best to be prepared for the worst," stated Amaryllis as she stroked one of the hens, "and get nothing than do nothing and get the worst."

"Oh."

Barry took the chickens into the barn while Lacey sat on the patio and watched. Two men and two of the women came out of the barn and walked over towards her. They took chairs, boxes, and art supplies off the patio and put them into the new shed. She overheard one of the men telling the others to remove anything that could blow over. Large potted plants were all that remained by the time Lacey's mother returned.

"Lacey, come help me please," Camille called from the back door.

Lacey followed her mother out the front door. Her grandmother's van doors were open wide. Inside were coolers filled with bags of ice, cases of water, and bags filled with canned goods, matches, charcoal, and batteries.

"The grocery store was a mad house," stated Camille as she handed Lacey a bag.

"Why?"

"Everyone is stocking up on hurricane supplies."

"Why? Gramma says it probably won't come."

"Hurricanes are unpredictable but…."

"It's better to be prepared for the worst," recited Lacey. "That's what Gramma said."

"Good girl."

Lacey took each item out of the bag, placed them one by one on the kitchen counter while thinking hard about the storm. "Mommy?"

"Yes Lacey?"

"Where will all the homeless people go?"

"Barry, of course," began Camille, "will stay here. Lucas, I believe, will be putting up everyone else at the church building."

Lacey felt better. "Oh, okay."

Two days later, the sky darkened. Low, black clouds in large swirling patterns brought stronger, steadier winds and then a light rain began to fall. Lacey sat by the window and watched the tree limbs sway from side to side then steadily to one side as the winds blew steadily. All of the wind chimes had been packed away so the only sounds were that of the raindrops splashing against the window panes. If this was a hurricane, Lacey didn't think it was such a big deal. She had seen harder rain than this.

After lunch, then rain stopped.

"Is the hurricane over?" asked Lacey.

"Not according to the weather radio," answered Amaryllis. "Now, don't you worry, little one. Why don't we find you something to keep you busy. I know, let's build birdhouses to put by the pond."

Lacey followed Amaryllis around the house. They gathered sticks, glue, paint, pine cones, pine needles, seashells, paintbrushes, scissors, acorn hats, a small saw, and other odds and ends. Amaryllis set up a card table away from the window near the center of the living room and began the bird house project. Lacey became so engrossed, she didn't notice when the rains returned and the winds picked up.

"I'm going to go take a quick bath," stated Amaryllis when the lights flickered.

Barry looked out the window at the darkened sky. The rain had slowed again. "I'm gonna check the barn."

"I'll go with you," stated Camille.

"Can I come?" asked Lacey.

"No. You stay and keep your grandmother company. We will only be a minute." Camille kissed her daughter on the head, slipped on the bright yellow rain slicker by the door, and followed Barry to the barn.

Lacey stood by the window until they were out of sight then began to wander around the kitchen looking for a snack. She reached for the refrigerator door then remembered being told not to open it unless necessary. Unclear what that meant, but wanting to be obedient, Lacey picked up a banana and sat at the kitchen table. A howling wind startled her. The room darkened and the lights flickered on and off then on again. Lacey pulled her knees up close to her chest and sat motionless except for the slow chewing of the banana. Alone, in the dim light, the little girl began to shiver in fear. A loud sound made her jump and drop the banana peel on the floor.

"Stupid phone," she said to herself. Her grandmother's house phone was ringing. Lacey sat for a moment then got up and followed the sound to a coffee table in the living room. Under the table, on the floor, sat the phone. "Hello?"

"Hello?" said the voice on the other end of the crackling phone line. "Hello?" The phone line made a popping sound. "Can you tell me if Camille Andreas and Lacey Andreas are there? Hello? Can you hear me?"

"Yes," answered Lacey. "I hear you. Me and Mommy are here and…" Lacey started to say more but the phone line began to hum then the sound stopped. "Hello?"

The back door flew open just as the lights flicked off. Lacey dropped the phone and hid behind the couch.

"Lacey!" Camille called out. "Lacey, quick, bring me some towels."

The terrified little girl jumped up to see her mother and Barry. They were soaking wet. She ran up the stairs, grabbed a handful of bath towels, then ran back to her mother.

"What's all the noise?" asked Amaryllis emerging from her bedroom dressed in cut-off shorts and a tank top. Her hair was in a soaking wet ponytail and dripping down her back.

"The barn is secure," stated Camille. "All the animals are inside, including the dogs. The wind has picked up tremendously so we need to stay away from the windows."

"Where is the plywood for this window?" Barry asked.

Amaryllis pointed to the garage. Barry hurried and retrieved the large sheet of plywood and set it in place.

"It's dark, Mommy," said Lacey near tears. "I don't think so that I like this hurricane."

Camille pulled her daughter close and they sat together in an armchair near the stairs. Together, they listened to the wind that sounded like a far away train whistle as it roared through the trees and over the rooftops. Rain beat the windows as if a band of men were aiming pressure washers at them, trying to break in. An hour passed without anyone speaking a word. From time to time, Amaryllis got up and turned on the weather radio. She turned the volume low so only she could hear. On returning to her seat she would nod or shake her head. Lacey screamed when she heard a loud banging on the front door.

"I'll see," said Barry. He jumped up and ran to the door.

"We need shelter," yelled the man at the door over the deafening hurricane-force wind and rain.

"Lucas? Is that you?" Camille gently slid Lacey off her lap and ran to the door. "What's happened?"

"The church has been damaged," stated Lucas. "Trees fell and the roof flew off. I've brought a busload. We had nowhere else to go. Shelters are full. Finn took them into the barn. They brought everything they need with them. He's going to stay in the barn."

"Where's your family?" asked Camille.

"In the car." Lucas motioned to the driveway.

"For God's sake man," hollered Amaryllis. "Bring them in."

A strong wind blew open the front door and in ran Morgan and Fiona Ridgeway followed by Lucas Ridgeway. He leaned on the door with all his might then bolted it closed. Amaryllis handed dry towels to each of the soaked evacuees.

Lacey studied the wet little girl and saw fear in her red, swollen eyes. Forgetting her own anxiety, she picked up a flashlight and took Fiona by the hand. "Come to my room. You can dry off and change."

Fiona looked at her mother who was slumped on the couch, wrapped in a towel and blanket, then towards the dark staircase. "It's dark."

"The lights went out, little one," said Amaryllis. "Good thing I have candles. Camille, take Morgan into my room to dry off. Lucas, help me. Barry, keep watch."

Another banging on the door stopped everyone in their tracks. Barry answered it again.

"Is my mother home?" yelled the voice behind the door.

A strong wind blew the door open wide. Barry grabbed the soaking wet woman by the arm, pulled her inside and pushed the door closed.

"Willow?" Camille said, completely shocked to see her sister.

"I tried to call but the phone was dead," Willow said, wiping wet hair away from her face. "It was barely raining when I left home."

"Well, well, look what the cat drug in. If I knew it would take a hurricane to get you to visit, I would have prayed for one years ago," said Amaryllis, only partly joking.

"Really, Mom," Willow said with a stomp of her foot. She crossed her arms and looked around. "No lights?"

"They just went out," answered Camille. "Come on. I'll get you a towel and some dry things." She led Willow and Mrs. Ridgeway into

Amaryllis' bedroom.

The two frightened little girls crept up the dark staircase dodging boxes and baskets that cast eerie shadows along the wall. The sounds of the tree branches slapping the roof in time to the wind gusts got louder with each step. Once inside Lacey's room, Fiona dropped to the floor and began to cry.

"You okay?" asked Lacey.

Fiona shook her head. "No, I'm not! I'm scared."

"Me too," stated Lacey. "I've never been in a hurricane before."

"It's not that," said Fiona, eyes to the floor. With a jerk of her eyes towards Lacey she asked, "Are your parents divorced?"

Lacey's stomach jumped. That question in the middle of the storm was confusing. "No."

"Where is he?"

"Why?"

"Well...it's just," Fiona wiped her nose and blurted out, "I think my parents are getting a divorce."

"Why?"

"I don't know. They used to yell all the time. At home. Never at church or anywhere else. Daddy's gone a lot. Then, a few weeks ago Mommy and Daddy stopped yelling at each other."

"That's good, right?"

"No, because, now they don't talk at all. Just now, a while ago, he got a call about the church and he almost left us at home. Mommy got really upset and started crying. Daddy got mad and told us to get in the car." Fiona looked up at Lacey with tears streaming down her face. "He didn't talk to Mommy at all. Left us in the car at church. I saw the roof blow off."

Just then there was a loud crack and the sound of a thud as if something heavy had fallen from the sky, bounced off the roof, and onto the ground. Lacey dropped to her knees, grabbed Fiona, and they both let out screams. They held onto each other and shivered in fear.

"What? What's wrong?" called out Lucas and Camille as they ran up the stairs.

"We heard a noise!" cried Lacey.

"Daddy! Daddy!" cried Fiona.

The two girls dove into their respective parents' arms seeking shelter and safety from the storm.

"Fiona, you're soaking wet." Lucas pulled his daughter away. He scowled and said angrily, "You were supposed to change clothes."

"I didn't have time, Daddy," she whined.

"It's okay, girls," stated Camille. "Lucas, go see what fell. I'll stay here and help Fiona."

Lacey slowly got up, retrieved her flashlight and found something for Fiona to wear. It wasn't what she was used to, but it was dry. Lacey looked out the window while the girl changed. Outside was a blur. The black sky and rain pelting the window made it very difficult to see, however, there was one distinct shape on the far left between the house and the fence. A large tree lay on it's side. Lacey watched in horror as another tree fell, away from the house, and blew out of sight. A low rumble began, quiet at first then gradually louder. Lacey thought it reminded her of a jet preparing for takeoff.

"Downstairs, now!" Lucas Ridgeway called from the bottom of the stairs.

Lacey ran to her mother and the three ran as fast as they could down the steps. They stopped just inside the living room and joined the others near Amaryllis' bedroom door. The couch and chairs were pushed forward creating a small fort-like area. Lacy sat in her mother's lap against the wall. Fiona huddled between her parents next to them. Amaryllis, Willow, and Barry sat side by side, leaning against the couch. No one spoke a word. The rumbling continued and the house began to shiver in time with the pulsating wind. It again reminded the terrified little girl of the sounds of jet planes at the last air show she had attended with her father. Lacey felt her stomach begin to churn. She covered her ears and buried her head against her mother's chest. Tears welled up in her eyes as fear swept over her body.

The storm continued to rage on for hours. Fiona did not stop crying despite her father repeatedly telling her to settle down. Her mother, who was also in tears, was of little help to comfort her daughter. Lucas Ridgeway, appeared to be embarrassed by his family's behavior the way he kept fidgeting and shushing his wife and daughter. Lacey and her family sat without speaking, simply watched and listened to the storm. Rumbling, groaning, howling wind continued without letting up well into the night. Amaryllis, who had weathered many storms, tried to offer everyone something to eat after several hours of sitting. No one took her up on the offer so she walked around the house with her flashlight collecting pillows in preparation of sleeping in the living room while the wind and rain continued to batter the house.

Lacey awoke at dawn. The household had all fallen asleep in their respective places inside the furniture fort. The air was still and smelled of sweat and body odor. No one else was awake. Lacey felt all around her until she found her grandmother's flashlight. She turned it on and aimed it towards the doors and windows. Everything seemed intact. She didn't see anything out of the ordinary, except for the boards over the windows. As quiet as a mouse, Lacey pulled herself free of her mother's arms, crept towards the back door and as carefully as possible turned the knob.

Dark rain clouds in a circular pattern were still low and ominous, however, the wind and rain had ceased. Lacey took one step outside onto the patio, squeezed through the smallest opening she needed, then shut the door. Leaves, pine needles, and small branches littered the yard in every direction. Several pine trees at the edge of the forest were bent over. The section of fence with Amaryllis' art had been blown over and broken in half. One section of fence in the pig pen had blown off and now rested against the bench near the pond. Several large branches of the old oak tree near the barn were on the ground.

All of a sudden, the barn door opened pouring out the two dogs, Finn, and the men and women who had been bussed in. Finn ran towards Lacey.

"Is everyone all right inside?" he asked.

Lacey nodded.

"We're fine," stated Camille from the doorway. "No electricity, but we're all safe. Lacey, if you're going to be outside, go put on boots. Not sandals. Boots."

"Okay, Mommy," she answered. Lacey ran up the stairs, grabbed a pair of boots from the closet, and ran back outside. "Everybody's still sleeping," she said to her mother and Finn while stuffing her feet into the boots.

"Not everyone." Willow stepped out behind Lacey onto the porch. She pushed her curly auburn hair behind her ears and said, "Hi, I'm Willow, Cami's sister." She stuck her hand out to Finn.

"Finn," he answered. "Wow, you two look like twins."

"I assure you, we are not," stated Willow.

"We heard trees falling last night," began Camille before her sister could say anything else. "Towards the neighbor's house."

"I'll do a house check. See if there are any injuries," stated Finn.

"I'll help. My medic bag is in the truck," Willow offered much to her sister's surprise.

"You a doctor?" asked Finn.

"EMS paramedic," she replied.

"Finn's a doctor. I'll lead the way," stated Camille.

"I'm coming too, Mommy." Lacey latched onto her mother's arm and refused to budge. There was no way she was leaving her mother's side.

Lacey followed as Camille walked around the house, between the barn and the garage. A half dozen or so of the men picked up tools including a wheelbarrow, wagon, rope, and saws before joining the search party. Fallen branches blocked the driveway, yet miraculously none had hit any vehicles. Willow got the bag out of her truck then quickly caught up to Camille.

"How long have you been here?" Willow asked.

"A few weeks. Surprised to see you."

"I've been busy."

"Sure."

"I have. Two guys quit last month. The weather is causing heat stroke to all the idiots who refuse to drink enough water and the elderly who can't afford to turn on their AC. I had to get special permission to come last night. Told Captain it was a medical emergency after I called."

"Was that you?" asked Lacey.

"Was that me what?" said Willow.

"Somebody called yesterday. They asked if me and Mommy was here and then the phone died."

"When was this?" asked Camille.

"Yesterday." Lacey thought for a minute then added, "When Gramma was taking a bath and you and Danny was outside."

"You mean Barry?"

"Uh, yeah."

"No," said Willow. "That wasn't me. No one answered when I called."

Lacey shrugged, looked right towards the lake. The water had risen covering the beach, the playground, and had made it all the way to the bath house but stopped at the creek bed. She could not see the bridge or the road that led to the lake. An enormous tree branch blocked the road where it turned. Water drained down the hill on the road and in the ditches towards the lake. Frightened, Lacey hung onto her mother's arm as Finn instructed several of the guys to drag the branch to the side of the road. They then turned left. More branches littered the roadway blocking their travel. A few feet further, an entire tree had fallen over. The roots stuck out of the ground on one side and the top of the tree lay on the opposite side, tangled in the brush. Several power poles on the opposite side of the street had broken and lay in the ditch or dangled from trees with their broken lines hanging loose.

"That house is damaged," stated Finn. He pointed to the Jackson's home. "Does anyone live there?"

Lacey looked in horror. The roof of the porch lay on the ground, collapsed like a deck of cards. A giant oak tree that was once in the back yard, now lay across the house, over the collapsed roof, splitting the house in two. The windows by the front door were shattered and the front yard, where the flower bed once was, now looked like a pond.

"Yes, an older couple," answered Camille. "I don't know if they evacuated or not. Lacey. Stay here in the driveway. Don't move!" Camille ran with Finn and Willow close behind towards the front door. "Beverly! Lamont! Anyone home?!"

"Guys, help me clear the porch!" Finn called out. Finn and two men pulled the porch roof clear from the door. "Watch for live wires."

"I'll see if I can reach 911," stated Willow. She opened her bag and pulled out a hand radio. "Mayday, Mayday. This is Willow Blythe, Fire Station 17. We need help in Wildwood, southern sector. Possible injuries. Power lines down. Trees blocking the roads. Flooding at the lake."

"Beverly, can you hear me?!" Camille called out again.

"Willow!" yelled Finn from the front door. "I think I hear voices. Bring your bag. I may need help."

"Be careful," stated Camille. "Beverly and Lamont are Mom's age. Lacey, you've been inside. Which way are their bedrooms?"

"That way, I think." Lacey pointed to the right.

"Want us to go down the road?" asked one of the younger men who had joined them. "Look for more folks?"

"I think that's a good idea," answered Camille.

"We'll clear the roads," stated another of the men who was carrying a saw. "This way, guys. Keep an eye out for downed power lines."

Lacey hopped from one foot to the other in nervous anticipation while her Aunt Willow and Finn Ryan pushed open the front door and made their way into the dark house. Her attention bounced back and forth from the house to the road where the homeless men and women who had been sheltered from the storm in her grandmother's barn were now busy clearing the road, making their way to the houses down the street.

Several minutes passed without any sounds coming from the house. People further down the street began to emerge and join in on the street-clearing efforts. High-pitched sounds of emergency vehicles off in the distance startled Lacey. She turned and watched in anticipation for them to round the corner. The sound did not come any closer. Glued to her spot, Lacey craned her neck to see what had happened.

"Cami, give me a hand," Willow called out from inside the house.

"Mommy, they aren't coming," stated Lacey. She pointed towards where she heard the fire trucks stop.

"They'll get here when they can," answered Camille. "Stay there."

Lacey nervously watched her mother disappear inside the damaged house. As much as she wanted to go inside, follow her mother and help, she did not move from her spot on the edge of the street.

"Here we go, Mrs. Jackson, steady now," said a voice from inside the house.

Mrs. Jackson, in her nightgown and her hair in curlers stepped out onto her broken porch. Finn had his arm around her waist, holding her up. He led her carefully down the steps towards Lacey. Right behind them was Camille and Willow escorting Mr. Jackson who was also in his pajamas. He had a bandage on his forehead and dust from head to toe.

"Oh, Mrs. Jackson!" cried Lacey as she ran up to the woman. "Are you okay?" Lacey put her arms around the woman who appeared to be in a state of shock and hugged her with all her might.

Finn sat Beverly down on the ground then helped to lower her husband to sit beside her.

"They don't need hospital," stated Willow, "but they can't stay here. The roof is collapsed."

"Do you have family nearby?" Camille asked.

Mr. Jackson shook his head no while his wife simply stared at their destroyed home.

"They can stay with us and Gramma," said Lacey. "She has room. I can move in with you, Mommy, and we can clean out the guest room."

"I will not step foot in that woman's house," Mrs. Jackson said in monotone with a blank stare.

"At this point, Bev, we don't have a choice," her husband said. He patted her hand and added, "I don't want to leave the house to looters. And I'd rather not go to a shelter."

"Please, please," begged Lacey. "I can take care of you. I know Gramma won't mind."

"Do you have injuries?" called out a voice from down the road.

Lacey turned and there were two firefighters running towards them.

"Just minor," answered Finn. "Willow, come with me." Finn motioned and they got up and joined the other rescue workers.

Lacey watched for a moment then she, her mother, and Susan who had just joined them escorted the Jackson's away from their home. Beverly turned every few steps to look back and Lacey was certain there were tears in her eyes. When they reached the driveway, she ran ahead to inform her grandmother who, with a controlled voice, approved of the invitation. Lacey rushed in to help take sheets off her grandmother's bed and replace them with clean ones before the couple entered the house.

"You may take my room, Beverly," stated Amaryllis with as much dignity as she could. "It's downstairs. I've just changed the sheets. Go lie down and I'll bring you something to eat."

Beverly and Lamont, obviously filled with mixed emotions, nodded and did what they were told. Holding onto each other, with stooped backs and their eyes to the floor, the couple navigated in the dim light to their room.

"Lucas, what about our house?" asked Morgan. "Shouldn't you go check on it?"

"The road is flooded," stated Camille. "You can't get out unless it's an emergency."

"And this isn't an emergency? I don't know what's happened to my house! Don't you care? What about cell service?" she shrieked, panic and shock overtaking her usual controlled demeanor.

"Cell service is down," answered Lucas with a shake of his head. "I've been trying. Try to stay calm, Morgan. Getting upset will not change anything. There is nothing we can do right now, but wait."

"There's plenty to do," corrected Amaryllis. "We have people to feed, roads to clear, homes to repair, neighbors to check on. Morgan, you come with me."

"Mother," said Camille as they headed to the kitchen. "We've got to clear the living room and the rooms upstairs to make room..."

Amaryllis put her hand up to silence Camille, stopped in her tracks, turned, surveyed all of her belongings taking up space in the dark and said with an authoritative wave of her hand, "Move everything to the shed. There's plenty of room. Everything."

"I'll help," said Barry. "Mr. Lucas, can you help, too?"

Lucas nodded and grabbed a box.

"I'll take the neighbors something to eat and then me and Fiona can put water in a wagon and take it to the people on the street," suggested Lacey.

"Oh, no," whimpered Morgan. "It's dangerous out there."

"We'll be careful, I promise," said Lacey.

"It's yucky outside," whined Fiona.

"Better than being in the dark in here," stated Lacey with a brave puff of her chest and an upward tilt of her chin.

"They'll be fine." Camille patted Morgan on the arm for reassurance and nodded for the girls to go.

"But, don't we need the water here?" asked Morgan. "I mean, if you give away all of your water, what will we drink?"

"Really?" Camille shook her head in disbelief.

Lacey understood what her mother meant. Now was not the time to be selfish. Lacey took the tray her grandmother prepared to the room Lamont and Beverly Jackson were now occupying. After a light knock on the door, she crept in. The older couple were lying on the bed, motionless. She paused for a moment, a bit afraid to enter because they looked so unreal, out of place, and very uncomfortable. Mrs. Jackson still had the curlers in her hair and her husband, covered in dust, seemed lifeless laying on the bed.

"I brought you something to eat," Lacey whispered.

"No thank you," Beverly stated in a monotone, robotic voice as if 'no' was preprogrammed.

"You need to eat, Bev," stated Lamont. He sat up and helped Lacey place the tray between them.

"I'm sorry about your house," Lacey said. She walked over to Mrs. Jackson's side of the bed and laid her hand gently on the old woman's.

Beverly flinched, but didn't retract her hand. She opened her eyes, took a deep breath then closed them again, as if to fight her conflicting emotions.

"Please tell your mother thank you for coming to find us," said Mr. Jackson. He put the muffin to his wife's lips to encourage her to eat. "Eat something, dear."

"Those are good muffins," stated Lacey. "My mother bought them at the store. I brought you water, in bottles, too. Me and Fiona are going to take water to all the workers outside now. There is a washcloth under the sink if you want to clean the dust off your face, Mr. Jackson. I'll come and check on you when we get back."

"Who is Fiona?" asked Mr. Jackson.

"She's Mr. Ridgeway's daughter," answered Lacey. "They came last night in the middle of the storm. So did a whole bunch of other people. That's how we got you out. My Aunt Willow and Mr. Finn came, too. You can open that window, if you want." Lacey pointed to the lone window in the room. "My gramma has the other windows open."

Beverly opened her eyes and looked at Lacey. A single tear rolled down her cheek then she turned her hand over and folded her fingers around the little girl's tiny hand. She looked into the child's eyes without speaking, yet they both understood. The family she had been feuding with all these years had saved her life. Beverly didn't expect kindness from anyone, especially Amaryllis. "I'd like to speak to your grandmother, when she's not busy," she said in a kind, gentle voice.

Lacey nodded then ran towards the kitchen. "Gramma," she shouted half way there, unable to contain her exuberance. "Gramma, Mrs. Jackson wants you."

"What for?" asked Amaryllis.

"I dunno, but she's being nice," answered Lacey.

Amaryllis let out a grunt of disbelief. "Humph, I'll bet."

"Maybe she wants to say thank you, or apologize," suggested Camille.

"My daddy told me a long time ago, 'forgive your enemies, it messes with their heads' so I did. I don't need an apology," boasted Amaryllis.

"She isn't your enemy, Mother."

"Maybe not, but she seems to think so."

Lacey led her grandmother by the hand to the bedroom. "Here she is," she said, flinging the door open wide.

Mrs. Jackson, lifted her hand and motioned for Amaryllis to step closer. With the help of her husband, she sat up, wiped her eyes, then said, "Amaryllis…thank you…I…" she lowered her eyes and wiped her eyes again.

"Well, now don't that beat all," stated Amaryllis. She leaned over and put her arms around the woman. "You and I are way too much alike. Stubborn as mules and we want our own way. Bad thing is, our ways are very different."

Lacey watched the two women come to terms with their differences and put them aside. She wasn't sure if Mrs. Jackson was being nice because she had no other options or if she was really affected by Amaryllis' generosity. She also wondered if her grandmother's generosity was genuine, and she had really wanted to say "no". However, now they acted like old friends, smiling and comparing storms.

"Is there any way someone can go in our house and get us a few things?" asked Mr. Jackson.

"Possibly," answered Amaryllis. "What do you need?"

"The pictures of the boys," said Mrs. Jackson. "Lacey knows the ones."

Amaryllis gasped involuntarily, turned her face away, then said to Lacey, "Can you ask someone when you go out with the water wagon?"

Lacey nodded her head "yes" then left the room. Fiona was sitting at the kitchen table watching their mothers work when she emerged. She found the wagon in the garage and began filling it with bottles of water. Lacey pulled while Fiona pushed, sort of, the wagon to the street. She could tell Fiona wasn't used to doing any kind of physical labor by her whimpering and constant need to stop and rest. Down the street, on the other side of the Jackson's house, people were working hard to clear a large tree that had fallen over. Neighbors that had not come out of their homes and talked to one another in years were now working together to clear the debris.

"Fiona, you hand out the water, and I'll pull the wagon," Lacey instructed.

"Okay," she answered with a huge sigh. "It's hot. How long do we have to be out here?"

"If you can't help, you can go home!" stated Lacey with a stomp of her foot and a look that dared her to leave.

"I can't," she answered. "Mommy said the street is flooded."

"For all you know, your house looks like that." Lacey pointed to a house that had been crushed by two old oak trees.

Fiona covered her mouth and burst into tears. She dropped the bottle she was holding back into the wagon and fell to the ground.

"I'm sorry," said Lacey. She was angry that the girl was so oblivious to the need around her, however, she didn't mean to upset her. "I didn't mean it. I'm sorry. My Gramma's house didn't get hurt. Maybe yours is okay too." Lacey looked at the house and then saw the people who lived there. "Look," she pointed to the couple, standing in their yard talking to Finn and Willow. "Those people. Look at those people. The lady has a bandage on her arm and on her head. Do you?"

Fiona shook her head in embarrassment.

"Then maybe we can help them. Maybe you can take them some water."

"Okay. I will. My daddy sometimes says the best way to forget your problems is to help somebody else." Fiona stood up and wiped away her tears.

"Really?" asked Lacey. "He said that?"

Fiona nodded. "It's just…well, Mommy doesn't like me to get dirty."

"Too late," Lacey giggled. "Dirt washes off, most of the time."

Fiona gritted her teeth, took two bottles of water, and marched right up to the couple. They gratefully accepted the gift. She then ran back to the wagon, got two more bottles and handed them to Finn and Willow. One of the homeless men asked her if he could have a drink and she nodded, skipped to the wagon and became the water girl with Lacey as her driver.

Chapter 12

"What can we do now, Mommy?" Lacey asked after emptying the wagon. "I got the pictures for Mrs. Jackson. Aunt Willow found them."

"That was very nice. Why don't you take them in. Fiona, I could use some help cleaning," stated Camille. "I have all the windows open upstairs. Lacey, when you come back, you girls very carefully pick up everything that is on the stairs and move them to the back door."

"Okay," stated Lacey.

"I'm tired," Fiona whined. She plopped down onto the couch defiantly.

Lacey rolled her eyes and stomped off with pictures in hand. "Hi," she said after a brief knock on the door. "My Aunt Willow found your pictures. They aren't broken or anything." Lacey handed the two framed photographs to an eager Mrs. Jackson.

"Thank you so much, child," Mrs. Jackson said. She studied the prized pictures, smiled a sad, longing smile, and leaned in towards her husband who patted her gently on the arm. "It's all I have left of the boys."

"What happened?" Lacey asked cautiously, remembering what happened the last time she asked.

"None of your…" began Mrs. Jackson.

"Tell her, Beverly." Mr. Jackson took his wife by the hand and said in a somber tone, "You need to talk about it. I miss the boys, miss reminiscing about old times, happy days when they splashed in the ocean, dug holes in the back yard with their toy trucks." Tears welled up in his eyes as he spoke of his children lost so long ago.

"It's too painful," stated Mrs. Jackson. "I'll never forgive that man for taking my boys."

"My gramma said," began Lacey, "that you should forgive your enemies because it…uh…because their heads get all messed up. I think that's what she said."

Mr. Jackson laughed. "Amaryllis would say something like that."

"My Sunday school teacher told us once that if we don't forgive people it makes our hearts hard. Is that what causes heart attacks?" Lacey said with a shrug.

Mrs. Jackson stifled a laugh then began to cry. She reached out to grasp Lacey's hand and held it tight. "Oh child," she said, "what an angel you are." Beverly lifted her head and studied the girl's face. "We were coming home from church one night. The boys were 6 and 9, just a little bigger than you. They were laughing and talking about upcoming events and I don't remember what all. I remember them laughing in the back seat. We…we were hit by a…," she stopped and in tears, motioned for her husband to finish.

"A drunk driver ran a red light. Hit the rear of our car going 80. They were killed. The man didn't have a record, had never even had a parking ticket. He was an off-duty cop and got fired and probation. Killed two little boys and got a slap on the wrist. The man never even apologized. Beverly and I weren't injured, but she went into depression. We moved here a few years later, to get away from it all. Nobody from back home contacted us. Well, I think the preacher did a few times." Mr. Jackson stopped and looked up towards the door.

"Why didn't you tell me?" asked Amaryllis.

Lacey looked over at her grandmother who was wiping away tears. She didn't know what to do or say. All these years her grandmother and her neighbors could have helped each other, but chose anger and bitterness instead. "So you're not mad at Gramma for something she did?"

"No, not really," stated Mrs. Jackson. "I wanted to be left alone and she, I felt, wanted to pry in my business."

"I knew you were hurting, Beverly. I'm sorry I didn't do more."

"Well," Mrs. Jackson said with a sigh and a slight smile, "it's all in the past now."

"Meanness don't happen overnight," stated Amaryllis, "but it can be wiped away with an apology and forgiveness. I forgive you." Amaryllis took a giant step into the room and hugged her new friends.

Lacey smiled, backed up out of the room and shut the door. She found Fiona and insisted the sniveling girl help do what they had been asked. The stairs were just barely light enough to see, however, after going up and down them for weeks, Lacey knew where everything was. Starting at the top, one basket at a time, they cleared each step. A large basket with a lid which had sat untouched caught Lacey's eye. She peeked inside then carried it to the kitchen.

"Mommy, I think this one has mail in it." Lacey dropped the basket onto the kitchen counter then pulled out a handful of unopened envelopes.

"Let me see that." Camille took the letters from Lacey and read the return address of each of them. She then opened the lid and rifled through the mail. "Mother!" Camille called out. "Lacey poke your head in the bedroom door and ask your grandmother to come in here," she instructed.

"What? Is there a fire?" asked Amaryllis, obviously annoyed.

"Mother, why haven't you opened your mail?"

"What are you talking about?" asked Amaryllis.

"This basket." Camille pointed and held up a handful of letters. "You have mail in here from as far back as last year. Some from last week."

"Oh, Lordy. I forgot all about that." Amaryllis looked, but didn't touch the letters. "Most of my bills are paid automatically by the bank. Set that up years ago because I travel so much. You can clean that out if you want to," she said with a wave of the hand. She turned to go outside.

"Wait, Mother," Camille ordered. "There are checks in here. Made out to you. This one says rent for May. Who pays you rent?"

"Well, now, let me think." Amaryllis sat down at the kitchen table and looked at the check. "This one is for across the street."

"You own rental property?" asked Camille.

"Well now my dear, how do you think I pay my bills?"

"Honestly Mother, do you even know?"

"Yes, no need to get your tail feathers all ruffled," Amaryllis said. She slammed down the bill and stood up. "I may be losing my memory but I'm not stupid."

"That's not what I meant, Mother. If you have rental property, and the people pay you by check, you have to keep track, put the money in the bank, so you can pay your bills."

"I know that, Camille. Most of them are what do you call it, direct deposited."

"Most? How many rental properties do you own?" Camille took her mother by the hand and led her to sit down. She dumped out the basket and began to sort the mail. "Mother, think. This is important. You have stacks of checks here, unopened bills, and bank statements. I know Dad bought the land and built this house. I know he set you up financially before he died. Tell me, exactly, how much land do you own? Is it free and clear or do you have a mortgage?"

Morgan Ridgeway stepped forward and whispered, "I know her banker. He's an elder at the church."

"Really? Is he honest?" asked Camille.

"Of course he is," stated Amaryllis indignantly. "He's an elder."

"Actually, he's my cousin," stated Morgan. "But he is honest. He's been taking care of Amaryllis' finances since her husband passed."

"Not very well by the looks of this," Camille said, fuming as she inspected each piece of mail again.

Lacey looked at the women in the room. Her mother looked shocked, grandmother looked angry, and Mrs. Ridgeway still looked as frightened as she did the night before. "Did I do something wrong?" asked Lacey. She didn't understand what all of it meant.

"No, of course not, honey." Camille pulled Lacey close and gave her a gentle hug.

"Is Gramma rich or is she in trouble?" Lacey thought it had to be one of those.

"Neither, honey bunch," stated Amaryllis. "Your father left me some money when he died. He told me to keep watch on the real estate market. If the property values dropped, I should buy. It dropped a lot. The golf community, those houses and the empty lots were going up left and right. They were constantly building. Over here, cobwebs on the for sale signs. So, I invested. Bought as much land as I could afford. I asked the young deacon, at the time, to manage things for me. He's done a great job, Camille. The rent pays my taxes and insurance and a little left over. Some of the renters pay me directly. I guess I forgot." Amaryllis nodded to finalize her statement.

"So, how much land do you own?" Camille asked again.

"Seventy-five acres total," answered Amaryllis with a definitive slap on the table. "I don't own the Jackson's property but I own everything around them, including across the street."

"Do they know this?" asked Camille.

"No siree they do not!"

"Good grief," stated Camille. She put all of the checks together. "Mother, as soon as we can, we've got to get to the bank. You have thousands of dollars in checks here."

"Did Lucas get the generator out of the garage?" Amaryllis said with a sudden change of expression. As was her custom, when finished with a conversation, she quickly redirected.

"What generator?" asked Camille.

"Generator? What generator? Where?" Lucas asked when he came in the door behind Barry.

Lacey watched as the adults scrambled to find the generator buried somewhere in the garage. Her grandmother pointed them in the approximate direction where she thought it and a suction pump to siphon gasoline from cars might be then went outside to 'look around'. Lacey and Fiona followed her to the pond. The girls stood and watched while Amaryllis picked up twigs and debris from the recently cleaned pond.

"Well girls," she said. "I guess this is how the pond got buried in the first place."

Lacey picked up a branch, motioned for Fiona to help then said, "We won't let it happen again, Gramma." She watched her grandmother's face for a few minutes. It seemed tired and sad and all of a sudden her grandmother looked old. "Are you okay, Gramma?"

Amaryllis slumped down onto the bench, patted the spot next to her for Lacey to sit, then said, "Honeybunch, you never know where life will take you. Every path has a puddle from time to time. This is one of those times."

"What does that mean?" Fiona whispered to Lacey.

"I'm an old woman," stated Amaryllis. "My mind is older than I think it is and I don't much like it. Your mother is right, I'm alone too much. I've been in my own little world doing my own thing and I've missed the forest for the trees."

"Huh?" said Fiona with a shake of the head.

"What's your name, little one?" Amaryllis asked.

"Fiona."

"That's a very pretty name. Now, listen up. Your parents aren't perfect. They may try to fool people, but you know they aren't. Love 'em anyway."

"They fight a lot," Fiona said.

"That's their business. Has nothing to do with how much they love you."

Fiona, with tears in her eyes, shrugged, sat on the edge of the pond with her back to Lacey and Amaryllis. "Sometimes I just want to run away. When they fight, they forget about me. Like when the storm came. Daddy wanted to go to the church and leave me and Mommy at home. Mommy got really mad. I went and sat outside on the porch for a long, long time. They didn't even know."

"Times like this brings out the worst and the best in people," said Amaryllis. "Hopefully, your folks will lean on each other and remember that they love each other."

"I don't think they do. They are always mad at each other," whimpered Fiona. "I just wanna go home. Do you think I can go home tomorrow?"

"Is Aunt Willow mad at you?" Lacey asked before her grandmother could answer. She didn't want to completely ignore Fiona, however, did not have anything to say to the girl, thought her whining was annoying.

"Your Aunt Willow has been mad at the world her whole life. She's been ornery since the day she was born. I think she's mad at her father for not leaving her any property. So, she takes it out on me."

"So, what now, Gramma?" Lacey asked. She looked around at the bent-over trees and the garden covered with leaves and pine needles. All their hard work to get her grandmother's property cleaned up and now they have to start the cleaning process all over again. The hurricane had not destroyed anything on her grandmother's property, by the grace of God, and now it seemed to be turning into a refuge for those who's homes had been damaged.

"Now, we put one foot in front of the other and keep moving. Help those who need it, and just take one day at a time."

Near dinnertime, most of the neighborhood had gathered in the back yard. This included Beverly and Lamont Jackson, the Ridgeway family, all of the homeless who had been bussed in, Finn and Barry Ryan, Willow, and four other families from the neighborhood who had to evacuate their homes due to damage. The group gathered to make plans for the future of their section of the community. Rainwater continued to flow downstream into the overflowing lake then towards the golf community. The water level continued to creep up and into the riverbed. Most of the water, once it hit the creek, flowed down and away from the uphill homes. Most, but not all. It's depth prevented the water from getting too close to the homes, however, if it were to rain again, even the creek would not save them. Willow, through her dispatcher, informed them that it was too late and too dangerous to clear the debris in the creek. The upstream creek was also flooded and emptying into the lake. Cleaning the south end of the creek would have to wait until the lake crested.

Amaryllis Blythe's house, even though closest to the lake, was the least damaged. Lucas and Finn both believed it was due to the trees on the east side of the property. They had, they speculated, served as a shield from the heaviest winds. The land, the newly renovated barn, and the location made it ideal for the little community that had been dying off to congregate.

Over a dinner prepared on Amaryllis' BBQ pit with the contents of darkened refrigerators, the adults discussed repairs. Since it was nearly impossible at this point to get in or out except by boat, they would have to make do with the supplies they had on hand and help each other out. Plywood and other materials intended for remodeling the barn and other repairs on Amaryllis' property was delegated out to the homes that were the least damaged and most easily fixed. Many of the homeless men were able carpenters and gladly volunteered to help. The homeowners were grateful to accept and a plan was drawn up to tackle one house at a time.

"Where will everyone sleep?" Lacey asked her mother.

"Let's see. The Jackson's have Mother's room. You, me, Mother, and Willow will sleep upstairs in your room. That leaves two rooms. Lucas and his family can take one and Finn and Barry the other." Camille stated. "That leaves the living room for…"

"I can sleep in the barn with Dad," interrupted Finn. "Give that room to the other women and children. Your mother has several good tents in the garage. Dad and I are going to set those up now."

"I'll help," offered Willow.

"I can sleep outside with the men," offered Lucas. "That way the women and children can all stay inside."

Morgan and Fiona looked at him in surprise.

"Daddy," whined Fiona. "Don't leave us."

"Lucas Ridgeway," Mrs. Jackson nearly shouted, "You stay with your family. They need you. You've done enough do-gooding to last a lifetime. Don't wipe it away by forgetting what's most important. You act like they will always be there, waiting for you. Well, life doesn't always work that way."

Fiona ran over to her father, stopped, then turned to look at her mother. "I'll show you which room," she implored.

Lucas nodded reluctantly and followed his wife and daughter inside.

"When will the generator be turned on?" asked Lacey once they were out of sight. "It's really hot."

"At bedtime," Camille answered.

"When's that?" asked Lacey.

"Soon. We have to get the bedding out for everyone."

"I can help," offered Mrs. Jackson.

"This way." Amaryllis led Beverly into the house.

Lacey followed her mother and grandmother around and helped where she could. Three tents had been pulled out of the garage and set up near the patio by several of the men. One of the new guests repaired the fence then returned the pig and horse to their pens so the barn could house more people. One family was settled into an upstairs room while the other family and several of the women were given space in the living room. The air conditioner and every available fan plugged into the commercial-grade generator almost made the house bearable. No one was allowed to take a bath so the air smelled like a gymnasium locker room. Finn Ryan made explicit instructions regarding water usage since the pumps worked sporadically. Boil first, use for cooking and drinking only until the health department gave the all clear.

"I smell smoke," said Rona who was helping to set up the bedrooms.

Lacey stopped half way up the stairs on her way to bedroom and sniffed the air. She looked at her mother and said, "Did Gramma forget to put out the bar-be-que?"

"No, I did not," said Amaryllis from the bottom of the stairwell. She opened the front door and stepped outside. "Smells different."

Lacey followed her mother and the inhabitants of the living room out to the front yard. Just above the tree line she saw a huge plume of black smoke, blacker than the evening sky. When they reached the street, Lacey gasped and pointed. Not far beyond the lake was a line of flames. Lacey listened as the adults speculated on what was on fire and how it got started. Some thought a gas leak, others outdoor fire pits for cooking that had gotten out of hand. Sounds of fire engines off in the distance roared towards the blaze. The lake, they all agreed, would prevent the fire from spreading to the south, however, if it were to get out of control and go around the lake, there would be no way for the fire trucks to get to them.

"What's that smell, Mommy?" Lacey asked. She held her nose against the sickly sweet aroma wafting in from the smoke.

"Oh my God!" a scream came from an upstairs window. "Our house is over there! Lucas, do something!"

Lacey looked up. Lucas Ridgeway slammed the window shut but she could still see Mrs. Ridgeway's mouth moving and her arms waving wildly. Lucas had his cell phone in his hand, apparently trying to call out. He raised his arms in exasperation then pulled his wife away from the window. Fiona must still be upstairs, Lacey thought, as she looked around at the people standing in the road. Willow and Finn stood the closest to the lake. Willow was talking to someone on her radio. When news came in, the neighbors moved closer to her to hear.

"What's going on, Mommy?" asked Lacey.

"Sounds like a gas leak sparked a fire," answered Camille.

"Listen up, everyone!" Willow called everyone to come over to her. "The fire is going to have to burn itself out. Gas has been turned off. The roads are blocked and until they are cleared the engines can't get to the houses. Fire lines are going to be made to prevent spread. Water may have to be shut off so we need to go fill up as many buckets, pitchers, coolers as we can now."

"Stay away from the lake and standing water," added Finn. "If gas leaks into the river, the lake could catch fire."

Finn and several of the neighbors organized the water. Several others worked on moving downed trees away from the lake and other low-lying areas filled with water. Wood useful for the BBQ pit was carried to the back yard and laid out to dry. Amaryllis, Camille, and several other women prepared a light snack for the exhausted evacuees. Even after a long, hot day of work, the group worked together without complaint. All, that is, except Lucas and Morgan.

On her way up the stairs for a much needed rest, Lacey heard the arguing. Their voices were low and muffled, but it was obviously an argument. A high-pitched whine intermingled with a low, gruff and angry voice. A few seconds of silence seemed to only allow them time to catch their breath then the quarreling began again in earnest. Lacey tried her best to ignore them as she and her mother and grandmother got ready for bed. Doors upstairs and downstairs opened and closed, voices throughout the house died down. The house, inside and outside, became still, however, all was not tranquil. The arguing continued. A box fan in the corner of the room turned to high to quell the stagnant air did not provide enough noise to muffle the angry voices.

"I'm going to go over there and smack the fire out of those two," Amaryllis said under her breath.

"Maybe we should let Fiona sleep in here," Camille suggested.

"That won't stop 'em from fighting, or from her hearing them."

"She's used to it," Lacey said with a yawn.

"She told you that?" asked her mother.

"Yeah, she said…," began Lacey.

"Shh, they've stopped. Let's get some sleep," said Camille.

Lacey and her mother said their prayers then they all fell fast asleep. It didn't last very long. Dogs barking frantically woke her from a nice dream. The one she often had but stopped talking about. The air smelled heavily of smoke. Fear gripped her in the stomach and she sat up and began coughing.

"What is it? What's wrong?" Camille and Amaryllis jolted out of bed.

"The dogs woke me," stated Lacey. She put on her boots and followed her mother and grandmother down the stairs.

"Is everything alright?" asked Rona who had been sleeping on the couch.

"'Bout to find out," stated Amaryllis.

The two dogs, Troy and Diaz, barking with frantic attempts at communication, ran around in circles in the front yard. Troy ran up to Amaryllis then down the driveway to the road. Diaz did the same. Lacey ran down the driveway to the road. The two dogs licked her hand then ran ahead of her, turned to make sure they were being followed, then continued toward the lake.

"Lacey, stop!" Camille called out. "Mother, get some flashlights!"

Lacey stopped where the street turned to the right. The fire was still burning, lighting up the night sky and filling the air with smoke making it difficult to breathe. The two dogs ran back and forth towards the water line, near the creek. A loud wail from the house drew her attention quickly away from the dogs.

"Fiona!! Fiona!!!" Morgan Ridgeway cried out over and over again.

The little girl suddenly understood. "Fiona!" she called out. "Fiona where are you?"

A group of bouncing lights approached Lacey while the dogs continued to bark frantically. Lucas Ridgeway appeared from the shadows and stopped beside Lacey.

"Did you see her?" he asked.

"No."

Lacey stood, frozen in fear as the men advanced toward the water line. The black sky made it impossible for them to see beyond the surface. One wrong step and they could either be up to their ankles, their necks, or worse. Every available flashlight pointed to the water. The lights bounced off the debris and the flat surface of the now still waters. Troy ran up to Lacey then off towards the right, towards the bridge. She stayed glued to her spot, thanks to the strong hand of her grandmother. Lucas ran after the dog followed by Willow, Finn, and the other men. Behind her, in the dark, a faint crying slowly came closer and closer.

"Morgan, what happened?" Camille asked.

"The dogs woke us up," she sniffled. "I turned to check on Fiona, and she was gone."

"You and Lucas were arguing all night," began Camille.

"Oh, you heard?"

"Everyone heard," stated Amaryllis.

"I'll never forgive him if anything happens to my little girl," said Morgan.

"Maybe you should've thought about that sooner." Amaryllis turned to face Morgan.

"She said she wanted to go home," said Lacey. "She was sad."

"What would make her run away in the dark?" asked Morgan. "She's never even disobeyed me. Ever. I don't understand."

Sirens broke in on the conversation. Lacey and the crowd that had gathered looked toward the fire that was still burning as hard as it had hours before. The fire line had grown wider but not any closer. Heavy smoke and an odor thought to be gas filled the air. The lights on the fire truck broke through the dense darkness. It stopped on the opposite side of the lake. A bright search light began swaying back and forth across the water, crept closer and closer to the bridge. Men's voices called out.

"I think I see her!" someone yelled.

"Where's Morgan?" Willow shouted as she ran towards them.

"Did you find my baby?" Morgan asked.

"Come with me, ma'am," Willow stated in a calm, controlled voice.

Morgan nodded and followed obediently.

"What's happened?" asked Lacey. She looked over towards her mother and grandmother who stood silently. The dogs returned and sat and Lacey's feet.

"We should go back in now," stated Amaryllis.

Chapter 13

Confusion filled the little girl's head. Did they find her? Was she okay? Why didn't Aunt Willow tell them anything? The awful feeling of not knowing turned her stomach. Lacey tried to stay behind to watch the rescue but her mother picked her up and carried her up the hill and into the house. No one said a word. She attempted to stay awake and listen, however, lack of sleep, exhaustion, emotional turmoil took over and drove her into a deep sleep. Hours later, Lacey groggily opened her eyes. The room was bright, even through the closed curtains. She stared at the ceiling and listened. Like the night before Christmas, the house was still and silent. More quiet than even the first night she had slept in her grandmother's house. Realizing she was alone, Lacey jumped out of bed and ran to the window. She pushed the window frame open wide and smashed her face up against the screen so she could see as far in either direction as possible. Smoke continued to billow high in the sky reaching the noonday sun. Lacey sniffed the polluted air and slammed the window shut. With no electricity still and smoke from the fire, breathing inside was nauseating and outside it was hazardous.

After pulling on her boots, Lacey ran down the stairs. No one was in the living room or kitchen. She ran to the back door and threw it open. She was surprised to find there on the patio the same people who had been busily working the day before. Now, they sat silently picking at their lunch, heads down, backs slumped over.

"Mommy?" Lacey said in a whisper from the doorway.

"Come, baby girl." Camille put her plate down and opened her arms inviting her daughter in.

When she felt her mother's embrace, Lacey knew something had gone terribly wrong. She looked at all the faces. The Jacksons sat together, holding hands. Finn and Barry sat quietly next to Willow and Amaryllis. The two neighbor families and their children sat in silence with the mothers holding their youngest in their laps. Everyone was accounted for except the Ridgeway family.

"Is Fiona okay?" Lacey asked. Stifled cries answered the question. "Where is she? Where are her Mommy and Daddy?" Lacey tried to pull away from her mother.

"Lacey, honey. Look at Mommy, Lacey." Camille turned her daughter so she could look her in the eyes. "Fiona tried to cross the bridge. She didn't make it."

"But…the firemen found her, right?"

"Yes, but…" Camille began. Not knowing the right words to say, she darted her tear-filled eyes towards her own mother.

"She drowned?" Lacey looked at all the faces around her. Parents hugged their children a little tighter. Fathers comforted their wives. Everyone looked so distraught, yet somehow their closeness comforted the usually emotional little girl. "She's not sad anymore, Mommy. She's with Jesus now." Lacey gave her mother a kiss on the cheek then said with child-like innocence, "I'll miss her. Maybe her parents will stop arguing now."

In her little-girl mind, Lacey saw the good, the potential good, in the tragedy. A child no longer had to bear the burden of her parent's actions which had driven her to run away, and now was in the hands of a kind and loving father where there no longer is any pain. Looking beyond the grief, not only that due to death but also due to the devastation brought about by the hurricane, this young girl was able to see unity in the strangers who had been thrown together through disaster for a common purpose. Lacey had been more downhearted over the fact that her grandmother's neighbors not only didn't know one another but also did not like or even care about each other. Yes, they knew each other's business, or so they thought, but did not have neighborly love for one another.

"That's one way to look at it," Amaryllis said with a heavy sigh. "We've been praying for Morgan and Lucas all morning. They've lost everything."

"What's that mean?" asked Lacey.

"Their house was destroyed in the storm," stated Camille.

"What about the fire?" Lacey pointed to the plume of smoke still rising in black spirals over the tree tops. "Is it going to burn up all the houses?"

"It won't come here, if that's your worry," stated Amaryllis. She stood up and looked at everyone with a shake of the head. "Sitting around being sad isn't going to change anything," she said with as much authority as she could muster. "We've got work to do, people. Barry, you're in charge of the garden and the animals. Russ, carpentry. Finn and Willow, since there are no medical issues y'all lead a team to clean out the creek. And I mean clean it out completely. Make it better than the original. Rona, you get the girls together to help me with meals. Mr. Farley and Mr. Munoz, get a team together to salvage what can be saved in the neighborhood for food, clothing, and whatever else you can think of."

"What can we do?" asked Mr. Jackson.

"We can help keep things tidy inside," stated Mrs. Jackson. "I have a washing board and tub in the shed out back. We can do laundry in the lake water, if it's safe, and hang things to dry."

A smile of satisfaction crept over Lacey's face as she watched the community come together. Her personal pain, her sadness melted away seeing her grandmother take charge while working side by side with the neighbor she had been feuding with for decades. Barry, forgetting his shyness, hand picked several men and women and got right to work. Willow even smiled and gave her mother and sister a hug before heading out to the lake.

In total, 37 people had gathered in the little section of Wildwood on Amaryllis Blythe's property that day then at dawn the next for prayer and a meal before breaking into work groups. The creek, once cleared of debris, flowed freely downstream from the lake lowering the water level almost back to normal. The bridge, however, was damaged. It's wooden pillars had been cracked by the force of the water and debris pushing against it. Only foot traffic could cross until the county could come and repair it. With the help of Willow's two-way radio, supplies were found and trucked in as far as the bridge. The fresh food and water, medical supplies, and gasoline had to be carried by hand or wagon up to the house. The fire eventually burned itself out in three days reducing to ashes everything it touched including the Ridgeway's home and the golf course club house. Given the all clear by the health department several days later, the group flocked to the lake to rinse off the dust, smoke, and a little stink. The men inspected the bathhouse which was found to be filled with debris. The water in the sinks and showers as well as the toilets thankfully were in working order. Several of the homeless men and women cleaned out the debris and scrubbed it from top to bottom. They were given the special honor of first bath with soap.

"When will the 'lectricity come back?" Lacey asked that evening after dinner while the group lingered before heading off to bed.

"There's no way to know," Camille answered.

"Thank God for the gas for the generator," stated Mr. Munoz. "We'd be in trouble without that."

"Ain't that the truth," stated Russ. He picked up a 5-gallon can and shook it. "Empty. I'm gonna fill up the generator with the last of the other'un and run 'em down to the bridge."

"Seein' those gas cans are a sure sight for sore eyes," Amaryllis said with a nod. "Anyone know who's sending them?"

"Maybe someone from your church?" suggested Rona. "After all you've done for us."

Amaryllis shrugged. "Could be."

"No one has seen who picks them up or drops them off," stated Finn. "We've kept watch, but never see anyone."

"It's a blessing," said Mrs. Jackson while fanning herself with a paper plate. "That's for sure. A blessing, indeed."

***

"Finn and I are going to take a walk towards the club house to see if we can find out anything more about what's going on," stated Willow a little over a week after Fiona's death. Most of the work that could be done had been and everyone was anxious to get to the world outside their little section of Wildwood. The clubhouse had burned down, however, a make-shift shelter was erected for centralized information and rationing of food and water. "The radio dispatcher is too busy to check the power company for me."

"Just you and Finn?" Camille asked with a wink.

"You can come," Willow said with a shake of the head. "Don't look at me like that. I may have to go back to work and Finn needs to check on his patients every day possible. I've only been given permission to stay for the safety of the residents. Cell towers are down here but they might be up further towards town."

"See what you can find out about Lucas and Morgan," Camille asked with a bit of a hesitation. "They are welcome to come back here. Please let them know that."

Willow nodded her head then joined Finn for the long walk.

"I think Aunt Willow likes Mr. Ryan," stated Lacey.

"You noticed that did you?" said Amaryllis with a sly grin.

Willow returned that evening after dinner. Finn was not with her. "Mom," she called out from the entryway. "You in here?"

"In the kitchen," answered Amaryllis.

Lacey looked up from the card game she was playing with the other children. Aunt Willow looked tired. Her eyes had dark circles under them, her shoulders drooped, and her voice was different, calmer than before.

"How'd it go?" asked Amaryllis. She put a sandwich on the kitchen table then took Willow's backpack out of her hands.

"Rough." Willow took a bite of the sandwich. "Power is out in about 80% of the county."

"Still?" asked Mr. Jackson. "Even in the city?"

"Yes. The worst hit area was an hour east of us," answered Willow.

"That's near the power station," he stated.

"Exactly."

"How is your place?" Camille asked her sister.

"No power, trees down. Carport was blown away. Other than that, there doesn't seem to be any damage. Looks like the water came within inches of the house."

"You're lucky," stated Mrs. Jackson.

"My neighbor wasn't," Willow said with a slight laugh. "The carport landed in her pool, after knocking down the fence she built last year."

"Were you able to find out anything about the church? Lucas and Morgan?" asked Camille.

"From what I was able to piece together, she left him."

"What's that mean?" asked Lacey, suddenly interested in the conversation.

"Finn and I went to the hospital. We asked about Fiona. Finn was told they couldn't hold her because of the power and suggested cremation. Apparently, they refused and Morgan took or rather had Fiona transported to Houston."

"Why Houston?" asked Camille.

"Beats me," said Willow with a mouthful of sandwich.

"I heard tell a while back that she has family there," stated Amaryllis. "Where is Lucas now?"

"My captain told me he took Lucas to what was left of their home. It was demolished. Except for a car in the garage. Captain Willoughby told me Lucas picked through the rubble and packed some things in a duffle bag. One bag, his things only. He asked Captain to keep an eye on the house and that he would call in a few days. Wouldn't say where he was going except that he wasn't going to join Morgan in Houston."

"Well, I'm not a bit surprised," said Amaryllis. "At church Morgan oftentimes looked madder than a wet hen and her face like a corked up Coke that's been shook to kingdom come."

"Mother," Camille said with a shake of the head. "I thought you didn't know who she was."

"Well, after she come here that day, I remembered. And it's true. Those two barely tolerated each other. You saw when she popped in that day. Well," Amaryllis said, patting her chest, "I had hoped this tragedy would wake them up and bring them back together. Looks like the opposite. Well then, I reckon all we can do now is pray for them."

"We should stop speculating," said Mrs. Munoz. "I don't take kindly to gossip."

Amaryllis quickly changed the subject. "Did you go by the church? I'd like to thank them for the generator gas."

"It wasn't from them," Willow said with a wry grin.

"How do you know?" asked Amaryllis.

"I stopped in at the only gas station open for a soda." Willow waited until she had everyone's full attention. "There was a man pumping gas into your gas can. I could tell because it was old." She paused for purposeful dramatic effect.

"Well, don't keep us hanging, girl!" exclaimed Amaryllis.

"It was Byron Ridgeway himself," she said, enunciating every syllable.

"That snake in the grass? I don't believe it," Amaryllis said with a bitter scowl on her face. She stood up and started to march off towards the pond.

"Hold it right there, Mother," began Camille. "What's that all about?"

"Oh, Lord have mercy," began Mrs. Jackson. "Those two hate each other."

"Spill it, Mom," stated Willow.

Lacey glanced from person to person. Everyone appeared to lean in just a little. By the frown on her grandmother's face, it was obvious she was not happy with the news. Willow had a funny smile on her face and her mother's forehead furrow told her something was about to happen.

Amaryllis picked up an unfinished basket by the door and began to fidget. "I can't remember exactly," she said without looking up. "Shortly after your father died…I already told you the real estate market went south and I bought a few tracts. Then the weather went sour. Several tropical storms. One after another. The developer on this side had already gone bust. Byron and his cronies were busy pumping money into the golf course. He was the original investor in Wildwood. Initially him and the other guy were partners but split after disagreeing on plans.

He, Byron I mean, built the road to town and traffic stopped coming down the first entrance."

"Lack of traffic equated to no buyers?" asked Mr. Jackson.

"I guess," answered Amaryllis. "Anywho, the storms dumped a lot of rain and the lake water rose significantly."

"I remember that," stated Mrs. Jackson. "That's when the creek was dug out deeper and the bridge raised."

"Yep." Amaryllis put the basket down. She put her hands on her hips and continued, "I noticed we were higher up. I don't exactly remember, but I had some money that your dad left me or an investment paid off or something. That's when I bought the land across the street and around the house. Your father had suggested I invest in land. I heard talk about the golf course flooding and the possibility of them buying land over here to put in a new 9-hole golf course. Lucas or some other people in the church is the ones who told me. Lucas was working close with his father so he knew what was going on. News spreads like wildfire in that church. So, I quickly bought up several more parcels before Byron and his golf developer cronies could get it. My husband knew the owner well and we got on. They worked together or something. Wonder what happened to him? We kept in touch for a while."

"Mom, focus," stated Willow who was becoming agitated.

Amaryllis ignored her daughter's comment but did get back on track. "Once the rain stopped and everything dried out, the golf course was still wet. Byron started hounding me about selling. I refused. He kept after me, threatened to close the main road and fill in the lake so I put up some land for lease to bring in money then bought the store, you know the one, Wildwood Pit Stop. It had closed after the new road was built."

"You own that?" Willow stood up and faced her mother with a shocked look on her face.

"Why would people lease when they wouldn't buy?" asked Camille. Nothing her mother did surprised her. "You didn't tell me all this a few weeks ago when I asked about the mail."

"It was cheaper," answered Mr. Munoz. "No mortgage or loans to deal with."

"Well, I forgot. That blocked his doing anything with the lake," Amaryllis continued. "He sued. I won. Don't remember how but I did. That's when all development on this side stopped over here. They stopped the construction on the second bridge. Lake maintenance stopped and everything went silent. The golf side continued to grow. Byron quit bothering me and I haven't put a foot on his side since. Well, that's all she'wrote!"

"That's quite the story, Mother," said Willow. She shook her head as if she didn't believe it.

"Well, now. Now you know. At least, that's what I remember. So there's no way Byron is buying us gas."

"Perhaps he's grateful to you for taking care of Lucas and his family," suggested Mrs. Munoz.

"I highly doubt it, that man is meaner than a hornet." Amaryllis crossed her arms and stomped her foot. "There's not a kind bone in his body. His son's house got blown away and his gran'baby died and he didn't even come to check on 'em."

"I have half a mind to do something for that poor girl," said Mrs. Jackson after a long pause. "Perhaps we could have a memorial service at the bridge once it's safe enough. Wouldn't that be lovely?" Mrs. Jackson said to her husband. "Perhaps we could make a memorial of some kind to place on the creek bed, to remember her by."

"Do you know if any other lives were lost?" Mrs. Munoz asked Willow. She had been sitting quietly in the corner listening. "We could include them."

"One in the fire and three in town, from what I was told," answered Willow. "I don't know about any others."

"We should add their names to a plaque," stated Amaryllis. "Or just put in the date and the name of the hurricane. We can use the supplies in the shed to construct something."

"Fiona liked butterflies," said Lacey. "We can make a big butterfly and maybe one for every person…"

"A butterfly sculpture," interrupted Amaryllis. "I love that. Very symbolic."

"I want to help," offered Barry. "We could plant a tree in her honor."

Lacey listened intently to all the ideas being tossed around. The butterfly garden with evergreen trees were her favorite.

"Why do you think God let her die?" Lacey said to no one in particular when the conversation died down.

"I don't know," her grandmother answered.

"I believe God has a plan for everyone," Camille said sounding reverential similar to when she studied the Bible with Lacey. "Maybe she had fulfilled that plan. Maybe it was to get our attention. Maybe because her parents hadn't given her the love and devotion they should have."

"Whatever the plan, Lacey," Amaryllis said after wiping her nose, "it's His plan. We have to learn, understand, accept, then use it for His good. We can get angry, reject God, let it tear our lives apart, or we can try to understand."

"I wish someone would have said those words to us." Mrs. Jackson stepped forward. "We let our sons' deaths make us hate the world, and God."

"I'm sorry we weren't there for you," said Amaryllis. "By us, I mean me and the whole neighborhood. I hope you can forgive us."

"You didn't know," Mrs. Jackson said. "We didn't tell anyone. Let our life teach you what not to do." The formerly crotchety old woman reached out and wrapped her arms around Amaryllis.

Lacey put her hands under her chin and watched the new friendship blossom. The adults, including her mother and aunt, were crying and laughing all at the same time which comforted Lacey, who was hot and sweaty in a cramped house that was not her own, surrounded by people who she didn't really know. For the first time in a long time, Lacey felt safe and secure and happy. A song she learned in Sunday School came to mind and bounced around in her head well into the night. She awoke to it the next morning.

"Mommy, can I sing a song at Fiona's 'morial?" Lacey asked at breakfast.

Camille looked at her daughter in amazement. "Sing? You want to sing? In front of people?" She studied her daughter's serious expression then stated, "Of course you can, if that's what you want to do."

Lacey skipped outside to find Barry. The two little girls she had played cards with the night before followed close behind. She discovered him at the shed with her grandmother, Rona, Susan, and Mrs. Munoz. Supplies for the butterfly garden memorial were pulled out and sorted. Amaryllis instructed the group in exactly how she wanted everything done. Lacey and the children were given cut-outs of butterflies to paint while Barry did the metal work then set off to find trees to transplant. By evening, the project was ready to be installed at the creek.

After breakfast the next morning, the group gathered outside by the shed. The sun was shining for the first time in weeks which helped wipe away a bit of the gloom that had descended upon them during the hurricane and its aftermath.

"Where are we going to put it?" Lacey asked. She ran her finger over the sculpture, pleased with the final product.

Amaryllis led Lacey and the others down to the creek bed. "If we clear this section," she pointed to an area accessible from the lake side of the creek, "we can put it there, and build a bench to go next to it."

"I'll go get a rake," said Barry.

"I'd like to plant some flowers, ones that attract butterflies," stated Mrs. Munoz. "What if we planted in the shape of a butterfly? Would that be too much?"

"Very creative. I have seeds in the garage," stated Amaryllis. "You and Rona mark out the area we need to clean. Girls, follow me."

Lacey and the two girls searched the garage with Amaryllis until the seeds were found. They loaded up the wagon with as much of the project as they could carry, headed back to the creek, walked carefully over the bridge, then set to work. Logs and debris were cleared by Barry then the whole area raked clean. Some of the larger branches were cut down to size and laid out in the shape of a butterfly. As they were working, the rest of Lacey's family and neighbors trickled in to watch the garden take shape. With Amaryllis' permission, the bench from the pond was brought down and placed near the tail, facing the sculpture at the head.

"It's going to be so pretty when the flowers are all in bloom," said Lacey.

"It's pretty," chimed in the little girls.

"Who's hungry?" called out Mrs. Jackson after a long silence. "Dinner is at the pavilion tonight."

"It's dinnertime already, Mommy?" Lacey asked.

"It is," she answered. "You've been very busy today."

"Mommy, look!" Lacey pointed down the road to three large trucks coming towards them.

"It's county," stated Willow. "They told me they'd be out today to fix the bridge."

"Does that mean the power company will be right behind them?" asked Camille.

"That's what I'm told," she answered. "Power is now back on in some parts of town. Finn's office is open, hospital has power. It's coming.

Slowly but surely, it's coming."

While the men from the county worked, the meal crew prepared dinner. They made sure there was enough to feed everyone including the county workers. Mrs. Munoz and Beverly Jackson brought a tray to them right after Mr. Jackson said a blessing on the meal. The weary men were much appreciative. At sunset, all work was brought to a halt, including those working on the bridge. Finn arrived in time to eat a quick dinner before the few leftovers were put away. Amaryllis gathered her family, neighbors, the men and women living in the barn, and the county workers around the memorial garden where the children lit white candles they had placed around the outline of the butterfly. Several more white candles hung from tree limbs by horsehair ropes. They swayed in the gentle breeze hovering over the memorial while the light from the candles on the ground flickered in the night sky, illuminating the metal butterfly making it appear to dance and float upward into the heavens. To everyone's surprise, Barry stepped forward.

"I want to share this passage from Ecclesiastes," he said in a reverent, bold voice that he had not used before this day. He stood up tall, pulled a small book from his breast pocket and began, "For everything there is a season, a time for every activity under heaven. A time to be born and a time to die. A time to plant and a time to harvest. A time to kill and a time to heal. A time to tear down and a time to build up. A time to cry and a time to laugh. A time to grieve and a time to dance. A time to scatter stones and a time to gather stones. A time to embrace and a time to turn away. A time to search and a time to quit searching. A time to keep and a time to throw away. A time to tear and a time to mend. A time to be quiet and a time to speak. A time to love and a time to hate. A time for war and a time for peace. Ecclesiastes 3."

"Wow, didn't expect that," Willow whispered.

"Dad was a chaplain in the military," Finn explained.

"Some things you never forget," said Amaryllis.

Barry paused, held out his hands, took Lacey by one and Rona, who stood nearest to him, the other. He nodded for everyone to do the same.

Once the entire group was joined together, he continued. "What do people really get for all their hard work? I have seen the burden God has placed on us all. Yet God has made everything beautiful for its own time. He has planted eternity in the human heart, but even so, people cannot see the whole scope of God's work from beginning to end." (Ecclesiastes 3:1-11) Barry looked around at the group then down to Lacey. He nodded and she understood.

Lacey let go of the hands she was holding and stepped forward. She took a deep breath then began to sing in an unexpected, sweet soprano voice, "I've got peace like a river, I've got peace like a river, I've got peace like a river in my soul." She heard several men echo while she continued the next verse. "I've got joy like a fountain, I've got joy like a fountain, I've got joy like a fountain in my soul."

The men echoed the last phrase then everyone who knew the song joined in. "I've got love like the ocean, I've got love like the ocean, I've got love like the ocean in my soul. I've got peace like a river, I've got joy like a fountain, I've got love like an ocean in my soul."

After the last verse, Lacey sang alone, "I've got peace, I've got peace, I've got peace in my soul, in my soul."

As soon as the last note drifted off into the heavens the community fell into a respectful silence. Sounds of the night with the chirping grasshoppers and occasional hoot from an owl gave everyone a sense of hope and renewal. The worst was behind them. Tomorrow was a brand new day, a day for new beginnings and a time for healing to begin.

After several minutes of silence, when the children began to squirm, Barry whispered to Lacey just loud enough for everyone to hear, "My mother used to sing that song."

"You remember?" asked Lacey. Her face lit up with a broad smile.

Barry nodded.

"Are all your memories coming back?" she asked with a hopeful heart.

"Some," he answered. "Here and there, a memory pops up. Thank you for all you've done for me. You may be just a child, but God gave you a precious gift."

"I want to thank you, too, Lacey," Finn said. "For taking care of my father."

A loud "Amen" erupted from Mr. Jackson. "Thank you for reaching out to this crotchety old man and bringing love back into our lives."

Lacey was given hugs by nearly everyone, including Mrs. Jackson, who's hug felt most like her mother's. The young men politely gave a sideways hug or a pat on the shoulder along with "good job". When the revelry died down, those who had livable homes to return to began the long walk back. It had been a very full day and everyone was exhausted. The heat, lack of electricity and all the comforts that came with it were beginning to wear each and every person down, young and old. Lacey and her family stayed behind to watch the bridge repairs until all the candles burned out and the only light was from the generator-driven spotlights directed onto the bridge.

"When the bridge is done, will everyone leave?" Lacey asked her mother. She got up and walked a little closer to get a better look at what the workers were doing.

"Some will," stated Camille. "Depends on whether or not there is somewhere for them to go. Most likely, people will be going back and forth and return at night. They have to get back to work, like Mr. Ryan and Aunt Willow."

"Where will Rona, Susan, Russ, and the others go?" asked Lacey. "They never had homes to go to before the hurricane."

"They can stay here as long as they want," stated Amaryllis. "Maybe we can build a proper house on the land across the street."

"Eventually though," Camille continued, "everyone will get back to their own lives pretty much as it was before."

"That's too bad," stated Lacey.

"Why do you say that?"

"They might forget."

"I don't think so," Camille said with a shake of the head. "Not for a long time."

"That is why we have the memorial garden," stated Amaryllis. "Every time we cross that bridge we will see it and remember."

Lacey looked over her shoulder at the garden, now shadowed in darkness. Tears welled up in her eyes at the realization that Fiona was gone. She had never known anyone her own age that died and wasn't sure how she was supposed to feel. There had been a few tears shed during the ceremony, but nothing like some of the scenes she had seen on TV where the parents were wailing uncontrollably. Fiona wasn't exactly her best friend, she told herself to justify her feelings. "Do you think Fiona's parents are sad?" she asked her mother.

"Of course," answered Camille.

"Did they know about the 'morial?"

"I believe Willow did her best to tell them about it."

"Willow what?" asked Willow. She stepped over towards Lacey. "I heard my name."

"Were you able to let the Ridgway's know about tonight?" asked Camille.

"I left a message with the church secretary," Willow replied. "She told me he resigned. I couldn't reach his father. No one from the church could come because of the curfew."

"Curfew?" asked Amaryllis.

"Yeah. Didn't say anything because it didn't really apply here. We can't go anywhere anyways."

The women nodded in understanding. Lacey thought for a moment then said, "We should take a picture and send it to them."

"Great idea, little one," said Willow. "She's so sweet."

"That's my girl," stated Camille. She bent down and scooped up her daughter, gave her a big bear hug before Lacey could object, then set her gently back down.

The little girl's cheeks flushed red with embarrassment. A lot had changed since her arrival at Wildwood. It had never occurred to her how instrumental her actions had been in bringing about healing in the lives of everyone she encountered. A laugh brought her eyes up to witness such a change. Her mother, aunt, and grandmother were huddled together chatting and laughing – an event she had never seen in her short lifetime. She recalled how the others had behaved that night. Barry had stood straight and tall with his arm lovingly on his son's shoulder while they talked with the men and women from King's Hero. These men and women were no longer called 'homeless'. They were friends. The rest of the neighbors gathered together to watch their children play with the dogs as if it was something they did regularly. Most significantly, Mrs. Jackson, Mrs. Munoz, and her grandmother had worked together without a single argument that day.

Lacey looked up. Headlights in the distance slowly traveled up the dark road. It stopped, hesitated, then continued until halting behind the county trucks. The driver's side door opened and a man wearing a tattered straw cowboy hat stepped out. She looked over at the women who were not paying any attention. The man looked up but didn't see the family hidden by the shadows created by the bright flood lights illuminating the bridge. Curious, and fairly sure who the man was, Lacey remained still and watched as he lifted two large gas cans. With the help of the county workers, he transported the cans to the opposite side of the bridge. The flood light touched the man's face, revealing his identity.

"Gramma, look." Lacey pointed towards Byron Ridgeway who stood motionless, staring out towards Amaryllis' house.

"Well if that don't beat all," Amaryllis said with a sudden gasp. "Byron Ridgeway!" she called out. "What in tarnation brings you my way?"

The elder Mr. Ridgeway jumped, turned to face Amaryllis, and started to walk away.

"Don't you do it!" she said, apprehensive and confused at the man's presence. "Don't you walk away from me."

"Yes, ma'am," answered Mr. Ridgeway. He waited until Amaryllis was within arm's reach then said, "I didn't want you to know it was me. I figured you wouldn't accept it."

"Darn right!" she stated with all the bitterness that once was within her. Amaryllis felt a hand on her arm. She looked down and saw Lacey. "I am very grateful that you kept it secret. You saved our lives."

Mr. Ridgeway blinked and his head did a little shake. "Excuse me?" he said with great confusion.

"Oh, don't make me say thank you," Amaryllis said with feigned indignation.

He nodded his head and said, "The lights should be on in a day or two. Is there anything you need?"

"Do you wanna see Fiona's 'morial?" asked Lacey.

The little girl flinched when the old man's hand jumped up to cover his eyes. His chest began to heave and he nodded in short jerky motions. Lacey took Byron Ridgeway by the hand then led him to the butterfly garden. She sat with him alone in the dark silence while he wept. He never let go of her hand even when they were joined by Amaryllis who placed her hand gently on the man's shoulder. Lacey looked up to see tears in her grandmother's eyes. It was then that she knew her grandmother had forgiven him.

Chapter 14

"Who's ready for ice cream?" Byron Ridgeway called out from under the newly constructed pavilion by the lake. His new Stetson covered his bald head and prevented anyone from seeing his frequent glances towards Amaryllis.

"You scoop, I'll hand 'em out," stated Amaryllis. She gave Lacey a squeeze then said, "Scoot, baby girl and go round up the kids."

Lacey smiled then skipped off to the lake. She was thrilled when the electricity finally came on and her mother informed her they would be staying, moving in permanently with her grandmother. Whether it was really her grandmother's idea or not didn't matter. Lacey was staying with her family and friends and that was all she cared about. The day after Mr. Byron Ridgeway was found out, the bridge was completed and opened to cars. Two days after that, a foot bridge was built directly across from Blythe Road, across the creek, to give better access to the memorial garden and the lake. Somehow, he got the cable company to install internet the day after the lights came back on. He made sure the cable guy set up their computers so that Lacey could return to school and her mother could go back to work. Time had flown by after the storm, so much so that they were a week behind. This Labor Day week-end picnic was a celebration.

"Ice cream! Ice cream!" Lacey called out to the children at the lake. "Follow me to ice cream!"

A dozen or so children fell in line behind their new friend and followed her to the pavilion where they were served by her grandmother's former enemy. He was no one's enemy now. With Amaryllis' permission, he built two houses across the street for Russ, Susan, and a few of the others from King's Hero. Barry moved into a cabin built in the woods behind the garden. He was determined not to leave Amaryllis or 'his' home.

Much to everyone's surprise, Barry took over Lucas' job at King's Hero. The plan of teaching the homeless skills – gardening, crafts, building, and so on continued with the help of the church and a promise of a job from Ridgeway Oil and Gas. Barry, with the help of Byron Ridgeway, paid it forward by finding Rona's family. She was surprised when Lacey led her by the hand into a room filled with her family who welcomed her home. Thus, life began to return not to normal but a better version of what it had been before the storm.

"Thank you for the party, Mr. Ridgeway," said Lacey at the end of the day. "It was fun."

"You're welcome," he said with a genuine smile. "I'm glad you had fun. Wish Lucas could have joined us. He's yet to see the memorial."

"He will, when he's ready," stated Amaryllis. "Hope you're not working him too hard."

"Just hard enough," answered Byron. "After losing a child and his wife…she's not dead of course…but he needs to keep busy."

"Is the divorce finalized then?" asked Amaryllis.

Byron nodded.

"Hey, Mom, we're taking off." Willow ran up and gave her mother a hug. "Thanks for the party, Mr. Ridgeway. Me and Finn are going into town and then we both have to work in the morning."

"Have fun, darlin'," stated Amaryllis.

"We should get you in the bath and in bed," Camille said to her daughter.

Lacey, with eyes drooping said, "I'm not tired, really. It's not even dark yet."

"Well I am," Camille replied with as much authority as she could muster. "Let's go."

"But my friends are still here," she argued.

"You can play tomorrow."

"Barry and I can cart the coolers up," Byron Ridgeway offered.

"Thank you, much appreciated," said Amaryllis, obviously weary herself.

Lacey drug herself over the bridge and up the hill. She stopped at the bottom of the stairs and said, "Can I say goodnight to Mr. Ridgeway first? He's awful nice."

Camille let out a long sigh then said, "I suppose so. Help me unload the cooler while you wait."

"Okay, Mommy."

Lacey wasn't so much tired as she was unhappy about leaving the lake. Since the debris had been removed from both ends of the creek, the lake water began to circulate and clean itself out. The beach and the pavilion had become a meeting place for her new friends from both sides. It was now her favorite spot. She played there, swam there, did her homework there, and even had picnics alone with her mother from time to time.

"I'll get it," Lacey quickly offered when the doorbell rang unexpectedly. Barry and Byron Ridgeway almost always let themselves in through the back. She skipped to the door hoping to see a new friend who had moved in down the street.

"Good evening," said a familiar face at the door.

Lacey's heart skipped a beat and her stomach began to knot up. Standing on her front porch was Mrs. Norma and two men in uniform. The woman had the usual plastered smile on her face while the men were somber and at attention. One of the men, the taller of the two, held a package wrapped in brown paper. Lacey heard the back door open while she stood staring out the door.

"Mrs. Blythe, a big black car just drove in the driveway," said Barry. "Oh, they're already at the door."

"Who is it?" called out Amaryllis.

"Sweetie, please let your mommy know I'm here," Mrs. Norma said in her sickly sweet voice.

The fearful little girl held tight to the doorknob and backed away to let them in. "Mommy!" she cried out with her eyes glued to the man holding the package.

Camille came running out of the kitchen. "What, what is…" she stopped and froze the moment she laid eyes on the visitors.

"Camille, dear, you look wonderful," Norma said with her usual false bravado. "I've been trying to reach you for days and days. You don't know how upset I was when my best friend in the whole world up and disappeared."

"Friend? Friend?" Camille grew angrier and angrier with every word. "You are not my friend. You never have been. You only call me when you want something from me. What is it this time? Before you even ask, the answer is no."

"What?" Norma took a step back. Her face grew red. "I don't understand. Of course we're friends. Oh, I know. It's the shock, I'm sure." She pointed to the two men. "Seeing these gentleman."

The shorter of the officers stepped forward. "Ma'am, I apologize for the intrusion on your holiday."

"We have news," Norma said with a dramatic change in her face from embarrassment to sadness.

The officer shot her a look which forced Norma to retreat. He cleared his throat then continued, "Mrs. Andreas, your husband has been recovered."

Lacey looked from face to face. Her mother sat abruptly onto the ottoman flanked on either side by Amaryllis and Barry. In shock and unsure of what the man meant, she left the entryway and joined her mother. Just when the man was about to speak again, the front door flew open and in ran Willow followed shortly by Finn. She ran to her sister's side.

"I saw the car in town," she whispered.

"Go on," Amaryllis motioned to the officer.

"Mrs. Andreas, your husband did survive the initial crash. When exactly he passed away is unclear." He paused then asked, "May we sit?"

"Of course," answered Amaryllis.

Barry moved furniture and brought out a few chairs from the kitchen so everyone could sit down. Norma tried to squeeze herself into a spot next to Camille, however, Mr. Ridgeway gently escorted her to a seat across the room.

While the adults were seating themselves, Lacey fell to the ground with her head in her mother's lap. Tears flowed, suddenly realizing what was going on. Her father was dead. He was not coming back, ever. The dream, the hope was gone for good.

"While a small squadron was on a separate mission," continued the officer, "a grave outside a remote village was discovered. Upon questioning, an old woman took the presiding officer to her house. She told the story of a foreign man in torn clothing stumbling into the village. I say village, it was probably a few small huts and a garden. The woman said they took the man in and cared for him until he died. They did not know who he was or where he came from so they told no one. This," he pointed to the package, "is all that remains. The woman said they could not communicate at all except for basic hand signals but he wrote on paper every day. She kept it but of course could not read it."

The officer with the package held it out towards Camille. Lacey grabbed it and carefully began to unwrap the cherished last things her father had touched. Unfolding it, layer by layer, the unwashed uniform was revealed. Tears began to flow from everyone in the room. Lacey handed the torn and stained shirt to her mother. Underneath, on top of the pants lay a faded, small, spiral pocket notepad. She carefully picked it up and dropped the rest of the package. Amaryllis bent down and lovingly picked it up while Lacey began to open the notepad. Her fingers shook, tracing the words while her heart, shattered to pieces, tried to beat enough to force her mouth to read aloud.

"To the two women I love most in the world," Lacey began slowly. "Camille my amazing wife, and the sweetest, most loving child I have ever known – my daughter Lacey. I hope to live so you don't have to read this. I want you to know how much I love both of you. When the aircraft crashed, I was able to crawl out. When I awoke I was in someone's home. I don't know their language, but they are kind and loving people. They tend to me and meet my every need, except to return me to you. In a time of war, in enemy territory, they could have turned me in or left me to die. I want you to know that there is kindness, love, and God in this house. They may not call him God, but I see him in their faces." Lacey stopped reading, unable to control her emotions and go on.

"I will read it for you," offered Barry. "I pray for you and for them every day. I love you and miss you.

"It's been a while since I wrote. I love you both. I try to communicate with these good people. Either they don't understand or they know it's not safe for me to leave.

"I hear things at night. Bombs. Jets. Things don't look good. I love you Camille. Take care of Lacey.

"My love, my life, if I don't come home, Live. Live for me. Be happy. Love Lacey. Tell her how much I love her. I'm not in pain. I'm sorry.

I'm sorry I could not keep my promise to take care of you forever. Yes, I remember our wedding vows. Remembering them and reciting scripture and songs we used to sing at church keep me going. You, Lord are a shield around me. My glory. The one who lifts my head high. I call out to the Lord and he answers me.

"Even though I walk through the valley of the shadow of death, Camille, I will always love you. I won't be coming home. Lacey, I love you. I'm sorry I won't be able to see you grow up. I pray you will grow up to be a woman of God, marry a man who loves you as much as I love your mother. I'm not afraid to die. I only wish I could see your face one more time.

"I love you."

"No, no, no!" cried Lacey through sobs. "I want my daddy! I want my daddy!" She jumped and ran as fast as she could out the front door, down the road towards the lake. Her body shook with emotion as the tears flowed. The gut-wrenching sobs continued as she ran across the foot bridge to the memorial garden. She stopped and fell face-first into the center of the now-flowering garden. "No, no, no!" the little girl continued to cry. "You promised. You promised." Lacey continued to cry even after hearing footsteps approach and hands pressing on her head and back. No one spoke. Lacey recognized the sobs of her mother and reached out her hand. The two united and gave each other a knowing squeeze.

Mixed in with the chirping grasshoppers and hoot owls were the sounds of phones beeping as messages were sent back and forth from the people who had gathered at the memorial garden. No one wanted to be the first to speak, to break the respect needed while the family grieved. Car doors opened and closed so as not to disturb.

When Lacey emerged from her resting place, she looked around to see everyone who had been at the Labor Day picnic and more. Holding her mother's hand, she stood to face those who came to comfort them. "It's really true, Mommy?" she asked.

Camille nodded, tears still running down her face.

Amaryllis stepped forward to hold her granddaughter's free hand. She, too, could barely hold back her emotions.

"I knew," Lacey began, "a long time ago. I didn't want to."

"I know, honey," said Camille.

"Life goes on, right Mommy?" asked Lacey. "Isn't that what you said after the hurricane and Fiona died?"

Camille forced back a sob and nodded.

"You won't leave me, will you?" she asked, remembering how Morgan Ridgeway and Lucas reacted to Fiona's death.

"No, of course not," her mother answered.

"Neither will I," said Amaryllis.

"Or me," added Willow.

"Me, neither," said Barry. "You brought this community together. There's no way we will abandon you. We will be by your side, yours and your mother's, let you cry on our shoulders, and help you in anyway we can."

"Just like you helped us," said Mrs. Jackson.

"Amen," chimed in Mr. Jackson.

Lacey wiped away her tears, gave her mother a hug, thought for a moment then said, "I think so that I'm going to like living in Wildwood."

ABOUT THE AUTHOR

Colleen Wait began her writing career in elementary school. As a shy child she developed her vivid imagination writing short stories and telling her dolls and pets her dreams. She is an avid reader, especially the classics. Every book began as a dream or a daydream, something to keep her mind occupied, so even though it seems like she writes fast in actuality the books have been written in the recesses of her mind over the span of many years.

When her children were young, she was very involved in her church's youth activities including children's musicals where she stage managed, directed and even wrote a short play, Daughter's of the King, SonQuest and various other youth events including a local mission trip with her church's youth group. Colleen continues to be active in her church through card ministry, life groups, and pretty much whatever God puts in her path. Colleen's son Devin, is in the Air Force. His photograph graces the cover of 'Mount Mission', which is loosely based on that mission trip. Colleen's mission in life is sharing the Good News of Jesus Christ through the written word. "In the beginning was the Word, and the Word was with God, and the Word was God." John 1:1.

Feel free to contact me with comments or questions here:
www.facebook.com/cewait

Discover other titles by Colleen Wait

Sanctuary

Lessons Learned at Summer Camp

Black Purple Sky

Love on the Run

Mount Mission

Captured

Freedom Race

Man in the Mirror

Remnant

Jacob's Well

Made in the USA
San Bernardino, CA
01 August 2019